JOURNEY

TO

VENGEANCE

DWIGHT HOOD ROBERTS

COVER BY

DOUGLAS HOLLEMAN

DOGRIDGE PUBLISHING

BELTON, TEXAS

Copyright © 2014 Dwight Hood Roberts
All rights reserved.

ISBN-10: 0615987192
ISBN 13: **978-0615987194**
Library of Congress Control Number:
LCCN

DEDICATION

I WOULD LIKE TO DEDICATE THIS BOOK

TO MY SISTER, SHIRLEY ROBERTS HOLLEMAN,

AND MY FOUR BROTHERS

RONNY ROBERTS, GERALD ROBERTS, STEVE ROBERTS

AND RANDY ROBERTS.

WE ARE FAMILY AND I LOVE YOU ALL

This is a work of historical fiction. The actions and dialog of historical characters in the book are purely the imagination of the author.

CHAPTER 1

It was still thirty minutes until sunrise when Roy Smith and his boys, Alf and Charley, began their day. While the boys did their chores, Roy hitched old Bell to the plow and began turning over the soil in the field down by the county road. He was plowing the fifth row when the boys and their two sisters, Cordie and Jenny, yelled good-bye to him on their way to school. Roy stopped and watched them until they were out of sight. He was proud of his kids. Charley, the oldest at fifteen, was going to be the farmer of the family. He liked farming and working with the animals. Alf, on the other hand, was a good boy who never complained about doing his chores, but he read a lot and was always talking about the places he wanted to go to and see. Roy shook his head and smiled. No telling what Alf might do when he grew up. Roy's thoughts turned to his two girls, Cordie and Jenny. Cordie was a worker and never complained. She would make some man a good wife someday. Jenny…it was too early to tell about Jenny. She was real smart and she had a temper. Only time would tell what she'd do with her life.

Suddenly Roy popped out of his thoughts and remembered he was plowing. He snapped the reins and Bell obediently began to plod ahead. By noon and too many rows to count later, Roy was plowing the last row.

"Whoa, Bell," Roy yelled as he pulled a dingy white handkerchief from his back pocket and began wiping his face. Then, out of the corner of his eye, he saw movement on the road. He squinted to see what had caught his attention, but the bushes and trees that lined the road were in the way. He cut his eyes to an opening in the trees and waited. A few seconds later, four scruffy-looking horsemen rode into view. Roy felt a cold chill move up his back and slowly stepped back behind Bell. As he watched them ride closer, he realized the horsemen were out of place in this Illinois farming country. They all rode on Mexican-style roping saddles and wore big roweled spurs and wide-brimmed hats. They must be the cowboys he had read about in the newspapers. He had never expected to see any in this area. He stepped out from behind Bell and started walking toward the road.

The cowboys noticed him and waved, then stopped their horses and talked among themselves for a minute. One of them eased off his saddle and walked over to the split-rail fence next to the field. He put his boot on the bottom rail and waited.

"Hello, sir, my name's Jude Brown," the man drawled when Roy was in hearing distance. "We were wondering if you had a place where we could get some water and maybe buy a little corn for our horses." He stuck his hand over the fence and grinned.

Roy, who was naturally suspicious of strangers, studied the man for a second. He was a few inches taller than his own five-foot-eight, but thick boned and muscular. Carrot-red hair spilled out from under his hat, and a few freckles dotted his grinning face. Roy decided to trust him. Besides, he was curious and wanted to know more about the cowboys. He reached for the man's hand. "Sure, mister, I was just heading to the house to put up my horse. Stay on the road until you get to my gate, then ride on down to my barn. There's a pump where you can get some water." Roy turned and began walking toward Bell.

"Much obliged, mister. What did you say your name was?"

Roy stopped and turned. "Smith, My name is Roy Smith." Roy watched as Jude walked back to his horse and mounted. Jude said something to the other three men, and then they rode on up the road. Roy still had a bad feeling about the four cowboys as he unhooked the plow. He felt menaced by their presence and hoped they wouldn't be a nuisance.

He flicked the reins and Bell turned toward the dirt road that ran by the fence, turned and followed it until they reached the barn. Roy put the horse in her small pasture and then hung the harness on pegs driven into the barn wall. As he walked back toward the house, he saw three of the men over by the pump, filling their canteens. A slight feeling of uneasiness stirred again as he watched them. He shook it off and walked toward the men. Jude, their apparent leader, spoke to him when he got closer.

"Nice place you got here, Mr. Smith. How many acres do you work?"

Roy tilted his chin. "Well, thank you, Mr. Brown. I believe in keeping my place neat and clean." He grabbed the pump handle and pumped it until a stream of water flowed into the water trough. "I farm a hundred and forty acres. Do you farm back where you're from?"

Jude cast his eyes around the farm. "Nope, I have a small ranch in Texas, over close to Waco. It ain't near as neat and clean as your place. Looks like you're doing right good. You got men working for you?"

Roy tensed for a second at Jude's words. His uneasiness returned but his pride brushed it aside. "Nope, it's just me, my wife, and the kids. Ain't none of 'em afraid to work."

Jude gazed around the farm. "I'm forgetting my manners. Mr. Smith, this cowboy here beside me is Willy James, and that one leaning against the fence is Stinky Sholt. The one with the horses is Duce Rangle."

Roy studied the four men. All of them were dressed about the same, in dungarees and calico shirts. Willie was shorter than Roy but wider. He had a large, sandy-colored mustache to go with his long sandy hair. Stinky was around Roy's height and slim. His hair was gray and he had a gray beard stained with tobacco juice. Duce was taller than Roy, probably over six feet. His hair was long, black, and greasy; black stubble colored his lower face. Roy reached out to shake their hands. "Roy Smith pleased to meet you. If you want some corn for your horses, get some ears out of the crib. There's a tow sack hanging on the wall."

"Much obliged, Mr. Smith. Stinky, you and Willy go get about a half a sack of corn." Jude looked over at Duce, who was tying the horses to the fence, then back at Roy. "I guess you farmers help each other out at times. Back at my place, the nearest neighbor is five miles away."

"My closest neighbor is about two miles away. Sometimes we help each other out at harvest time, but usually it's just me and the boys." Roy was beginning to enjoy the conversation. He didn't get a lot of chances to talk to strangers, especially ones from Texas. He had noticed all of them were wearing identical boots, each with a red star on the front of the shaft, and he was curious about them. "Mr. Brown, I was noticing your boots."

Jude smiled. "It's the symbol of our unit during the war. We were all in the Calvary Regiment with Bell out of Texas. We had these boots made down in San Antonio one time when we were on leave."

"Nice boots—looks like they've been wearing well. The war's been over pert' near six years." Roy's thoughts went back to his own service during the rebellion. He had joined a local company right after Fort Sumter and ended up with Grant when he was still just a major. He fought some in Tennessee, and then they marched to Vicksburg and camped around it for months until the Rebels had nothing left to eat. He had grown sick of the war after seeing all the carnage and destruction. "I was with the 63rd Illinois myself; saw a little action at Vicksburg. I was glad when it was over."

"We had it pretty bad in Texas after the war," Stinky interrupted angrily. He spat tobacco juice between him and Roy.

Jude turned to Stinky. "Like the man said, the war's been over for six years. Let's not talk about it if it bothers you that much."

Roy noticed the tone of Jude's voice as Stinky quickly lowered his eyes. The man seemed afraid of Jude. Roy hoped they would hurry up and leave. "Well, I need to get back to work anyhow. I'll go up to the house and see if my wife has some corn bread you can take with you." He turned and started toward the house.

Jude followed after him. "I'll go with you if you don't mind, Mr. Smith. I'd be glad to pay you for the food."

"No, that's okay. Glad to do it." Roy hurried his steps; he didn't want Jude in his house. He arrived at the back door several steps ahead of Jude. "Just wait here and I'll see where my wife is." He entered the house and called, "Cordelia, we have some men out here. Do you have something for them to eat?"

"I'm in here," Cordelia called from her sewing room. "I'll be there in just a second."

Roy met her at the door to the dining room and drew her to one side. "There are four men outside and I don't like their looks. Fix up some food in a flour sack so they can be on their way."

Cordelia's face turned ashen. She peered into the kitchen, and then went in with Roy following. "Who are they?" she asked as she grabbed a sack and began filling it with corn bread.

Jude figured he had been waiting long enough. He pulled out his Colt and pushed open the back door. Roy and his wife looked up at him in surprise.

Roy saw the gun in Jude's hand and stepped in front of his wife. "What is the meaning of this? We're getting the food for you."

"I think we want a little more than food." Jude looked past Roy at Cordelia. "You got a mighty handsome wife, Roy."
Cordelia's eyes opened wide as she stepped back against the cabinet; the corn bread in her hand fell to the floor. Roy, his face a mask of desperation, grabbed a knife from the counter and lunged at Jude.

Boom.

Roy jerked back as the forty-four-caliber bullet slammed into his body. A surprised look appeared on his face as he looked down at his chest and the blood spurting out of it. He turned to his wife and tried to speak but slowly he collapsed to the floor.

Cordelia screamed as she knelt beside Roy and put her hand over his wound, but the blood still flowed around her hand. She turned to Jude with tears in her eyes.

"You've killed him! Why?" Tears flowing, she turned back to Roy and caressed his face.

Jude holstered his gun, walked over, and grabbed her by her hair just as Duce burst through the door. "You and the boys search the house for loot. I'm going to take care of this Yankee bitch." Jude pulled Cordelia to her feet. She screamed and he slapped her. Seeing a bed through an open door, he carried her to it and shoved her down. She screamed and fought as he began tearing her clothes off, but he slapped her again and again until she finally stopped struggling and only lay crying. Jude crawled onto the bed.

Later Duce took his turn and Jude went to check up on his men. He found Willie looking through the shelves and drawers in the kitchen. Piled on the table were several pieces of silverware and silver dishes along with candlesticks and couple of gold watches. "You found any money yet?"

"Not yet, but I found a lot of silver and a little gold."

"I can see that. Keep looking."

"I am, I am." Willy paused for a second. "How was the woman? I'm next, right?"

"Just like always." Jude made a sour face. "Nobody wants to go after Stinky." Jude looked around. "Where is he?"

"He was in the front room. He hollered out a while ago that he found an old gun and a sword in there."

Jude walked back through the house. He could hear the squeaking springs from the bedroom and he grinned. This wasn't the first time he had raped and killed. When he joined the Confederate Army in sixty-one, he had thought it would be a glorious war and the South would end it in a few months. As the fighting dragged on through the years, he became frustrated and then angry at the Yankees. When he was punished for killing some civilians close to Gettysburg, he deserted his unit and joined Quantrill and his bunch of cutthroats. After the war ended, he rode with the James boys for a while, but when things got hot and the law was close on his trail, he scurried back to Texas and bought a ranch.

A loud crash brought Jude out of his thoughts. "What the hell is going on?" he shouted as he hurried to the front room where the sound had come from. "What are you doing, Stinky?"

Stinky looked up from where he was digging through a pile of books lying on the floor. "I thought it would be easier to look through these if I unloaded them from the shelves."

"What the hell do you think you are going to find, Stinky? We don't have time to look through every one of them books. We got to find their money and get out of here."

Duce hurried through the door with his pistol in his hand. "What's going on, Jude?"

"It's just Stinky. He thinks we have time to look through all these books. Stinky, put all the things you found in a sack and go look in one of those other rooms."

"Ain't nothing in there, I done looked."

Duce pulled aside the curtains and looked out toward the road. "If they have kids, they may be here pretty quick." He turned and looked at Jude. "The money's probably hidden in the Yankees' bedroom."

"Let's look." Jude headed for the door with Duce close behind him. When they got to the bedroom, Willie was crawling off the bed. Cordelia was turned over on her stomach and not moving.

"Willy, go tell Stinky to get in here and take his turn. Then you go find some kerosene." Jude moved his eyes about the room. A huge closet as tall as the ceiling stood against one wall. A chest of drawers sat against another wall, with a dresser close beside it. "Duce, you check the closet," Jude said. "I'll search over here." He began riffling through the contents of the dresser. He found a small box containing some jewelry and stuck it in his pocket. There was more jewelry in the middle drawer. Desperately he looked over at Duce. "You find any money?"

"Nope, nothing but clothes." Duce slammed the door "How about you?"

"Just some old jewelry." Jude scanned the room again. He rushed over to some shelves high on the wall and pulled down a canning jar full of coins. Duce rushed over as Jude poured them on the bed. "Pennies and nickels," Jude said disappointedly. He looked up as Stinky entered.

"You find some money?"

"Just some change, how about you?"

"No money, just the silver from the kitchen. Did you men think to look under the mattress?"

"Hell, no," Jude said. Duce grabbed Cordelia's arm and pulled her off the bed. With Stinky's help, Jude flipped the mattress. At first Jude didn't see anything, but then a patch of cloth the same color as the mattress caught his eye. He pulled out his knife, cut the thread on one side of the cloth, and ripped it off. A stack of brown-backs met his eyes.

Stinky's eyes lit up. "Look at all that money—them's tens and twenties!"

Jude's hands shook as he pulled out the bills. "There's some fifties and hundreds too. This is it, boys. Pack it up and let's get out of here."

"Not without my turn," Stinky grunted as he pulled the semiconscious Cordelia back onto the bed.

Jude was impatient to leave but he couldn't ignore Stinky. The old man had had his back for a long time. "Hurry it up, old man. We got to get a fire started pretty quick. When you're through, take care of the woman and don't leave any marks. Duce, go help Willy find some kerosene, then bring Smith and put him in bed with his wife. Dose 'em real good, and then set 'em on fire."

7

Duce grinned as he walked to the door. "Yes, sir, boss."

Jude was excited as he hurried out to the horses. When he led them back to the house, Duce was waiting for him with the lumpy sacks of loot in his arms. Jude scanned the road as Duce tied the sacks to the horses.

Jude untied his saddlebags and put the money in them. Then he asked Duce, "Did you get us some food?"

"Naw, I just grabbed these sacks while we were waiting on Stinky. I'll go get some now." He hurried back into the house.

Jude looked nervously up the road. If anyone came upon them now, he would have to kill them too. Their plan to cover up the robbery and murder depended on making it look like an accidental fire. Losing patience, he rushed back toward the house. He would have to make sure they did it right. He met them coming out the door—Willy first, with a sack of food, then Stinky, buckling up his gun belt. Jude could already smell the smoke along with the strong smell of kerosene as Duce came out with a cavalry sword in his hand.

"Look what I found, boss. It's a Confederate sword. It's got the name of a unit from Texas on it."

Jude glanced at the sword. "I'll look at it later. Right now we've got to ride." The house was in flames now and smoke was billowing into the sky. He wheeled his horse toward the lane and then spurred him into a gallop.

CHAPTER 2

Even with the windows open, the classroom had become hot and stuffy and the children had grown more restless with each hour. The day seemed to drag on forever until sometime after lunch the air stirred and a gentle breeze from the south carried the sweet fragrance of apple blossoms into the schoolhouse. Almost in unison the students forgot about their lessons and gazed out the windows at the changing scenery of the arriving spring. Alf Smith, twelve years old, stared at the budding trees and blooming flowers and sighed. He wished he were out there enjoying the warm weather. He glanced back down at his arithmetic test. He was still unsure of some of his answers but he had to turn it in before class was over, so he hurried to the front and placed it on the teacher's desk.

"Class dismissed," called Mr. Roberts, looking at his pocket watch. "I will see you Monday morning."

The words were hardly out of his mouth when the thirty-three once-silent children all began talking at once and gathering up their books. The younger ones, their pent-up energy ready to burst, were the loudest as they hurried to the door. The oldest were slower to leave but just as excited as they maneuvered to talk to their friends or get close to someone they fancied.

Like the rest of the older students, Alf began stuffing his things into his school bag, but he paused when he saw Susan Higgins walking toward his desk. His eyes cut to the front of her pink gingham dress, where two large lumps had mysteriously appeared over the summer months. She used to be one of his best friends, but gradually over the summer she'd quit hanging around with him and started spending a lot of time with his brother, Charley, who was fifteen.

"How did you do on the test?"

"Okay," she answered as she kept walking.

Alf watched her until she reached Charley, who was talking to some other boys. With a deep sigh, he shoved the rest of his stuff into his bag and headed for the door.

"Alf, you want to play baseball?" Sonny Higgins called from the base of the schoolhouse porch steps. He was holding his bat and gesturing toward the school baseball field.

"Sure, who all's playing?" Alf asked as he came down the steps.

"A bunch of the guys and some of the girls said they would play."

Alf frowned as he looked over toward the ball field. Several kids were already there, throwing a ball around. "I can play for a little bit, but I got chores to do before dark."

Sonny grinned. "I got chores too, so let's hurry and choose up sides." He took off running, Alf close behind him.

Sonny and Alf, being both twelve and the oldest, were team captains. Alf picked Ronald Harbin, who was a good hitter, but then had to pick his own sister, Cordie, who was eight. Sonny picked Gerald Royce and Linda, who was a good fielder. There were two kids left—Alf's sister Jenny, and Shorty Boyd. Alf picked Shorty and Jenny was left to play with Sonny, which was okay with her.

The game had been going on about thirty minutes when Alf noticed Charley and Susan walking toward him, holding hands. A tinge of jealousy crept into his mind, along with anger toward his brother.

"We need to go on home, Alf," Charley said. "Get the girls and come on."

Alf clenched his teeth then turned to get his book bag. "Cordie, Jennie, get your things. We got chores to do."

The ball game over, all the children began to pick up their things and scatter, some on the road toward town, while others took the shortest way home through the fields and pastures. Alf and his siblings, along with Sonny and Susan, who lived on the farm next to theirs, started on the road away from the town.

They had only gone a little way when Sonny called out, "Hey, there's someone coming down the road." They stopped and watched as four horsemen approached them. They were rough-looking men, strangers. As they got closer, Charley herded the little ones off the road to let the horsemen pass. Alf felt a wave of caution as the strange men approached and he pulled Jenny closer, but his unease changed to excitement when he noticed their unusual attire. They looked like the cowboys he had read about in dime novels. They had big hats, carried pistols, and their saddles had big horns with coiled ropes tied to them. Alf had always dreamed of being a cowboy, and he stood in awe as the men rode by him. One of the men smiled at Susan as he rode by her, but he turned away when one of the men in front spurred his horse into a lope and the others followed suit. The kids watched the cowboys until they were out of sight.

"Did you see that? They were real cowboys!" Sonny exclaimed as he stepped back into the road.

"We seen 'em just like you did, Sonny," Charley replied. "I wonder what they were doing around here."

"Did you see their boots?" Susan said to no one in particular. "They had a red star on them."

"I didn't see that. I was looking at their guns." Sonny waved his hands around, mimicking pistols.

"I saw their boots," Cordie said. "They were pretty."

"They had pretty horses," Jenny said in a low voice.

Cordie looked back at her sister. "Jenny, you are such a baby."

"I am not."

"You are too."

Alf started walking again. Father would be waiting for them. Maybe he'd seen the cowboys too.

"Alf, one of them had a sword," Sonny said.

"I didn't see one."

"It was on my side of the road. They cowboy in front had it tied to his saddle."

Al didn't know if he was telling the truth or not. Sonny had a bad habit of making stuff up. "Did you see the rifles in the saddle boots? They all had one."

"No, were they Winchesters?

"Yeah, and they all had Colt pistols too."

Alf felt a hand on his arm. "I see smoke," Cordie said, pointing up the road.

Alf looked. A large plume of black smoke was visible just over the trees. Suddenly he felt cold and he shivered.

"Looks like a big fire," exclaimed Charley.

"Maybe someone is burning brush?" Sonny said casually, but he looked worried.

"It looks like it could be close to our place, Alf," Charley said. "You stay with the girls." He took off running. Sonny looked at Alf and then he too began to run.

Alf had a funny feeling in his gut. He couldn't wait—he needed to see what was on fire. "Come on, girls, keep up with me." He grabbed Jenny's hand and began to run. Cordie and Susan followed close behind him. They had run for almost a mile before Jenny, her little legs going slower and slower, finally had to stop. Alf tried to urge her on but she sat down in the road and wouldn't move, so he squatted and told her to get on his back. He carried her piggyback until the road started up a small hill. Setting her down, he waited for Cordie and Susan to catch up to him.

"Susan, would you help Jenny and Cordie? I want to run ahead to the top of the hill and look. I'll be able to see our farm from there."

Alf didn't wait for an answer. He took off up the hill. As he neared the top, he slowed, shaded his eyes, and looked toward the smoke. His heart skipped a beat and he couldn't seem to catch his breath. Their farm was still a mile away, but he could see something there was on fire. Desperately he looked for Charley and Sonny, but they were out of sight. He looked back toward Susan and the girls, who were only a stone's throw away. The fear on their faces reflected the fear he felt himself. At least he could relieve Susan's fear that it was her house afire.

"Susan, the fire is at our place. I'm going on, I need to help."

Susan grabbed the younger girl's hands. "Go on, Alf, hurry, I'll bring the girls as fast as I can."

Alf ran, the fear pushing him faster and faster. He reached the bottom of the hill where the road turned to the left. His side began to hurt and he couldn't seem to get enough air in his lungs. He slowed to a jog, trying to catch his breath. Finally he had to stop and rest for a few seconds, but as soon as he was breathing regularly he began to jog again. By the time he got to the lane that turned to his house, the smoke was all around him. He began to cough and his eyes burned. He circled wide around the house, trying to escape the smoke, and suddenly Charley and Sonny were in front of him. Both were staring at the flames.

Charley shook his head. "We can't get any closer."

Alf didn't say anything, refusing to believe that it was his home. How could all of his things be burning? His clothes, the bed he shared with his brother, the twenty-two rifle he had gotten for his birthday…Maybe Dad would buy him another rifle. He moved his eyes to the barn and then to the sheds behind it. He turned and looked at Charley. "Charley, where's Dad?

"I don't know. Surely he would see the smoke from the fields." Charley swept his eyes across the barnyard. "Daddy, Daddy, where are you?" He waited and then called louder, "Daddy, Daddy!" No one answered.

Alf felt another wave of fear and took off toward the barn, screaming his father's name. The smoke thinned as he entered the barn, but all Alf saw was Bossie anxiously pacing in her small stall, her calf scrambling to keep up with her. Without thinking, Alf unlatched the door to her stall, and then ran out to the pens, Bossie and her calf close behind him. Alf saw Charley near the water trough and heard Sonny's voice too, but he couldn't see him. Suddenly Alf remembered his dad had been planning to plow today, so he turned toward the corral. Bell was there, running up and down the fence. "Daddy, Daddy," he called, but there was still no answer. Where was he? He must have come in for dinner. Fear gripped his heart again as he turned his eyes toward the house. He screamed, "Daddy!"

CHAPTER 3

Sheriff Jake Boone clenched his teeth as he stood in the middle of the black pile of rubble and thought of the house it used to be before the fire. He had stood watch with some of the neighbors all night waiting for the ashes to cool, hoping not to find the Smiths bodies, but knowing they probable would. He picked up a piece of twisted metal that had once been a shotgun. It was a rarity that he could even tell what it was; other pieces of metal he had found gave no hint as to their original form. He pitched the twisted gun out into the yard, and then glanced toward the two burnt bodies in the middle of the rubble. He had been in the house several times through the years and was good friends with the Smiths. He had been in the war with Roy, and he remembered the times that had brought them closer than brothers. He frowned at the charred remains in the Smith bedroom. Something about this fire just didn't look right. He could understand why Roy and Cordelia might be in bed in the middle of the day. It made sense to make love when the kids were at school. It was the other things that didn't look right. The house looked like it could have been ransacked and things could be missing.

Jake turned to Tom Higgins, who was helping him dig through the ashes and melted metal where the kitchen used to be. "Tom, I've seen a few house fires in my day, but this one seems different. It looks like things are scattered too much. What do you think?"

"I hadn't noticed, Jake, but it's hard to tell unless you find something you know is out of place, and then you still really don't know if maybe the Smiths had a reason to move it."

"In a way you're right. I need the boys to look and tell me if anything is out of place."

Tom looked over toward the barn, where Charley, Alf, and some of the neighbors were waiting for the sheriff to finish his examination and call them over. "Do you think the boys are ready for this, Jake?"

"It doesn't matter if they're ready for it or not. It's happened and they have to face it. That's the way life is, Tom. In the war we had to get used to a lot of things we didn't want to do or see." Jake turned toward the waiting boys. "Charley, come on over here." Charley slowly came toward the burnt-out house that used to be his home. Jake could see the tears forming in his eyes as he got closer, and he wondered how the boy was going to react. "Charley, you have to be a man about this." He put his hand on Charley's shoulder.

"I'll try, Sheriff." Charley sniffed and wiped his eyes. He glanced toward his parents' bedroom, swallowed, and then carefully made his way to the blackened remains of his mother and father. He looked down at the charred bodies among the ashes. "I know they're in heaven now. I know they're in a better place…but I sure wish they hadn't gone so soon. Do you think they suffered, Sheriff?"

"No, Charley, I'm sure the smoke got them before the fire did."

"I guess we'll bury them out by Granma, sir." Charley looked toward a gravestone under a large oak tree a stone's throw behind the barn. "I don't think the girls need to see them, Sheriff. Maybe Alf can look if he wants to, but not the girls."

"That's what I think too, Charley. No one else needs to see them either, Charley, so I think we need to go ahead and bury them."

Charley nodded and picked his way through the rubble toward his brother. Jake turned to Tom. "We need to get the Smiths into the ground. Can you and your neighbors over there help dig the graves?"

"Sure, Jake, we can put them in the ground today and have a service in the morning at the church. I'll send Sonny to tell the preacher."

Jake watched Tom go to his son, who was standing with Alf, and then walk over to where some of the men from neighboring farms were gathered. "I need some volunteers to dig two graves over there in the family plot," Jake heard him say. "We need to bury Roy and Cordelia. It won't do anyone any good to see them like they are."

Ben Wilhite, one of the farmers and a part-time carpenter, raised his hand. "What about caskets? I can make a couple if someone can help me."

"That would be real good, Ben, get someone to help you. The rest of you find some picks and shovels and meet me at the family plot over there under that tree."

It was nearly noon by the time Jake got back to his investigation of the ruined house. Judge Ivey had arrived, along with the undertaker, and they had examined the bodies. Later they wrapped up what was left of the bodies in blankets and laid them out in the barn until Ben could finish the caskets. Jake still had his doubts about what had started the fire, but he hadn't found any answers. It didn't make sense that the house could burn without the Smiths smelling smoke. Maybe they'd both gone to sleep after their lovemaking? He looked over to where Alf and Charley were still looking through the rubble for anything that might have survived the fire. Every once in a while one of them would pitch something over to the side, but most of it was useless junk now. Even the cast-iron pots were cracked, along with all the clay ones. The pewter pans had melted to shapeless gray globs of metal. Only the melted silver was worth saving, but there didn't seem to be much of that. Jake took one last look at the rubble, and then called, "Come on, boys. I think they're about ready for the burial."

Jake watched as people lined up to shake hands and comfort the children. He was glad the funeral was over. Preacher West had spoken beautifully to the children about how their mother and father were in a better place, and that one day they would see them again if they went to heaven too. He gave one of his best sermons as he reminded everyone that they could be next, and they had better be ready for Judgment Day.

Now Jake and Judge Ivey had to decide what was to become of Charley, Alf, Cordie, and Jenny. The children didn't have any kin that anyone knew of; Roy had come west in the fifties with his parents, but they had died years ago. Cordelia had come out of a New York orphanage and didn't have any siblings. It would be up to some of the neighbors to take them in. Charley, who was almost sixteen, had already said he wouldn't leave the farm. He would work it himself. Tom and Elizabeth Higgins were the first to say they would take the girls. Others had stepped forward, but Jake was a little leery of some of them. It wasn't uncommon for people to adopt orphans just for the free labor. Some of the people who had offered he didn't know very well, and that was why he was watching the line. He wanted to see how the people who had said they'd take the children acted with them. So far, most of them had quickly said their condolences and left the church. Only the Higgins's, who had been first in line, hovered about the children, reluctant to leave.

Finally the last person in line shook the children's hands and went out the door. The children looked around, wondering what to do. Jenny began to cry, and Elizabeth Higgins quickly wrapped her arms around her and whispered soothing words. Cordie too began to cry, and Elizabeth pulled her to her bosom. Alf looked at the girls, a longing in his eyes. Soon tears formed and he slowly sobbed. Charley pulled Alf to him and they cried together. Jake waited a few moments then walked over to Tom, who was standing by his wife.

"Tom, I need to talk to you."

"Sure, Jake, what's on your mind?"

"I need to talk to you about the children. Let's go outside."

Tom glanced at his wife, and then went out the door with Jake. They sat on a bench by a huge oak in the back of the church. "I'll put it to you straight, Tom. Are you and Elizabeth willing to take the girls and raise them as your own?"

Tom looked Jake in the eye. "We will. And we'll take the boys too."

"You know Charley wants to stay at the farm and work it."

"I know, he told me. I told him I would help him."

"What did he say?"

"He told me we should split the profit to help pay for the extra expenses I will have for taking his family in. I told him he didn't have to do that but he insisted. Besides, if he and Susan get hitched in a few years, it won't make any difference. He'll be part of the family."

Jake laughed. "I guess you're right. I know you're a good man, Tom, and I'm going to tell Judge Ivey to grant custody to you. I kind of wanted to let Alf come live with me and Martha, but it would be best to not break up the family."

"That's true, but we could give him a choice. Sometimes you never know what a kid really wants to do."

Alf's emotions slowly changed from sadness to anger as he searched through the charred and melted items that had once been part of his home. This was the third time he had searched the ruins, but this time his mind was clear and he didn't cry. Alf had looked through all of the scrap metal the day after the funeral and then again two months ago, but both times he had burst out in tears of anguish. Now it was six months past the fire and he was convinced it had not been an accident. He had found the pewter and the copper things from the house, but the sword his father had accepted from a Confederate captain was nowhere to be found. His mother's silverware and the silver pitcher and cups his grandparents had brought with them from Pennsylvania were missing too. His thoughts kept going back to the cowboys with the fancy Texas boots. He remembered Sonny said one of them had a sword. Maybe they'd stolen it and then set the house on fire. Alf brushed off his hands as he walked back to his horse. He would talk to Jake when he got back home, but now he had to go help Charley build a fence.

It was late in the afternoon when Alf got back to the Boones' house. Jake was in the kitchen talking to his wife, Martha, a kind and loving lady who had made Alf welcome in her home.

She smiled when she noticed Alf and gave him a big hug. "Alf, you're just in time. Supper will be ready in a few minutes, and I baked you an apple pie."

"Thank you, Martha; you know that's my favorite." Alf didn't care much for the hugs and kisses on his cheek, but he wasn't going to complain about it. He liked living with Jake and Martha. He had a few chores to do but nothing like when he was on the farm. Jake had got him a horse a few weeks after he moved in, and a few weeks later he had bought him his own twenty-two rifle.

"Jake, I need to tell you something. I think some cowboys from Texas robbed my parents and burned the house down."

Jake glanced at Martha. "What makes you say that, Alf?"

"I was thinking about how on the day the house burned, we saw four men dressed like cowboys riding down the road. Sonny said that one of them had a sword."

Jake thought for a minute, then asked, "What does a sword have to do with it, and how do you know they were from Texas?"

"I've been looking for Daddy's sword in the pile of metal from the house and I can't find it or any of the silverware, not even the Paul Revere silver set."

"I had forgotten about the sword Roy had from the war. Were these men coming from the direction of your farm, Alf?"

"Yes, sir."

Jake frowned. He had thought things didn't look right, but it was nothing he could prove. "Why haven't you told me this before?"

Alf thought for a moment. "I just didn't think about it, Jake, with the funeral and all."

"Well, of course he didn't think about swords and cowboys. He was hurting," Martha cooed as she went to Alf and hugged him.

Jake stared at them for a moment. "I'll look into it tomorrow, Alf. I'll ask around and see if anyone else saw the cowboys. They were probably heading for the river. I'll telegraph the sheriffs in both directions and see if they have had any problems with cowboys."

Alf pulled away from Martha and looked up at Jake. "Do you think the law can find them?"

Jake shook his head. "I don't know. It's been six months since the fire and these men could already be back in Texas, or anywhere else for that matter. I think the only way we could ever catch them is if they got caught doing something near here and were put in jail. And even then, we would have to prove that they did it."

Alf's muscles tensed as he clenched his fist. "I think they did it, Jake, and if the law doesn't catch them, someday I'll go to Texas and find them myself."

CHAPTER 4

Leaning forward in the saddle, Alf burst through the trees in a dead run, heading toward his target. Suddenly he pulled his black gelding to a sliding stop, jumped off, and drew his Colt. *Boom!* An old whiskey bottle hanging in a tree shattered into a hundred pieces. Alf grinned and looked toward Sonny, who had been watching a few feet away.

"How'd you like that shot, Sonny? I had Smokey in a dead run too."

"Damn it to hell, Alf, I bet you could outshoot Jesse James or Wild Bill Hickok."

Alf pulled a bullet from his gun belt to reload his pistol. Jake had given him the Colt forty-five for his fifteenth birthday, and he had practiced with it ever since.

It had been nearly ten years since he had moved in with Jake and Martha. He was a man now, six feet tall and slim, but wide in the chest. His hair was dark and he wore it long. His dungarees were stuck into his stovepipe boots, and his white shirt was open at the top button. A leather holster rig for his Colt forty-five was belted around his waist.

Alf reached up and rubbed his shiny badge. He was a deputy now and he needed to be good with a gun.

"I'm going to practice my fast draw, Sonny. You want to practice too."

"Naw, I ain't never going to be no good with a pistol; I'll just stick with this ol' rifle." Sonny pulled his Winchester seventy-three out of the saddle boot and brought it to his shoulder. *Boom.* A limb fell off a tree fifty yards away. "And I'm already pretty good with it."

Alf pulled his pistol and fired. Three bottles hanging in the tree shattered. "I'm pretty good with this pistol too, but you know what they say—there's always someone who's a little bit faster."

Sonny shook his head. "I guess in the law business you need to shoot fast, but I'm always going to be a farmer like my dad, so I don't need to be."

"You're right, Sonny, but remember you have Cordie to protect now."

Sonny pursed his lips and shook his head. "I know, you've told me a hundred times." He put his hand on Alf's shoulder. "Alf, I love Cordie and I'll protect her with all my being, but sometimes things happen like what happened to your folks that we have no control over. You are my best friend and I'm telling it to you straight: you need to get on with your life. What happened is in the past and there is nothing you can do about it." He squeezed Alf's shoulder. "You need to accept that, Alf."

Alf looked into Sonny's eyes. "I've tried to accept it, Sonny, but the nightmares still come. I can't get it out of my mind. I know those four men did it, and it will haunt me the rest of my life." Alf pulled his watch from his pocket and looked at the dial. "I have to head back to town. We have a man in jail who robbed and murdered his boss over in Clarksville." Alf mounted Smokey, and then turned to look back at Sonny. "Are you going back home?"

"No, I told Charley I'd come by and help him work on the house. He's anxious to finish that back room he started when he found out Susan was expecting again."

"Tell him I'll come out and help him one day next week."

Alf spurred Smokey and turned him toward town. He knew Sonny was right; he needed to stop worrying about it. His brother and sisters seemed to be doing okay. Charley had clung to the farm, plowing and planting the same crops their father had grown. With the help of Tom and his other neighbors, he had built a new house where the other one used to stand. He and Susan had married three years ago, and now they were going to have their second baby. Cordie had married Sonny last year and now they were expecting too. Jenny was sixteen, and half the boys in the county were courting her.

Alf sighed. He knew he wouldn't go help Charley. Every time he went to the farm, his eyes would eventually turn toward the three graves under the old apple tree, and a picture of his burning home would flash in his mind. There were just too many bad memories for him. He still couldn't get the deaths of his mother and father out of his mind.

Martha Boone had tried to be a mother to Alf and he had liked her a lot, but he could never call her Mom. She had caught the fever last year and now it was just him and Jake. Jake was okay, but he had taken it pretty hard when Martha died, and he just wasn't the cheerful man he used to be.

Alf sighed and turned his thoughts back to his job as he saw the town coming into view. Jake would be waiting for him to watch the prisoner while he went to get something to eat.

The sun was straight overhead when Alf rode into the horse barn behind the sheriff's office. He quickly unsaddled Smokey and turned him out into the small corral, then hurried to relieve Jake.

Suddenly two shots rang out from inside the jail. Alf pulled his Colt and raced toward the back door of the jail. He remembered seeing two horses tied in front of the jail but hadn't thought much about it at the time.

Another shot rang out as Alf pushed open the door. Jake was sprawled out on the floor and a stranger stood over him, smoke curling from his pistol barrel. The prisoner was out of his cell and rifling through Jake's desk. Both men turned to look at Alf as he burst into the room.

Alf didn't have time to think; Jake was down and the men had guns. He fired. The prisoner went down but the one standing over Jake jerked, and then slowly aimed his pistol at Alf. Alf fired again and the man spun around, then dropped to the floor. Alf stood ready with his gun cocked and waited for the smoke-filled room to clear.

"Jake, what's going on in there?" Alf swung his gun to the door but then realized it was Barney.

"Come on in, Barney, I think I got 'em all," Alf shouted as he hurried over to Jake.

Barney the jailer slowly pushed the door open and peeped in. He cut his eyes toward the three men lying on the floor. "Somebody get the doctor, Jake's been shot!" Barney shouted to some men behind him. He hurried over to examine Jake's wounds. Slowly he began shaking his head. He turned and looked at Alf. "He's gone." He turned to the crowd of men standing by the door. "Someone get Judge Ivey."

"I'll go get him." One of the men turned and hurried down the street.

Alf slumped down and his eyes welled. He felt weak and helpless as he leaned against the wall, and his tears began flowing freely.

Barney turned to Alf. "What happened here?"

Alf looked up and wiped his eyes. "I was out back putting Smokey in the barn when I heard shots in here. When I came in the door, that man on the floor there was standing over Jake and his gun was smoking. He turned it toward me so I fired. The prisoner was going through Jake's desk and he pulled out a gun and aimed it at me, so I shot him too." Alf glanced at the two men he had shot. "They're dead, ain't they, Barney? I've killed two men." Alf paused, thoughts whirling in his head. "Am I going to hell now?"

Barney didn't have time to answer as Dr. Scott and Judge Ivey rushed into the room and over to where Jake lay on the floor. Dr. Scott quickly knelt down and checked Jake's pulse; after a few seconds he shook his head. "He's gone." At a slower pace, the doctor checked the other two men. Both of them were dead too. "Somebody call the undertaker."

"I'm outside, Doc. Let me know when I can move them to my shop."

Dr. Scott looked over at Judge Ivey and nodded. Judge Ivey looked toward the jailer. "What happened here, Barney?"

"Apparently this man over here come in and somehow got the drop on Jake. He got the prisoner out of the cell and then for some reason he shot Jake. They were about to leave when Alf came in the back door." Barney looked over at Alf for a second, then back at the judge. "Alf shot both of them."

"Is that what happened, Alf?"

Alf wiped his eyes, swallowed, and nodded.

Judge Ivey rubbed his chin. "What do you think, Doc?"

Dr. Scott went back to Jake and examined his body. After a few minutes, he called the judge over. "Look at this, Judge. Jake has a lump and a cut on his head. He was knocked out first, then the man shot him in cold blood."

Judge Ivey shook his head. "Damn it, Barney, Jake didn't deserve this." He turned to Alf. "You did good, Alf, you got the bastards. You got them good."

Events passed quickly after the shooting. Jake's body was taken to the undertaker's, where he was cleaned up and put in a nice hardwood casket. The other two bodies were taken outside the jail and propped up with braces so the local photographer could take their picture. Alf found out later that the two men were brothers who'd had a pretty bad reputation over in Clarksville. Alf thought he was going to have to shoot two more of the brothers when they came to claim the bodies late that evening, but Judge Ivey calmed them down and sent them on their way. The day after the shooting, they had Jake's funeral. Alf was still upset and he cried for the man who had taken him under his wing and raised him. It was almost as bad as his parents' funeral, but this time he had nowhere to go, no one to take him in. Afterward, when the church members brought food, he went through the motions of fixing a plate but couldn't eat. Finally Reverend West sat down beside him and asked him if he wanted to talk.

Alf stared at his untouched food for another few seconds. "Reverend West, I killed two men, and the Bible says it's a sin to kill. Am I going to hell?"

Reverend West thought for a minute. "No, Alf. It's like war—they were the enemy and they would have killed you. During the War of the Rebellion, I saw a lot of what you're going through."

"I still feel bad about it, though. I wish I hadn't had to do it." Alf lowered his head and stared at the ground.

Reverend West hesitated. "I know it's a burden on your soul, Alf, but just pray to God and tell him how you feel. You'll feel better."

"Alf, you want to play baseball?" someone shouted.

Alf turned to see Sonny, carrying his bat and ball. He gave Sonny a slight smile. "Sure, I'll play." He turned back to Reverend West. "Thank you, Reverend; I guess I just needed to hear it from you. I think I'll be all right now. I'm going over here and play some ball and not think about it anymore."

Later that day, after the ball game broke up and everyone went home, Alf slowly walked back to the little house he and Jake had shared. For ten years it had been his home, but when he walked in the door this time, his heart felt like an anvil in his chest. He glanced toward Jake's bedroom and memories came flooding into his mind. He staggered over to the kitchen table and collapsed into a chair. He pounded the table with his fist, and then, with tears streaming from his eyes, he laid his head on the table and sobbed.

It was almost dark when Alf raised his head and wiped his eyes. He was a twenty-one year old man, not a twelve-year-old boy, and he needed to quit giving in to his sorrow. He took a deep breath as he looked around the room. The house was a mess. Alf lit a lantern, then walked over to the kitchen sink and pumped water into the dishpan. He washed his face first and then began to clean the house. When he was finished, he thought about fixing something to eat, but then he remembered he hadn't fed the horses and he hurried out to the barn.

Smokey nickered when he saw Alf come out the back door; it was past time for his daily ration of oats and he was hungry. The gelding quickly trotted to meet Alf at the gate, and then impatiently followed him to where Jake kept a barrel of oats. Alf filled a wooden bucket and gave half of it to Jake's horse, Big Red, and half to Smokey. He watched the horses eat for a few minutes, and then walked back to the house.

Alf sat down in Jake's old rocking chair on the small porch on the back of the cabin and pulled out the corncob pipe Jake had made for him. He filled it from a leather pouch, packing it tight with his finger. He stuck the stem into his mouth, then pulled a Lucifer from a small tin in the tobacco pouch and lit the tobacco. Alf sat and smoked for a while, trying to figure out what he was going to do with his life now that Jake was gone. The house belonged to the county, and when a new sheriff was elected, he would live in it and Alf would have to move out. Alf didn't want to move in with Charley and he didn't want to be a deputy under another sheriff. His thoughts turned to the one thing he couldn't seem to get out of his mind: the four horsemen he had seen the day his parents died. He had thought about it from time to time and a few things always stuck out as peculiar. In the first place, they were coming from the direction of the farm, so they would have had to pass right by the house, which could be seen from the road. The house was completely in flames when Charley got to it, and that was only about fifteen minutes after they saw the men. Giving the horsemen the same fifteen minutes since they'd ridden past the farm, they should have seen the flames or at least smoke. The men had to have started the fire.

Back when Alf had first told Jake about the cowboys a few months after his parents' funeral, Jake had scoured the countryside and all the towns in a hundred-mile radius, but there was no trace of the men. Jake sent a few telegrams to some of the larger cities' sheriffs but never received a reply. He did find out that some of the Texans in General Hood's Calvary had red stars on their boots. Jake finally told Alf that with the thin evidence they had, there was nothing else he could do.

As Alf mulled through his thoughts, a plan began to form in his mind. He had nothing holding him here; Charley and Susan were married now and had the farm. Cordie was married, and Jenny had a good home with the Higgins's. He could never settle down and live a normal life as long as the murderers of his parents went unpunished. He would go to Texas and search for the men with the red star on their boots. Surely someone would remember seeing such fancy footwear.

Over the next few days, Alf got ready to leave. Judge Ivey tried to talk him out of it but finally gave up when he saw that Alf was determined to go. Alf sold Big Red and Jake's saddle to Barney, then donated Jake's clothes and other things to the church. When he was ready to leave, he went by the Higgins's and told Cordie and Jenny he was going. They made a big fuss and cried, but after they settled down, they made him promise to write.

He left the Higgins place and rode over to Charley's house, where he left all his extra clothes and things. He said his good-byes and then left the house, but he stopped at the three graves up by the apple tree. The scent from the apple blossoms was strong as he stood by the graves of his mother and father. He remembered smelling the blossoms the day the house burned and his parents died. He stood in silence for a while, tears in his eyes, as he thought about the good times he remembered. Finally he knelt down, touched both headstones, and whispered, "Mom, Dad, I'm going to find them, and I'm going to make them pay. I hope you understand why I have to do this." He rose, mounted Smokey, and rode away.

CHAPTER 5

The nice weather Alf had experienced for the first two days since riding out of Marshall turned cold on the third day. A Canadian front laden with cold rain had moved in fast, and by the time he got his slicker out of his bedroll and slipped it on, he was already wet. He was miserably cold for the next few miles as he looked for a town where he could warm up and spend the night. His spirits lifted when he crossed the wooden bridge over the Shoal River and saw the town just ahead. It was still raining when Alf tied Smokey to the hitching rack at the Greenville general store. Still shivering, he hurried up the steps and opened the door. Inside were three men, all wearing overalls and flannel shirts, crowded around a glowing potbellied stove. They turned to look at Alf as he came through the door. One of them, a short, husky man with sandy hair sticking out from under his hat, hollered, "Hurry up and close the door, you're letting the cold air in."

Alf quickly shut the door and wiped his feet after he pulled off his slicker and hung it on a peg on the wall. He hurried over to the warm stove where the men had spread out to make a place for him. One of them was obviously the storekeeper; he had a dirty white apron tied around his thick waist and a visor set atop a head of closely cropped gray hair. He was taller than the middle-aged man who had shouted at Alf, but not as tall as the third man, who was rail thin. A wide-brimmed hat perched on his dark, lank hair. Thanking them, Alf thrust his hands as close as he could to the cast-iron stove. He relaxed as the heat slowly made its way up his arms and then to the rest of his body. He felt better now except for his wet clothes. Finally his shivering stopped and he looked around at the men beside him. He nodded to the man in the apron.

"Do you run this store, mister?"

"Sure do. What can I do for you?"

"I could use a new union suit. Do you have my size?"

"I have three sizes, small, medium, and large. You would take a medium. If you want to change clothes, I have a storeroom you can use."

"Thanks, mister. Let me warm up a few more minutes and I'll go out and get my bag off my horse so I can change out of these wet clothes."

Alf stayed a few minutes longer at the stove, then reluctantly hurried out to Smokey and grabbed his bag. He paid for the long johns, went to the back room, and changed. He felt a lot better now that he had on dry clothes, but the storeroom was cold so he hurried back to the stove.

"Where're you from, young feller?" the clerk asked him.

"I'm from east of here in Clark County, about a three-day ride."

The tall man turned and looked at him. "You're a long ways from home. You got business over here or you just drifting?"

For the first time Alf noticed the sheriff's badge pinned to the man's shirt. "Well, I'm not just drifting. I'm on my way to Texas."

The sheriff frowned. "Do you mind telling me why you're going to Texas? I'm Sheriff Bud Light, and this man beside me is my deputy, Bill James. I like to know what's going on in my county."

"Well, Sheriff Light, for one thing, I hear tell it's a lot warmer down in Texas, and right this minute that would be reason enough to go down there. But that's not why I'm going. I've got some business to take care of." He paused, and then added, "I'll only be in your county long enough to pass through it."

Sheriff Light cocked his head. "What's your name, mister? Where bouts in Texas you going?"

"My name's Alf Smith. I'm not sure where I'll land in Texas, Sheriff, but let me ask you a question. Did you know Sheriff Jake Boone of Clark County?"

Sheriff Light paused to think. "I knew of him but I never met him. I heard he was dead, killed by the brother of one of his prisoners."

"It's true, he is dead." Alf swallowed as he thought about what he was about to say. "Sheriff Boone took me in after my folks were killed nine years ago. I was his deputy when he was killed."

Sheriff Light pursed his lips then nodded and lifted his chin. "Are you the Smith boy who shot the two brothers?"

"Yes sir, I was out back of the jail when I heard shots from inside. I hurried in the back door but it was too late, they had already shot Jake. When they saw me, they turned their guns on me and I had to shoot 'em."

"I want to shake your hand, Alf," Sheriff Light said in a more respectful voice and stuck out his hand.

After they shook hands, Alf asked Sheriff Light about a place to eat and a place to stay for the night. "There's a hotel just down the street that has a café and a stable," the sheriff said. "My deputy and I were going to head that way to eat supper after we warmed up a little. I guess we're about as warm as we'll get, so when you're ready, I'll show you where it's at." He smiled as he raised his chin. "In fact, let me buy your supper."

Alf untied Smokey and followed Sheriff Light and Deputy James to the hotel. After he paid for his room and put Smokey in the hotel stable, he went to the café where Sheriff Light and his deputy were waiting for him.

The sheriff pointed to a plate of food. "I ordered the corned beef and hash for you. It's the daily special."

Alf sat down and picked up his fork. "It looks good to me, Sheriff."

The three men ate in silence for a few minutes. Then Sheriff Light cocked his head at Alf.

"Tell me, Alf, what do you hope to find in Texas that we don't have in Illinois?"

"It's a long story, Sheriff."

"I always like a good story."

Alf hesitated, wondering if he should tell him. He had to tell someone eventually if he was ever going to find out anything about the cowboys with the red star on their boots. Who better to tell than a sheriff? "Okay, Sheriff, this is my story."

Alf told them about the fire and the four cowboys he thought had killed his parents. When he was through, the sheriff looked concerned, and Deputy James seemed doubtful.

"I don't think you'll ever find them," the deputy said. "Texas is a big state. Besides, that was nine years ago. No telling where they are now."

"He may be right," Sheriff Light agreed. "I wasn't sheriff here back then. I was elected about four years ago and I never knew about any four cowboys from Texas being up this way. They're probably long gone by now."

"Well, thank you, Sheriff. I may never find them, but at least I'll be able to say I tried."

The sheriff looked at Alf sadly. "If you don't find them, Alf, don't be too hard on yourself. Chances are they will pay for their crimes, if not in this life, then certainly in the next. I was never a God-fearing man myself until a few years ago. I did some things I'm not proud of before I found the Lord."

"If I find them, Sheriff, I will exact my own revenge."

Later, after they had finished their supper, Alf thanked the sheriff again and went up to his room. He was tired but he needed to do a few things before he went to bed. First he checked and cleaned his pistol, then stuck it under his pillow. Jake had always told him that if he took care of his gun, it would take care of him. He washed out his socks and hung them up to dry, along with his wet clothes. The rest of his clothes he stuffed back into his bag so he would be ready to head out early in the morning if the weather was agreeable. When he finished with his chores, he felt sleepy and cold in the unheated room. Stripping down to his union suit, he placed his pants and shirt into the bed so they would be warm when he put them on in the morning. The heavy quilts were cold when he pulled them up to his chin, but in a few minutes his body heat had warmed them up. The last thing he remembered as he drifted off to sleep was the scent of apple blossoms in the air.

Alf was home from school and his house was burning. He ran inside, looking for his mother. She was in her bedroom, but every time he started into her room, flames would erupt and drive him back. He searched frantically for a way into the room when suddenly he was at the window and could see her lying on the bed. She looked at him and her lips moved. Faintly he heard her calling to him. He tried to understand her but the words were too faint. He watched her mouth and it looked like she was saying, "Wake up." Why would she want him to wake up? She opened her mouth again but he only heard a squeaking noise. What was happening? Then the house and his mother disappeared, but he still heard the squeaking.

He awoke. Someone was opening the door. He reached under the pillow for his pistol and rolled onto the floor. Against the moonlit window he could see the outline of a man aiming a gun at the bed.

Boom, boom. Flames erupted from the man's gun. Alf fired back from the floor. The man bent over as the heavy slugs knocked him down. He began to moan. Alf waited for a few seconds, and then rose to his feet. He saw the man's gun lying on the floor and kicked it away from him to the wall. He lit the lantern and held it over the man. It was Deputy James. He was conscious, but blood was spreading across his shirt at his belly.

Alf was puzzled. "What are you doing coming into my room?"

The man looked up, pain showing on his face. "You don't know who I am, but I was one of the four cowboys who killed your folks."

Alf opened his eyes wide. His mind filled with questions as he stared at the deputy. "Why did you try to kill me? I didn't know who you were."

Deputy James groaned and closed his eyes. "I thought if you found the others, they would tell you where I was. I was born near here, and when we went to Chicago on the train with the cattle, I had planned on coming back home."

Alf was still puzzled. "Did you think I would find them that easy? You told me yourself that Texas was a big state."

The deputy groaned again and pulled his legs up into a fetal position. "Can you give me some water?"

"I don't think you should have water. You're gut shot."

The deputy grinned for a second through his pain. "What's it going to do, kill me? I've seen enough of these kind of wounds in the war. I'm a dead man."

Alf frowned, then went over to the pitcher and poured a glass full of water. He carefully poured some of it over the dying man's lips. "Who was with you that day?"

Deputy James studied Alf's face and then spoke in a halting voice. "I'm going to tell you because this thing has been eating at me since the day we done it. I used to go to church when I was a kid, but the war changed me." He paused. "I was in Texas when the war started, and I joined up with my friends in the Texas Brigade. I got used to the killing and doing other things, so after the war I stayed with Jude and we robbed and killed to make a living. When we killed your folks, something happened. The look in your mother's eyes…it sickened me." He stopped as he closed his eyes and groaned, then continued. "I came back home but I couldn't get the images out of my mind. I started going back to church and it helped a little. I asked God to forgive me and that helped too, but when you showed up, it brought it all back and I panicked. I didn't want to live looking over my shoulder so I decided to get rid of you. But I think in the back of my mind I really wanted you to kill me."

"Did you rape my mother?"

Deputy James looked up at Alf with tear-filled eyes. "Yes. We all did. Jude Brown was the leader; in the war he was our sergeant. He is probably back home in Waco—his parents had a small ranch out west of there. Duce Rangle will be down in Galveston. The other man was Stinky Sholt. He was from down in Bell County— lived out in the cedar breaks and made a living stealing cattle. Half the herd we took to Kansas was stolen. You look out for Stinky. He's a coward but he's mean. He won't fight you fair."

He stopped talking as Sheriff Light, pistol in hand, walked into the room. "What happened here?" the sheriff demanded as he turned the gun toward Alf. Alf still held his gun but slowly lowered it and pitched it onto the bed.

"Your deputy tried to kill me, Sheriff."

"It wasn't his fault, Sheriff," James said. "I brought it on myself."

Sheriff Light raised his eyebrows. He put up his gun and knelt down beside his deputy. "What's this all about, Bill?"

Deputy Bill James slowly turned his pain-filled eyes toward the sheriff. "Would you send somebody to get Doc Velasquez?" he groaned. "Tell him to bring me some laudanum for the pain." The sheriff nodded to the hotel clerk, who was standing at the door. The clerk left and Sheriff Light turned back to his deputy.

"Doc'll be here soon."

"Bud, I'm one of the four men who killed this young man's parents. I don't think it was a coincidence that he stopped in this town. I think something led him here." Bill closed his eyes for a second, and then looked back at Sheriff Light. "I've been trying to live with the guilt ever since that day, but even going to church and asking for forgiveness didn't help. I guess I kind of snapped when I came up here and shot at him, but I just needed the guilt to go away, one way or another." He closed his eyes again. When he opened them, he looked back at Sheriff Light. "I'm glad I didn't kill him. That would have been just more guilt." He paused again. "I would like to talk to the preacher before I die, Bud."

The sheriff looked again at the door where other people stood watching and he nodded again. "I'll send someone to get him, Bill. Now tell me the whole story."

The next morning Alf, snug under the quilts, opened his eyes to a cold and dreary room. The fog from his breath confirmed the coldness and he was thankful he had put his clothes in the bed with him the night before. He quickly dressed, packed his bag, and hurried to the diner, where he knew there would be a warm fire. He took his time eating, knowing the trip to the outhouse out back would come next.

When Alf returned to the diner from the outhouse, Sheriff Light was eating breakfast. Alf asked him about Bill.

"He died early this morning. Preacher Kemp was with him at the time." He paused for a minute, thinking. "You know, Alf, war is a terrible thing. Bill was a good man, but the war changed him into another person. I hope we never have another war."

"I hope we don't either, Sheriff, but to be honest, there were a lot of men came home from the war who just went back to doing what they always did. My daddy was one of them and he didn't deserve to die like he did."

"You're right about that. You got a pretty good head on your shoulders, son. Don't let this vendetta change you."

"I'll try not to." He paused, then asked, "How's the best way to get to Saint Louis?"

The sheriff told him which road to take and where he could find places to stop. Alf liked the sheriff and was grateful for the good advice, but eventually he decided it was time to go. He said his good-byes, saddled Smokey, and headed down the road toward Saint Louis.

CHAPTER 6

Alf squinted as he gazed out across the valley, trying to decide if what he was looking at was real. It looked like a bunch of tall buildings, but if it was, they were the tallest buildings he had ever seen. He wiped his eyes and looked again; they were still there. The sight was unlike anything Alf had ever seen and he gazed at it for a long time in amazement, wondering what it was like and how many people lived there. He was almost afraid as he nudged Smokey back into a walk. He had never seen a big city, much less ever been in one. He was trembling in excitement as he slowly drew closer to it. The huge farms and plantations along the graveled road grew smaller and smaller, and soon it was just houses with big gardens behind them. Eventually Alf came upon shops and stores and the road became wider and better kept. The first brick building he came to was a huge mercantile full of more goods than he had ever seen in his life. A few blocks later the streets were made of brick too, and the buildings were so high that he had to crane his neck to see the tops of them. Alf forgot about everything else as he rode around the city, seeing something new every time he turned up a different street. He was fascinated by the crowds of people scurrying like ants up and down the brick sidewalks, entering and exiting stores. Most of them seemed like they were in a hurry.

Alf rode through the streets for several hours until finally he noticed it was getting dark and he didn't have a place to stay the night. By chance he found himself close to the docks, where several hotels lined one of the busier streets. He inquired at several, but they didn't have a stable for Smokey. He kept looking until finally he found one a few blocks from the wharfs. He paid for his room and then led Smokey around back to the stable. The hotel clerk had informed Alf that the stable had an attendant, but when he led Smokey into the small barn, no one was there. Alf let Smokey drink his fill at the water trough while he waited, but after a few minutes he pulled off Smokey's saddle and bridle himself and put him in one of the empty stalls. Not finding any oats, he forked some hay out of the loft to feed him. Alf hung around awhile, brushing Smokey and checking his hooves.

Finally he decided to go on up to his room. He was still a little worried about the unattended stable, but the hotel clerk had assured him that Smokey would be safe, so he grabbed his bag and went back into the hotel. He had asked for a bath when he paid the clerk, and a tub full of hot water was waiting when he walked into the room. Stripping off his clothes, he eased into the water until only his head was above the surface. He soaked until the water was lukewarm, then reluctantly he finished his bath. It was late in the day when Alf finished putting on his clean clothes, and he was getting hungry, so he left the hotel and headed toward a café he had seen earlier. Walking in, he paused for a minute to look for a table. Seeing that all of them were occupied, he started to leave, but a man in an odd-looking suit came up to him.

"Did you want to eat, sir?"

"Yes, but I see the tables are full and I didn't want to wait."

"Just wait here for a moment and I will see if I can find you a place." The waiter walked over to a table where only two men were sitting, waiting for their meal. After a short conversation, he came back to Alf. "Those kind men said that they would share the table with you, sir. Follow me and I will take you there."

Alf studied the two men as he followed the waiter over to their table. Both were middle-aged and dressed in nice clothes. One had bushy, graying hair and a large mustache. He was wearing an off-white suit that looked clean but rumpled. The other had mutton chop whiskers and a short haircut, and he wore a blue uniform with brass buttons. They halted their conversation as Alf slipped into one of the empty chairs.

"Thank you for sharing your table, gentlemen," Alf said with a smile. "I've been riding all day and I haven't eaten since breakfast."

"That's quite all right, lad, you must be famished," Muttonchops said as he held out his hand. "My name is Horace Bixby."

"I'm Alf Smith, sir, glad to meet you." He shook hands with Horace, and then turned to the other man, who also extended his hand.

"I'm Samuel Clemens, son. Perhaps you have heard of me?"

Alf searched his memory but didn't recall a Samuel Clemens. "I guess you have the better of me, sir, I can't recall the name."

Samuel's face showed a slight look of disappointment, but before he could speak, the waiter came over to get Alf's order. Alf remembered the menu in his hand. "Just give me whatever they ordered," he said.

"How would you like your steak, sir?"

"Well done," Alf answered hastily, and then watched as the waiter turned and headed toward the kitchen.

Samuel smiled. "I write books, Alf. Maybe you recall the name Mark Twain."

Alf paused for a second, then his eyes opened wide and his mouth fell open. "Great God almighty, you wrote *Tom Sawyer!*"

"Yes, I wrote that book, among others. But I'm not God almighty."

Alf was in awe. He had never met a writer before, and now he was sitting at a table with one of the most famous writers in America. "Please excuse me, sir, I didn't mean that I thought you were—I just don't know what to say. I've read *Tom Sawyer* at least four times and I enjoyed it every time."

"No, Alf, I was just kidding. I get this reaction all the time. Yes, I enjoyed writing *Tom Sawyer* very much, and I have to say that it has been one of my most profitable books."

"I've read *A Tramp Abroad* and *The Prince and the Pauper* too."

"How did you like those two books?" Horace asked.

"I liked them, but not as much as Tom Sawyer."

"Of course not, Horace," Samuel said. "I wrote *Tom Sawyer* for young people. Young people can relate to Tom and Becky and even Huck Finn."

"I think a book about Huck Finn would be popular, sir," Alf interjected. "When we used to play down on the creeks, most of the boys wanted to be Huck."

"Great Caesar's ghost, what a grand idea;" Horace exclaimed. "Have you thought of writing a book about Huck Finn, Samuel?"

"As a matter of fact, I started writing it several years ago, but I became distracted and now I can't seem to find time to finish it."

"You must finish it, Samuel. Your readers deserve it."

"I will at some time, but now I am working on a book about life on the Mississippi and I need to finish it first."

"Mr. Bixby, are you a writer too?" Alf asked.

Horace laughed. "No, lad, I'm a steamboat captain. Mr. Clemens is one of my passengers."

Alf's mouth flew open again. A steamboat captain and a writer at his table! Even though he thought of himself as a man, he still felt excited to meet men such as these. He wanted to ask them a thousand questions, but he didn't want to appear childish. He was glad when the waiter brought their food and they settled down to eat. Alf mostly listened to Horace and Samuel talk, but every so often he got in a question. Eventually the conversation turned to Alf.

"Alf, you commented that you had been riding all day. Do you not live here in Saint Louis?" Horace asked as he forked his last piece of his steak.

Samuel paused as he lifted his glass to his mouth. "Yes, Alf, you must tell us your story."

Alf weighed the question for a few seconds before he replied, "There isn't much to tell about me. I was raised on a farm up in Clark County, Illinois. My folks died in a fire when I was twelve and I went to live with the county sheriff. He died a little while back, so I decided to go to Texas."

Horace swallowed his steak and said in a kindly voice, "My God, Alf, it seems you have had your share of bad luck. How old are you, lad?"

"I'm twenty-one, sir."

Samuel frowned. "I feel you are leaving out some of the story, Alf. Why are you going to Texas?"

Alf looked at both men for a few seconds, and then decided to tell them the whole story. He began with the fire, the four cowboys, and his suspicions. He told them about his family, about Jake and the shootout at the jail. The two men listened in silence, their food forgotten, as the story unwound. Finally Alf told them about how he had accidentally run into Deputy James and how that had ended.

Horace shook his head. "That's quite a story, lad. You are a very resourceful man."

"I admire your bravery," Samuel said. "I don't know if I could have done what you did."

"I did what I had to do. I guess God was watching over me."

"Do you think you will find the other three men in Texas?" Samuel asked as he resumed eating.

"I know their names now and where they might be. I hope I find them. I don't think I can quit until I do." Alf picked up his glass of water. "So tell me, Mr. Clemens, what is your next book going to be about?

The three men continued talking until they finished their supper. Finally Samuel looked at his watch and announced that he was ready to go back to the boat. Horace called the waiter over to pay their bill. He waved Alf off when he tried to pay his share.

"Perhaps we will meet again," Horace said. "Next time it will be your turn to pay." They walked out of the café, shook hands, and all went their way, Alf off to his hotel room and Samuel and Horace to the steamboat.

CHAPTER 7

Alf slept well for the first time since he'd left Marshall, but he woke the next morning to a slow, steady rain beating on his window. Disappointed by the gloomy day, he dressed and made his way down to the hotel café to eat breakfast. He found a table by the window, and as he ate he watched the falling rain, thinking about how much he disliked riding in it. When he finished breakfast, he went back to his room and packed his clothes. He grimaced as he glanced out his window again and saw it was still raining. He didn't want to stay another day at the hotel, though, so he grabbed his bag and made his way down to the lobby desk to turn in his room key.

Rain was coming down in buckets when Alf stepped out the back door of the hotel and headed to the stable. He was a little apprehensive when he arrived and saw that again there was no one on duty. His fear increased when he couldn't find Smoky or his saddle. Frantically he checked every stall and corral, but all he found was an old mule. His frustration began to turn into anger as he hurried back to the hotel. The same clerk who he had taken his room key earlier was chatting with an older man dressed in worn-out overalls.

"My horse is gone from the stable. What did you do with him?"

The clerk looked annoyed. "What horse are you talking about, sonny?"

"When I checked in yesterday I put my horse in your stable. Now he's gone."

"Maybe someone took him by mistake. They'll probably bring him back later."

Alf couldn't believe what he was hearing. He felt his face grow hot. "When I checked in yesterday, you said your stable was safe, and now my horse is gone. I think someone stole him. What are you going to do about it?"

The clerk cut his eyes toward Alf's gun belt and the large Colt pistol stuck in the holster. "Now, sir, don't get all upset with me. Usually the stable *is* safe. I can't help it if someone took your horse. Things like that happen."

"What are you going to do about it?" Alf repeated. His patience was wearing thin but he didn't know what else to do. He didn't have enough money to buy another horse. Besides, he wanted Smokey back.

"I will send for the city police right away." The clerk turned to the man in the overalls. "Go find one of the policemen, Joe. Mr. Smith, a policeman will be here shortly and you can report your theft."

Alf stood looking at the clerk. It came to him that he probably wasn't going to get Smokey back. The splendor of Saint Louis had distracted him and he had let his guard down. He had forgotten there were people who had no reservations about stealing.

Twenty minutes later the policeman arrived at the hotel. Alf thought he was an army man at first, in his bright uniform with lots of gold braid and buttons. The officer spoke with the clerk for a minute, and then pointed to Alf.

"Man said you had your horse stolen. Where was he at?"

Alf could feel his temper rising again, but he answered in a calm voice, "I checked into the hotel yesterday and the clerk told me they had a stable in back. He said it was attended and safe. I put my horse and saddle in a stall and fed him. This morning I went to get him and he wasn't there."

The policeman wrote down Alf's statement down in a small notebook he had pulled out of his pocket. He was slow, and twice he had to ask Alf how to spell words. When he had finally finished writing, he looked up at Alf. "Who was working in the stable when you brought your horse in?"

"No one! No one was working there when I brought my horse in. I looked and waited, but when no one showed up, I took care of him myself. Then I went up to my room."

"Did you go back and check on him later?"

Alf frowned as he realized again how trusting he had been. "No, the hotel clerk assured me that the stable was safe, so I didn't worry about him."

The policeman shook his head. "We'll look for your horse, but I doubt we'll find him. Since no one saw you put your horse up, I can't fault the hotel for your loss." He pulled out his notepad again. "Now, what did your horse look like?"

Alf gave the police Smokey's description, but deep inside he knew he wouldn't see his horse again. He had been suckered by someone. It could have been the clerk, or it could have been the stableman, if there was a stableman. Maybe it was just someone who'd come into the stable and taken Smokey. Alf hadn't felt this helpless since his parents had died, and he swore he would never feel like this again.

The policeman wanted to talk to the clerk next, so the two of them went over to the desk. The man in the overalls was there again. The clerk said the hotel did have a stableman, and he happened to be the man in the overalls. When the policeman asked the man where he had been when Alf brought in his horse, he said he had been tending to some other business during that time. He swore that when he came back, there was no horse there. The policeman asked him and the clerk more questions, then finally put up his pad. "Mr. Smith, you can stay around a day or two in case we find you horse, but I wouldn't count on it."

Alf thought for a minute. "I can stay another day here. I'm not sure what I'm going to do, but I don't have the money to wait for something to happen."

"Come to the police station tomorrow afternoon. Maybe we can tell you something then. But again, I warn you, don't look to get your horse back. He is probably long gone by now."

After the policeman left, Alf paid for another night at the hotel. He went to his room and put up his bag, then began to walk around the city. He asked around to learn where the livery stables and corrals were located. Most were on the outskirts of town and far apart. By the time he had visited most of them, it was late and he still hadn't found Smokey. Discouraged, he headed back to the hotel. He had only gone a little ways when he found himself at the Mississippi River and the wharfs where the big boats docked. A thought came to him as he looked at the big steamboats. He thought about Samuel Clemens and *Tom Sawyer*. Alf had always been curious about the Mississippi. Maybe since he didn't have Smokey, he could take one of the riverboats down to Texas. Excitement built up in his mind the more he thought about it. He quickened his steps as he neared the docks. A bustle of activity greeted him when he stepped upon the first wooden plank of the first huge pier. Alf stopped the first man who would pay attention to him and asked if he knew Captain Bixby. Yes, the man knew him, he said, but he didn't know if Bixby was in Saint Louis or not. Alf, his enthusiasm undimmed, continued his search and he hurried from pier to pier. Finally his search paid off when he questioned a dockworker who was directing the loading one of the cargo ships.

"Yeah, I know Captain Bixby. That's his boat right over there, the big side-wheeler. I think he's going to pull out tomorrow."

Alf cheerfully thanked the man, and with lifted spirits he hurried toward the steamboat. When he reached the gangway that spanned from the boat to the dock, he saw a man in uniform sorting through a stack of papers, while another man who looked like a dockworker watched. Alf waited until the dockworker took the papers and went onto the boat. The uniformed man turned to Alf.

"Can I help you?"

"I was looking for Captain Bixby. Do you know where I could find him?"

"He's in his cabin. Is he expecting you?"

Alf thought for a moment, then answered, "He's not expecting me, but when I had supper with him and Samuel Clemens last night, he told me to come see him and he would show me his boat."

"Well, in that case go on up. Just ask any of the crew where the captain's cabin is located."

Alf thanked the man and walked up the gangway to a passage that went both ways along the rail of the ship. He was wondering which way to go when a sailor appeared from one of the doors that faced the rails.

"Sir, could you tell me the location of the captain's cabin?"

The man hesitated, but finally he pointed toward a staircase that went up to the next level of the boat. "Go up the next deck. Look for the cabin that has 'Captain' wrote on it." The man grinned as he walked away.

The deck at the top of the steps was smaller than the lower deck. At the front of the ship was a large cabin with windows on the front and sides. Levers, instruments, and a large steering wheel took up most of the room in the cabin. The rest of the second level was closed in, with several doors lining the passageway. At the rear of the boat was an open area with a large smokestack coming out of the middle. On the other side of the boat Alf could see the large paddle wheel that propelled the boat. Looking back at the doors, he saw the one with "Captain" stenciled on it. He went to it and knocked. A muffled voice invited him in.

Captain Bixby seemed surprised when Alf walked in the door. He quickly stood up from the desk where he had been sitting and reached out his hand. "Alf, what a surprise to see you! I thought you would be halfway to Texas by now."

"I did too, Mr. Bixby," Alf said as he shook Horace's hand. "But now I have a problem."

"What kind of problem?'

"When I got ready to leave this morning, my horse was missing."

"Great Caesar's ghost, what happened?"

Alf told Horace everything that had happened. When he finished, Horace sat in silence, frowning.

"It is a shame that there is so much unlawfulness in this city. It seems that you are the victim of chance, Alf. I think the policeman may be right. I don't think you will see your horse again. I am sorry."

"Thank you, Mr. Bixby. After looking for Smokey at every livery stable and place where horses are sold in Saint Louis, I have come to the same conclusion."

"What are your plans now? Do you have the money to buy another horse?"

"No. And besides, I don't think I want to travel by horse the rest of the way to Texas. I think I would like to ride to Texas on a boat."

"That could be expensive. Do you have the money for your passage?"

"No, sir, but I was hoping you might know how I might work my way down the river."

"I don't know, but let me make a few inquiries. Come back in the morning and maybe I will have found you something."

"Thank you, sir. I don't want to take up any more of your time. I'm going to the police station this evening just in case they found Smokey, but I'm not counting on it." Alf reached out his hand and the men shook again. "I will check with you in the morning."

Horace walked Alf to the stairs. "I'm leaving about noon tomorrow and heading upstream, so come early."

"I will, and thanks again, Mr. Bixby." As Alf turned to go down the stairs, he heard Horace call to someone going down the gangway. Alf hoped it was concerning his future. If Horace couldn't help him, he would have to find some kind of job to keep him going. He had left home with a little money, but now he was almost broke. Maybe he could spend the night in the stable and not have to pay for a room. He would ask the clerk when he got back to the hotel.

A man in a suit stood at the desk when Alf arrived. Behind him stood a woman with a frown on her face and a baby in her arms.

"I need this room, sir. My wife and child are with me, and we have been looking for a room all day. Maybe someone has canceled?"

"I am sorry, sir, but I have already checked twice. There is nothing available."

"Maybe I can help you, sir," Alf interrupted. "I have paid for a room, but if you will reimburse me for it, you can have it. That is, if the clerk will let me sleep in the stable."

"I will pay you double for it, sir," the man said quickly.

"No need for that. Just give me the two dollars I paid for it."

"I insist." The man pulled out his wallet and handed Alf a five-dollar brown-back bill. "Keep the change, my good man. You have done me a great service."

Alf looked at the bill, then at the hotel clerk. He started to speak, but the clerk interrupted.

"You may use the stable, sir. And I'm sorry about your horse."

Alf thanked the man, then got his bag from the room and went to the stable. This time the hostler was there, sitting at a table and reading a book. When he saw Alf, he said, "I'm sorry about your horse, son. I want you to know that I wasn't just slacking off. I live with my sister and she's very sick. I have to go see about her a lot because she has no one else who cares about her."

Alf sensed the man was telling the truth, but he had been lied to before. "She doesn't have children?"

"No, she never married," the man said sadly. "Her only true love died in Texas and she pines for him still." He paused as if thinking, then motioned Alf to a stool. "Let me tell you a true story, sonny. I heard you telling the policeman you were going to Texas, and I have been thinking of a way to repay you ever since."

"You can tell me the story, but you don't owe me. It was partly my fault for leaving him unattended."

The hostler smiled. "Let me tell you the story first and then we will talk about it." He settled himself in his chair, and then began his story.

"A long time ago my sister fell in love with a man by the name of Karl Steinheimer. They courted for a while and were very happy. She was willing to marry him, but he would have nothing of it. He told her that he wanted to make his fortune before he married, that he was going to Mexico to look for gold and silver. She became angry and said some things she didn't mean, and he left on a boat. She was sorry and tried to contact him, but she never heard from him until twenty-five years later, when she received a letter from him that told an unusual story. Steinheimer had indeed found his fortune and was on his way back to her when he encountered hostile Indians. He had with him ten jack loads of gold when he first saw the Indians. He quickly buried nine of them where three rivers came together, some sixty miles north of Austin. With the other jack load in tow, he tried to escape the hostiles, but they caught up with him about ten miles east of the three forks, where several knob hills rose above the prairie. Steinheimer and his two men fought off the Indians until dark. During the fierce battle, both of Steinheimer's men were killed and he himself was wounded. Believing it was his only chance to escape; he buried the remaining gold on the hill and sneaked away under cover of the dark moonless night. Later, after wandering the prairie for a while, he found a settlement and wrote the letter. He told my sister he still loved her and would come to her when he was healed, but if she didn't hear from him, she was to have the ten jack loads of gold. He drew a map of where he buried it and included it in the letter. That was forty years ago."

Alf's heartbeat had quickened as he listened to the story. When the hostler paused, he asked, "Did you find the gold?"

The old man looked sad. "No. We went to Texas, but we never found any trace of any it. We found the three rivers and we found the small hills, but we dug and dug and never found any gold."

"Did you find out what happened to Steinheimer?"

"Yes. He died from his wounds." The hostler reached into a bag on the table. He handed a piece of paper to Alf. "Here is a copy of the map. If you get a chance, look for the gold. If you find it, send me half of it and you can keep the rest. I wrote my address on the map."

Alf took the map and looked at it. The only city on it was Austin, and a few inches above it he saw where the three rivers came together. Just east of the rivers the map showed several hills. Two X's were on the map, one on the hills and one by the rivers. Notes on the map told of distances and depth. One mentioned a brass spike in a tree by one of the rivers.

"I think the gold is still there, son, but it's a wild land and the directions are not that good. Still, if you're lucky, you might find it."

Alf shook his head and half smiled as he put the map into his bag. He figured the old man was telling the truth, but he didn't think he would ever have a chance to look for the treasure. He looked up at the old hostler. "My luck will have to change a lot for me to find it. If I ever do, though, I will send you your half."

The hostler smiled. "I know you will, son. Now I'm going to check on my sister, and since you are here tonight, I won't come back until morning."

The next morning Alf woke to the sound of the old mule braying. He had been dreaming about Willy James creeping into his room, so when he heard the braying, he grabbed his pistol and almost shot the animal. Luckily he remembered where he was in time and didn't end up having to pay for someone's mule. It was still dark, but Alf pulled out a match and lit a candle he remembered seeing stuck to a fence post. As the candle illuminated the barn, he checked the pocket watch Jake had given him for his fourteenth birthday. It was a little after five and time for him to get up. Alf yawned, brushed the straw from his socks, and pulled on his boots. The morning was cold and he hurried to put on his coat. After hanging up the old horse blanket he had slept on, he washed his face in a horse trough and tried to comb his hair. The old mule brayed again and he forked some of the hay he had slept on to him to shut the animal up. The old man who ran the stable hadn't come back. There were two more horses in stalls, though, and seeing Alf feed the mule, they too began to fidget and neigh. Alf forked them some hay, then gathered his stuff and headed for the hotel café.

It was still dark and only three other people were eating when Alf walked into the dining room and sat down. He hadn't eaten much the day before, so when the waiter came over with coffee, he ordered flapjacks with his eggs. As he waited for his food to arrive, he thought of all the mistakes he had made since he'd left home. When he'd gone to the police station the evening before, the sergeant at the desk told him they still hadn't found his horse and probably never would. Alf vowed to be more careful and less trusting in the future. One of his mistakes had almost cost him his life, and another had cost him his horse.

His thoughts were interrupted when the waiter brought his food. Alf ate quickly, visited the outhouse, and took off for the docks.

At Horace's steamboat there was a message for Alf to go see a Captain Morgan on a steamer called the *Texas Star*. Alf got directions and found the boat just a few docking spaces down the pier. It was an old side-wheeler, small in comparison to some of the newer steamers, but it was neat and clean. Alf found Captain Morgan standing by the gangplank looking nervously at his watch. When he saw Alf coming, he put up his watch and said, "Are you the stoker Captain Bixby was going to send over?"

Alf hesitated. He didn't know what a stoker was. "Yes, sir, Captain Bixby said he might find me a position. My name's Alf Smith."

"How many steamers have you worked on, Smith?"

Alf cut his eyes to the steamer. "Including this one, sir? Just one."

"What!" Captain Morgan's face turned red. "Bixby said you were a stoker!"

"I'm sorry, sir. I didn't tell him I was a stoker, but I am a hard worker, sir, and I learn fast."

Captain Morgan clenched his teeth and looked at his watch again. "Okay, Smith. I've got to leave within the hour or the tide will be out and I will be forced to wait for half a day. Get on board and go to the coal bins and start shoveling. The fireman will show you what to do."

"Yes, sir," Alf said, and went up the gangplank. He didn't know where he was going, but he figured he'd better get on the boat before the captain changed his mind.

"And don't forget, Smith," the captain shouted as Alf neared the top. "You got 'til we get to Memphis. You had better make a good stoker or I dump you there."

Alf didn't answer but hurried to ask the first man he saw where the engine room was located. When he got there, a man was shoveling coal into the firebox. He threw Alf the shovel, and then looked at his watch. "About time you got here. Keep shoveling coal into the furnace until I close the door. When I open it, start shoveling again."

Alf looked at the shovel and then at the coal. "Just like shoveling corn," he murmured. He began to shovel the coal rapidly into the firebox. In a few minutes he was sweating. Thirty minutes later he was still shoveling, but his pace had slowed a little. Finally the fireman closed the door and told Alf to take a rest.

"I'm Richard Ryan, but everyone calls me Rick. There's water over there in that keg. Better get some now." He looked at his watch. "You've got about fifteen minutes until the pressure starts dropping. Then you'll have to start shoveling again."

Alf quickly laid down the shovel and went to the keg. He wasn't tired but his muscles were aching, and when he filled the tin cup, his hands shook so much he spilled some as he drank. He refilled the cup, and then downed another one after that. He felt better now, but it was hot in the engine room, so he pulled off his shirt and hung it over a pipe. His long johns were wet with sweat, so he undid the buttons, pulled out his arms, and let them flop down his back. That felt better; he was cooling off now. The fireman pointed to a stool and he sat down to rest his legs.

The minutes passed quickly, and all too soon for Alf the fireman looked at his watch and opened the firebox door. Alf wasn't ready, but he got off the stool and began shoveling again. He glanced over at the fireman. "That's a nice watch you got there, Rick."

"It's a railroad watch. My dad gave it to me on my last birthday." He opened the back and showed it to Alf. "See, it's got my name engraved in it."

Alf looked at the engraving. "Richard Ryan, July fourth, 1879, you were born on July fourth?"

"Sure was, back in fifty-four."

"That makes you twenty-five years old."

"Yes. How old are you, Alf?"

"I turned twenty-one on March seventeenth this year."

CHAPTER 8

Much to Alf's relief, his job as ship's stoker wasn't as bad as he had first imagined. He found out that after the firebox reached a certain temperature, the amount of coal he had to shovel into it was cut to only a few shovelfuls every fifteen or twenty minutes. The work was hard, but Alf wasn't afraid of hard work. To him it was just life as usual and he settled into it with a desire to learn all he could. Soon after they left Saint Louis, Rick showed him how to read instruments and what to do when they reached a certain temperature. Alf was a fast learner, and by the time they were halfway to Memphis, he could run the engine room by himself. Despite the hard work, Alf began to enjoy his journey down the Mississippi. He was always asking Rick questions about the river and the ship. He found out that the *Texas Star* carried freight from northern factories down the river to southern towns and cities, but it also picked up cotton to take to New Orleans, where it would be shipped to England. They docked at almost every town on the river, unloading items the merchants had ordered and then loading up their cotton bales. When night came, the steamboat would stay docked at whatever town they were until morning. The many hidden rocks and logs in the river could rip out the bottom of a vessel, and Captain Morgan wasn't going to risk losing his steamboat by traveling at night.

It was only when the ship docked that Alf got to see the river. Sometimes Rick would send him to town to pick up food or some other things he needed, and Alf would tour the town as he looked for the items.

As the *Texas Star* traveled farther south, the weather became warmer, and although Alf had a small bunk in the engine room, sometimes he slept out on the deck where the air was fresher and he could watch the stars. It was during these times that Alf learned a lot about the constellations from one of the old sailors who had sailed on the open seas. Alf ate his morning and evening meals in a small dining room on the lower level that was for the crew, but he ate his lunch in the engine room so he could keep an eye on the steam-pressure gauges.

When the steamboat reached Memphis, they had a two-night layover and the firebox was allowed to cool down so Rick and Alf could make some repairs. They were just finishing up when Captain Morgan came down to the engine room to talk to Rick about some concerns. Right before he left, he turned to Alf. "I hear you've been doing a good job, so I guess you get to stay."

"Thank you, sir," Alf replied. He hesitated for a second. "Sir, I was wondering, how far down the river we are going on this trip?"

Captain Morgan smiled. "All the way to the end, son, and then some. We're going to Galveston."
Alf watched him leave as he realized that at the end of this journey, he would be in Texas.

The journey down the Mississippi became less exciting after a few more stops along the wide river. Alf was becoming used to the routine of the steamboat, but he disliked being in the dark all the time. He loved the outdoors and he missed the sunlit days. He was beginning to wish they would hurry up and get to Galveston.

Finally, on a Friday afternoon, the *Texas Star* arrived at the port of New Orleans. The steamboat slipped into a vacant spot on the commercial pier and the crewmen hurried to secure her to the dock. Alf noticed the men seemed more excited than usual, and then remembered it was the first of the month, which was payday. Some of the crew members were talking about going to the red-light district in New Orleans and they asked Alf if he wanted to go, but he declined politely. He did want to see the sights of the famous old city, though. He had read about New Orleans and had planned on seeing it, but first he and Rick had work to do. They spent the rest of the day servicing and repairing the different parts of the huge steam engine that propelled the huge boat. It was already night when they finished the last task and Alf was tired. Rick, on the other hand, seemed excited as he entered his small bunk next to the engine room. A short time later he came out wearing clean clothes and smelling of bay rum.

"Alf, I'm going into town and I might not be back tonight."

Alf grinned and make a show of sniffing the air. "You got a girlfriend you're not telling me about, Rick?"

Rick smiled and turned red. "I have a girlfriend in every port, but this one is special. We're thinking about getting married."

The announcement caught Alf by surprise. He had worked with Rick for weeks and he had never mentioned anything about women. He had always been businesslike and serious. "Tell me about her. What's her name?"

"Her name is Fifi Savoy. I met her at one of the taverns." Rick beamed. "She worked there as a waitress, but she's not a prostitute. We talked about it and she swore she wasn't like that."

"That's great. I guess every man needs to get married. I may get married myself someday."

Rick's mouth stretched into a wide smile. "We've been saving our money to buy a house. We looked at one a few weeks ago and put a down payment on it. We're going to pay it off tomorrow."

"I'm glad for you, Rick," Alf replied, but in his mind he was wondering if everything was as it seemed. Maybe he would go to the tavern tomorrow and see for himself. "Maybe I can drop by tomorrow and buy you a beer. Which tavern does she work at?"

"Sure, Alf. She works at the Blue Pearl, but she doesn't go to work until six in the evening. Come by after then and I'll buy your supper." Rick looked at his watch, then turned and headed up the stairs. "I'll see you tomorrow."

"See you then."

Alf walked to the small washstand next to his bunk. As he washed up, his thoughts turned to his first love, Susan Higgins. She had been his best friend since first grade, but when they grew older he began to dream about her in more intimate ways. He had been devastated when she began to flirt with Charley, and he with her. When he saw them kiss behind the trees on the playground, he decided he hated both of them. He moped around for a long time before he got over his puppy love for Susan, but deep in a corner of his heart he still loved her. When his parents died in the fire and Susan's parents wanted to take in his whole family, he rejected them because he still couldn't stand to see the way Susan and Charley treated one another. Later, when they finally got married, it was like a door closing in his face. Maybe someday he would find someone to love, but for now, he had other business to take care of. He didn't need to complicate it with a girlfriend.

The next morning, after Alf checked the boiler and pipes, he went to the boat's purser to pick up his pay. He was turning to leave when Captain Morgan came in.

"Alf, I was just looking for you. How are things down in the boiler room?"

"Everything is just fine, Captain. We cooled it down last night and there are no leaks in the pipes to report."

"That's fine. I see you picked up your pay. Are you going in to the city?"

"With your permission, sir, I would like to see New Orleans while I've got the chance."

"Yes, that's fine, take the day off. It's a beautiful city—lots of parks and monuments." Captain Morgan paused, then added, "But be careful if you get into the rough part of town. You can get into trouble there if you don't watch out."

"I will, sir, thank you." Alf turned and went back to his bunk. He changed into his better clothes and strapped on his gun. The captain wasn't the only person to warn him about the crime in New Orleans, and he wasn't going to take any chances.

The weather was clear and warm when Alf walked off the gangplank into the dock area of New Orleans. As he began to stroll through the unusual city, a sense of adventure coursed through his body. Saint Louis had seemed like a regular American town with more people and bigger buildings, but New Orleans, with its strange buildings and French-speaking people, felt like a foreign city. He was fascinated as he wandered through its streets. It was only when he saw a tavern decorated with wrought iron that he remembered he wanted to check out the Blue Pearl. Needing directions, he approached two men conversing on a bench. He asked if they knew how to get to the Blue Pearl tavern, and one of them explained how to get there.

Alf found the tavern a few minutes later, just a few blocks from where the *Texas Star* was docked. He wasn't impressed. The sign above the door hung from rusted chains and was in need of repainting. The building also needed repainting, as well as repairing. The smell of stale beer and vomit greeted him as he stepped through the door. It was early and only a few men sat at the tables. Most of them were drinking coffee, but one of them was at the bar nursing a tall mug of beer. A tall, husky man with a dirty apron tied around his bulging belly was behind the bar, wiping a coffee mug with a stained rag. He looked up as Alf approached. "What can I get you, sir?"

Alf's first thought was to leave, but he decided the coffee smelled pretty good. "Give me a coffee."

The man filled a cup from a huge black pot that sat on a cast-iron stove and set it in front of Alf. "That'll be five cents."

Alf handed him a nickel and took a sip. It was strong and tasted a little old, but it would do. He took another sip as he glanced around the room. The place didn't look too bad inside, but a couple of the men sitting at a back table looked like the pirates he had seen pictured in storybooks. One even had a big knife in his belt. An idea came to him and he turned back to the man behind the bar. "Does Fifi still work here?"

The bartender frowned. "Yeah, she works here. Why?"

"I was just wondering. I heard she got married. I thought she might have quit."

The bartender sneered. "Fifi? Hell, she ain't going to get married. She likes her men too much."

"I thought she was pretty nice the last time I was here."

"Oh, she acts all goody-goody when she's working, but she still has her customers upstairs. Let me give you some free advice, sonny. Unless you're pretty good with that big pistol strapped on your waist, I would leave her alone. She's got a jealous boyfriend who controls what she does. When other men try to interfere, he goads them into a fight, and he hasn't been beat yet."

Alf had heard enough. He quickly finished his coffee and left the tavern. He felt sorry for Rick, but he didn't know what to do to help him. Maybe the bartender was lying about Fifi. Maybe she was a nice girl. All Alf could do was be there tonight and see how things worked out.

When Alf walked out of the Blue Pearl and away from the docks, he put Fifi out of his mind and concentrated on sightseeing. The tall buildings and numerous bridges held his attention for a while, but he was more amazed when he came to the cemeteries with their aboveground mausoleums and tombs. He stopped at a café for lunch and tried the local food. He liked the gumbo and the shrimp, but the crawfish he didn't care for. After lunch he investigated all the shops in the business district. At a clothing store, he bought new socks and underwear. He also bought some of the new thick denim work pants and a new belt to hold them up. He found a few other things he needed at other stores, and soon he was ready to go back to the boat. He backtracked 'til he found the main street that took him to the docks.

It was middle of the afternoon when he got back to the boat. He put his purchases in his locker and decided he had time to do his laundry. There was a laundry room on the boat, and Alf washed his dirty clothes and hung them up to dry. As he waited he cleaned his pistol, and then tried to read a book he had bought, but his thoughts kept going back to Rick. He wondered how he was doing with Fifi. Had they really bought their house, or was it all a scam? Even though Alf was young, living with Jake and working at the jail had exposed him to a lot of evil people. He knew what people were capable of and how far they would go to steal. He hoped Rick was okay, but he still had his doubts.

It was close to six o'clock when he was through with his chores and his clothes were dry. He took a bath then put on all new clothes. The last thing he did before he left the boat was check his gun. He still had a bad feeling about how this night might turn.

The Blue Pearl looked different in the dim light of the gas lamps that lined the streets. The shabbiness and dirt were hidden in the shadows. Inside was the same, only much dimmer. Most of the tables were occupied, but Alf saw one of his shipmates, a deckhand, sitting alone at one of them and sauntered over.

"John, have you seen Rick?" Alf asked.

John had been watching one of the barmaids and hadn't seen Alf walk up. He smiled when he saw who it was. "Hello, Alf. No, I haven't see Rick tonight." He nodded toward the table. "Have a seat. I'm here by myself."

"Thanks." Alf pulled out the chair by the wall and sat down. He didn't want his back to the crowd. "I was supposed to meet Rick here at six." He pulled out his watch. "It's not quite six, so I guess he will be here in a little while."

John held up his mug. "You want something to drink?"

"Yeah, I'll take a beer. Let me buy yours."

"Much obliged, Alf." John held up two fingers as the barmaid looked his way. In a few minutes she brought two mugs to the table.

"You men want to order food?"

"Not me, I'm going to drink awhile," John replied.

"I'm waiting on a friend. I'll order then," Alf said.

An hour passed and Rick still hadn't shown up. Alf noticed a young woman had begun working behind the bar. More time passed and John decided he would order supper, so Alf reluctantly decided to order too. He was getting hungry and he didn't like to eat late. John got the waitress's attention and they ordered, but just as she started to leave, Alf stopped her.

"Miss, who is the new girl at the bar?"

The waitress glanced at the bar. "That's Fifi, cowboy. You don't want to mess with her. You might get hurt."

"What do you mean, get hurt?"

"She has a mean ex-boyfriend. He's been known to cripple people who mess with her."

"Is he that tough?"

She nodded toward a table in the back of the room. "See that guy sitting alone at that back table? That's Jack Fontain, her ex-boyfriend. He's not big enough to be tough, but he's sneaky and he likes to use a knife. She would like to be rid of him but no one will take him on."

Alf studied the man for a minute. He was sickly looking, with a slight build. His hair was dark and slicked back. A pencil-thin mustache looked like it was drawn on under his nose. He wore a black suit with a gold chain leading to the watch pocket in his vest. Alf disliked him instantly.

Alf stood and walked to the bar. Fifi was busy drawing a beer for a one-legged sailor, so as Alf waited, he studied the girl. She had reddish-brown hair in a single pigtail down her back. She was a medium-size young woman with wide hips and ample bosom. She also had a black eye that she'd tried to cover with a dusting of face powder.

She handed the mug to a portly sailor and turned to Alf. "What can I get you, sir?"

"I want to ask you something. Where is Rick?"

Fear leaped to her face. "How do you know him?"

"I work with him on the steamboat. He's my friend."

Her fear turned to hope. "I don't know. I was with him last night, but he left this morning to go to the courthouse and hasn't been back." She turned her eyes toward the back table but quickly turned them back. "I think maybe Jack found him and hurt him."

"Do you think he might have killed him?"

"I don't know. Sometimes he just beats them with a club."

Alf returned to his table. "John, would you cancel my food? I'm going to look for Rick."

"Sure, but where are you going to look?"

"I saw a hospital today when I was exploring the city. I'm going to check there."

Alf left the Blue Pearl and hurried to the wide street that ended at the docks. He remembered the hospital was about six blocks away on that street, and in a few minutes he saw it in the distance. When he walked in the door, a nurse was working at the front desk.

"I'm looking for a man named Richard Ryan, who might have come in today with some injuries. Do you have someone here like that?"

"We have a few people who came in with injuries today. I can check the register. What is your name? Are you family?"

"No, we both work on one of the steamboats and we just came into port yesterday."

"Let me look." The nurse opened a big book and read the entries. After a few minutes she looked up at Alf. "We don't have a Richard Ryan, but we have an unknown man who came in today with multiple injuries, including a concussion. He hasn't regained consciousness. I can take you to him to see if you think he is your friend."

"Yes, please."

Alf followed the nurse to a large room full of beds at the end of the hall. She went to one of the beds where a man covered in bandages was lying.

"Is this your friend?"

Alf looked at the bandaged man and his heart sank. It was Rick, and he looked terrible. He could hardly see his face for the bandages, but he remembered what Rick was wearing when he left the boat. Both of Rick's arms were in casts, and so was one of his legs. His ribs were wrapped tightly in more bandages. "Yes, this is him. What happened to him?"

"He was brought in today about noon. Besides the concussion, both his arms are broken and his ribs are cracked. He was unconscious when the police found him in an alley."

"Do they know who did it?"

"No, and they probably never will."

"Is he going to be all right?"

"With head injuries you never know. He might never wake up."

As Alf stared at his friend, he could feel his anger growing. He was pretty sure Jack Fontain had done this to Rick. If it was just a robbery, they wouldn't have taken the time to break his bones. "Thank you, nurse. I'll inform our captain and he will make arrangements for his bill. I'll be back to check on him later."

As Alf left the hospital, he thought of ways to punish Jack Fontain. First he would go tell the captain what had happened, if he could find him, and then he would go see Fontain.

The captain was asleep when Alf got back to the ship, and it took a while for Alf to rouse him. Captain Morgan was agitated at first, but when Alf told him about Rick, he hurried to put on his clothes.

"Where is he, Alf?"

The two men hurried to the dock and turned toward the hospital. Alf walked with him for two blocks, and then touched the captain on the arm.

"I'll meet you there later, Captain. I have something I have to take care of now."

Captain Morgan turned to Alf with questions on his face. "Okay, Alf. I will see you there." He patted Alf on the shoulder, and then hurried on down the street. Alf watched him briefly, and then headed for the Blue Pearl.

When Alf reached the tavern, it was late and most of the crowd was gone. The few remaining patrons were sipping beer and telling stories when Alf entered the room. He noticed John was gone, but Fifi was standing behind the bar. Jack Fontain was sitting at the same table, fooling with his watch. Alf slowly walked to the bar.

Fifi looked up. "Did you find him?"

"Yes, he was at the hospital. He's all broken up and he's unconscious."

Fifi's eyes filled with tears as she looked at Jack. "That bastard; I know he did it."

Alf followed her gaze. Jack looked up as if he felt them watching him. Alf stared at the watch in Jack's hand and then at the chain on his vest. It was Rick's watch! In five quick steps he was at Jack's table. Before Jack could react, Alf grabbed the watch and flipped open the back to read the inscription. He only had time to read Richard Ryan's name before Jack rose from his chair and pulled a pistol from under his coat. Alf threw the watch at him as he went for his Colt. Jack flinched for a second when he saw the watch flying at him, but then he aimed at Alf. Two shots rang out. As the smoke billowed around him, Jack fell back onto the floor.

Alf stood there for a second, watching Jack to see if he would move. Then he whirled to scan the room for anyone else who wanted to join the fight. All the men watching slowly raised their empty hands.

"Does anyone in here think this wasn't a fair fight?" Alf demanded. All the men shook their heads. Alf's face relaxed as he walked over to the table and picked up Rick's watch. He held it up as he looked around the room.

"A friend of mine, Rick Ryan, was badly beaten today. I saw Jack Fontain with my friend's watch and I grabbed it to be sure. Jack went for his gun and I protected myself." He opened the watch and walked around, showing them the inscription. All the men nodded.

A few minutes later the first policemen came in the door, and once again Alf explained what had happened. The police chief and a justice of the peace came a few minutes later and the situation was explained to them. After examining the watch and taking statements from eyewitnesses, the judge ruled that the shooting had been in self-defense. It turned out that the law had been trying to get evidence on Jack Fontain for a long time, and they were pleased that someone had taken care of their problem for them.

An hour later the law departed, carrying Jack's body with them. The Blue Pearl closed and Alf escorted Fifi to the hospital to see Rick. When they got there, he was awake, and the doctor on call said he would be fine after all his broken bones healed. Fifi excitedly told Rick what had happened at the Blue Pearl. Rick smiled when Alf showed him his watch, but tears formed in his eyes.

"Thank you, Alf. You are a true friend."

"You're welcome, Rick."

Rick turned to Captain Morgan. "Captain, I'm sorry I won't be able to work for a while, but Alf could do the job. He knows what to do."

"Don't worry about the job, Rick. Whenever you're ready, it will be waiting for you." Captain Morgan looked at his watch. "It's almost midnight. We need to get back to the ship, Alf. Rick, I'll be back in a couple of weeks to check up on you."

Alf told Rick and Fifi good-bye. Fifi gave him a big hug and kissed him on the cheek. His cheeks felt hot as he followed Captain Morgan out of the room. As they walked back to the docks, Alf told the captain he would be glad to do Rick's job, but he was leaving the boat in Galveston.

"Yes, I knew you were leaving. Captain Bixby explained your situation to me. At the time I felt like I was doing him a favor by giving you a job on my steamboat. Now I'm thinking he did me the favor."

Alf didn't reply and the two men walked in silence the rest of the way to the dock. They would be leaving tomorrow for Galveston, and Alf was already thinking of the days ahead.

CHAPTER 9

It was a warm, calm day when the *Texas Star* slowly eased in alongside the dock in Galveston, Texas. The side-wheeler came to a halt, and sailors ready with mooring ropes pitched them to dock workers, who quickly looped the lines around dung-stained pilings and knotted them tight. The ship now secured, the gangplank was slowly lowered to the landing, where the Galveston harbormaster was already waiting to board the ship.

When Alf received word that the *Texas Star* was secured to the dock, he shut down the engine and closed the damper on the firebox. Mixed emotions of regret and relief stirred in his mind as he glanced around the boiler room. This had been his home for two months and he had made some friends, but he was in Texas now and he had a mission to complete. With one last look, Alf picked up his bags and walked out the door.

Texas was different than Alf had imagined, at least the Texas he was looking at now from the rail of the *Texas Star*. It seemed so ordinary. He hadn't expected cowboys shooting guns into the air and cattle running up and down the beaches, but he expected it to be somehow different. He did feel a new sense of adventure as he stood at the ship's rail. His long, hard journey was over and he was happy he was finally in Texas. He found it strangely exciting that one of the men he was looking for might be in Galveston, but the fact that he didn't have a job worried him. The money he had left from when he started out in Illinois, along with the money he'd earned on the boat, wasn't much and he didn't know a soul in Texas. Setting his bag on the deck, he pulled out his purse and counted his money for the third time that day. Twenty dollars, six quarters, eight dimes, five nickels, and twenty pennies—only twenty-two dollars and seventy-five cents. He sighed as he closed the purse and stuck it back into his pants pocket. Picking up his bag, he joined other people who were slowly making their way toward the gangplank. As Alf swept his eyes across the deck of the old paddle-wheeler, he again felt a little sad about leaving the captain and the rest of the crew. But he was in Texas now, and he would never be able to live a normal life as long as the men who had killed his parents were still alive. Maybe afterward when it was all over, he might settle down here in Texas, or go back to work on the riverboats. But for now he was on his own again and he needed a job.

The line of passengers waiting for their turn to leave the *Texas Star* moved slowly. Alf joined them but as he shuffled closer to the gangplank, he noticed that one of the officers over by the entrance to the ship's hold was handing some papers to a man who had come on the ship with the harbormaster. Seeing an opportunity for a job, Alf left the line and walked toward them.

"Sir," he said to the man when he saw him turning to leave the ship. "Do you know if they need any help unloading?"

The man looked at Alf. "Are you a farm boy?"

"Yes, sir, I grew up on a farm, but when I was eighteen I worked on the river docks for a while."

"Okay, you'll do. Follow me." The man started down the small workers' gangplank. He called over his shoulder, "My name's Smitty."

"Yes, sir," Alf replied with a grin as he grabbed his carpetbag. He followed Smitty to a huge warehouse across the street from the dock. A group of men sitting around stopped their conversation as Smitty and Alf entered the wide door.

"All right, men, the *Texas Star* is ready to unload, so let's get to work. Rig up the lifts and get that cargo on the dock."
Laughing and talking, the men jumped up and began to move, grabbing gloves and ropes and cargo nets. Alf watched for a second, then dropped his bag and rushed to help one of the men lift a huge net.

"Wait a minute, boy, what's your name?" Smitty asked.

"Alf Smith, sir."

Smitty spoke to an older, heavyset man with steel-gray hair. "Otto, keep Alf with you for a while and show him what to do." He turned to Alf. "Otto is the foreman. Just do whatever he tells you."

Otto turned to Alf. "They got enough help on that net." He pointed to a man sorting through a pile of coiled ropes. "I'll put your bag in the office. You go over there and help carry the ropes."

"Yes, sir,"
Alf hurried over to the ropes. He grabbed one of them, flung it over his shoulder, and reached for another.

"Take it easy, boy, don't kill yourself the first day," drawled a tall and extremely thin young man. He spat a brown stream onto the dusty floor. "Just follow me and I'll show you the ropes." Slim picked up the coil that Alf already had his hand on. He hesitated, and then grinned as he held up the rope in front of Alf's face. "You get it? I'm showing you the ropes."

Alf frowned for a few seconds, then grinned too as he understood what the man was saying. He followed the thin man out the warehouse door toward the ship. "My name's Alf. What's yours?"

"I'll give you one guess."

"It's got to be Slim or Skinny," Alf replied. "I'll say Skinny."

"Nope, you're wrong. It's Slim, Slim Phillip. But you can call me Slim."

"Okay, Slim." Alf followed him up the gangplank to where Otto was already rigging up the crane to the net. The foreman turned to Slim.

"Slim, you and the boy get down in the hold and spread out the net. We'll unload the hogsheads first, then the crates."

Alf followed Slim down into the cargo hold, where another man was already spreading out the net. He was a stocky young man of medium height, with heavily muscled arms. A thatch of tow-colored hair topped a heavily bristled and mustached face. Like Alf and Slim, he wore denim trousers and a cotton shirt, but unlike them he was barefoot.

"That there's Billy Karl," Slim said as he reached down for the net. "He's one of them square heads who came over here from Germany."

Billy glared at Slim. "I keep telling you, I was born here in Texas, which is more than you were. And besides that, my folks came from Austria, not Germany."

Slim winked at Alf. "It's all the same to me. And I heared him speak German."

Billy shook his head. "Just get to work before we both get fired. I don't know about you, but I need this job."

Alf and Slim pulled the net into position to be loaded, and then Slim showed Alf how to roll the hogsheads into it. It wasn't long before they had four of the huge barrels ready to be hoisted. The donkey engine began to pull the ropes, and three men guided the net into place as it tightened around the barrels. Then, with lines tied to the net, they guided the load through the hold door. As soon as the cargo net was out of the hold, another net was thrown down and the three men began filling it again with the hogshead barrels. Later they loaded the crates and boxes. For the next eight hours and well into the night, they toiled until finally the ship was unloaded.

Alf was relieved when Otto hollered down for them to come up to the deck. He hadn't worked this hard in a long time. Farm work was hard, but at least he could stop and rest when he was tired.

The three men made their way to the deck and helped coil the ropes and fold up the nets, then carried everything back to the warehouse, where Smitty was waiting for them.

"Okay, men, good job. Get a good night's rest and be here at the usual time in the morning. We have another ship to unload tomorrow."

Most of the men laughed and talked as they hurried out the door, apparently in a hurry to get somewhere. Others lingered as they piddled with their lunch pails and tool packs. Alf retrieved his bag and started to move toward the door, then realized he had nowhere to go. He looked around for Slim and Billy and saw them over by the door, talking to one another. Billy noticed Alf looking at him and motioned for him to come over.

"Alf, we were wondering if you had a place to stay."

"No, I didn't have time to find anything. I guess I'll just sleep down on the beach somewhere."

"You don't want to do that, Alf. It could be dangerous," Slim said seriously as he shook his head. "There's a lot of bad men in Galveston who would cut your throat for your clothes."

Alf frowned as the thought of someone cutting his throat while he slept entered his mind. "What do you boys think I should do? I'm open to any ideas."

Slim was the first to speak. "We're staying at Otto's bunkhouse. He charges two bits a night for a bunk and two meals. The foods all right and the bunks are clean."

"Yeah, it ain't nothing fancy but it's all we need," Billy added, as his face stretched out in a wide grin.

Alf hesitated. "I guess that would be okay, but I don't even know what I'm being paid."

Billy frowned. "Smitty always pays two dollars a day unless you're good at something, and then he pays a little more."

Alf did some quick math in his head. "That would leave me a dollar and six bits a day for other things. I think I'm going to like this job. Come with me to talk to Otto."

Alf stopped when Slim put his arm on his shoulder. "Just wait a minute. Otto don't like to be interrupted when he's talking with the boss."

"Oh. Thanks, Slim, I didn't think of that." He hesitated as he looked at Slim and Billy. Alf was usually a loner and wasn't quick to trust strangers, but the two men had been friendly with him all day and he liked them. "I want to thank you boys for all the help you have given me today. I really appreciate it. I was feeling pretty lonely and unsure of myself when I got here today, but you two have really made me feel welcome."

"Ah, 'weren't nothing, Alf." Slim cocked his head. "We have been in the same situation. I was raised over on a farm in Nacogdoches, and I came here looking for work because I didn't want to do no farming. Besides that, I wanted to see the ocean."

"Same with me." Billy spat a stream of tobacco. "I was born over in Schulenburg, a little town about halfway to San Antonio. By the time I was eighteen, I was ready to leave and see other parts of Texas."

Alf looked at the two young men, seeing them in a different way. They were much like him, searching for something new, something different and exciting to make their lives worth living. The only difference was he was looking for his parents' murderers. "I still appreciate you boys helping me. I hope I can return the favor someday. And I hope we can be friends."

Billy grinned as he stuck out his hand. "I'd be glad to be your friend, Alf."

Alf felt some of the weight lift from his shoulders as he shook hands with Billy and Slim. The cloak of loneliness lifted from his body and he relaxed.

"What are you boys up to? I hope you two yahoos ain't planning on taking Alf out and getting him into trouble."

Alf turned to see that Otto had walked up behind him. "No, boss, we were just talking about finding me a place to stay. Slim and Billy said that you may be able to help me out."

Otto smiled. "That's what I came over to talk to you about. Did the boys tell you about my bunkhouse?"

"Yes, sir. They said you charge two bits a night for a place to sleep and two meals a day. Do you have a bunk for me?"

"Sure do. But you boys need to hurry on over there before the beans get cold. Slim, take him to the bunkhouse and find him a bed. I got to stay here with the night watchman to help lock things up."

"Yes, sir." Slim turned to Alf and nodded toward the door. "Come on, boys, I'm hungry."

"Thank you, sir," Alf said to Otto as he turned to follow Slim and Billy. Slim led the way up a warehouse-lined street away from the docks, where the main part of Galveston was built. They had only gone two blocks when Slim turned down a side street lined with large houses and white picket fences. The street was dark and Alf was startled when a dog barked as it ran up to the fence at one of the houses. More dogs joined in until all the dogs on the street were in the cacophony. Billy and Slim didn't even seem to notice, but Alf was nervous. He hoped the canine guardians stayed behind their fences. Farther down the street he saw lit-up buildings and hoped they'd reach them soon. But then Slim stopped unexpectedly and opened the white picket gate of the next house on the street. Out of the darkness a huge, growling mastiff came running toward them. Alf reached into his bag for his pistol but paused when Slim held out his hand to the dog. The huge canine sniffed Slim's hand for a minute, and then began to lick it. Slim patted the dog's wrinkled head and moved past him toward the house. Alf watched as Billy went through the same ritual, then stepped aside as he motioned to Alf. Slowly Alf approached and held out his hand. The dog sniffed and a low growl issued from his mouth.

Billy quickly patted the dog and spoke softly to calm him. "It's okay Bruno. He's one of us so make friends."

"Pet him, Alf," Billy added in a low voice.

Alf slowly lifted his hand and lightly stroked Bruno's head. "Good boy. Let's be friends." He continued to pet Bruno for a few more moments. Suddenly the mastiff heard another dog bark somewhere down the street and he raced to the side fence with a loud, gruff bellow. The men watched for a minute. Then Billy latched the gate and Slim led them to a huge, barnlike building behind the house. They went through a side door into a large room. Small, single bunks lined the walls, except on one end where there was a counter, shelves loaded with dinnerware, and a huge cast-iron cook stove. A hand pump sat on one end of the counter over a large wash pan. Four men were sitting at a huge table that took up half of the center of the room next to the counter.

"What took you boys so long?" one of the men called out as the three men entered. Alf recognized him from the warehouse. He was a short, husky man with huge, hairy arms and a black beard and mustache that covered most of his face. A full head of curly black hair hung down to his shoulders.

"We were waiting for Alf to see Otto so he could get a bunk," Slim drawled. "I hope you boys left us some beans."

"You know Bear. He would eat them all if we let him," one of the other men answered. He was an older man, somewhere in middle age and clean-shaven except for a long handlebar mustache perched under a long, thin nose. He was taller than Bear but not as tall as Slim, close to Billy's height.

"I don't eat any more than you do, Harrison," Bear responded as he glared at Harrison.

"Truth is, I've had to keep both of 'em out of the bean pot while we waited on you guys," remarked another man at the table. Alf could see that he was short man of medium build, with light hair cut short and no facial hair. A smile covered his round face as he talked.

"Thanks, Herman, we appreciate it." Billy remarked. He nodded at Alf and Slim. "Let's sit down before these guys starve to death."

Alf sat down next to Billy. On his other side sat a small, dark man who looked like he might be part Indian. Alf stuck out his hand. "My name's Alf Smith."

The man looked at Alf's hand for a second and then grasped it. "Roberto Rodriquez, but you can call me Rod." He picked up a plate of what Alf thought were thin flapjacks. "Have some of these tortillas."

Alf took two of them suspiciously, and then Slim passed him some kind of squishy beans he had never seen before. He spooned some onto his plate, along with a big helping of diced potatoes.

Slim told him they'd been fried with lard in a flat pan. One of the men, Harrison, set a mason jar of tea in front of him. Alf slowly tasted the strange food and found out it was good. He quickly wolfed it down, then got seconds when Slim prodded him to take more. Alf had never tasted food like this at home when he was growing up.

As the men settled down to eat, they also talked, and Alf learned a little bit about each of them. Bear's real name was Bob Gilmore and he was from Alabama. Harrison was from Kentucky but had moved his family to northern Texas. He was working in Galveston for a while because he needed the money to keep his farm going. Herman Schmidt was also working at the docks temporarily to earn money, but he was saving it to buy a farm in Bell County. Rob was born in San Antonio. His was one of the original families Spain had sent from the Canary Islands to Texas.

Alf told them a little about himself, where he was from and about his parents dying in the fire. He didn't tell them he was looking for their killers. Later, after they had finished eating, he picked out one of the empty bunks and hung his clothes in a small open closet built next to it. It also had shelves for his other things. When he pulled his gun belt and pistol from his bag, all the men had to take a look at it.

"That's a nice pistol, Alf," Slim said as he examined it. "I like those new Colts. I still have one of those old converted Colts but it shoots good."

"My stepfather gave this one to me for Christmas a few years ago. He was the county sheriff and he wanted me to learn to use it."

Billy took the pistol from Slim's hand. "Are you pretty good with it, Alf?"

"I do all right. I usually hit what I aim at if it ain't too far away." Alf took the pistol back. "I don't want to carry it while I'm working. Where can I find a safe place to keep it?"

"Otto can lock it up for you in his house or at the warehouse, whichever you want," Slim replied.

"I think I'll carry it to work and then lock it up." Alf stuck the Colt back in his holster. "You never know what you might run into out on the streets."

Alf and his new friends talked for a bit more and went to bed. Alf was ready. It had been a long day for him and he was tired. He washed up and lay down on his bunk just before someone turned down the lamps. At first Alf couldn't sleep; his body was still used to the motion of the river. But eventually his tired body relaxed and he fell into a deep sleep.

CHAPTER 10

The days passed swiftly and Alf grew comfortable with life in Galveston. There were a lot of ships to unload in the fast-growing city, and soon Alf was a seasoned hand at his job. He grew closer to Slim and Billy as the three men spent most of their free time together. He found out that both of them had sweethearts back home, and one day they were going home to marry them. One day he finally told them of his search for the Texas cowboys who had killed his parents. They both instantly volunteered to help but Alf told them no, he didn't want to put them in danger.

"I have to save my money to buy a horse and saddle first. This will be a long and dangerous hunt. One of the killers may be in Galveston, but I'm not quite ready to look for him yet."

It was the second week of December and the weather was clear and mild when Alf, Billy, and Slim decided to go to the strand one Saturday night and take in all the sights. Saloons and gambling houses lined the street, with their hucksters and soiled doves doing their best to draw in the customers. They stopped at a couple of places and drank a beer, which put them in a playful mood. They had just come out of one of the saloons when one of the soiled doves on the boardwalk caught Slim's attention and he stopped to talk to her. Slim always liked to joke around with the girls, but Alf had never seen him go to the crib with one. Slim said he was saving himself for his sweetheart back in Nacogdoches. The woman looked pretty, but under her powder and rouge Alf could see her flaws. She put her arms around Slim and rubbed his arm.

"Why don't you come on in and buy me a drink?" She puckered her lips. "Later I'll show you my room…or anything else you might want to see."

Slim grinned and winked at Alf. "Woo-ee, what are you going to show me, honey?"

Billy laughed and slapped Slim on the back. "Go on with her, Slim, she might give you some lessons on what to do on your honeymoon."

Alf smiled as he nudged Slim's shoulder. "What's she going to show you, Slim?"

Slim was just about to say something when a man walked up, grabbed the woman's arm, and jerked her so hard she almost fell to the boardwalk.

"You bitch; you have customers waiting for you inside." He turned and glared at Slim. "Quit fucking around with these kids and get inside where the men are waiting." He started to reach for the woman's arm again, but Slim stepped forward and slapped him on the shoulder. The man drew back his fist, but Slim was quick and hit him with an uppercut that knocked him to the ground. As Slim stood over him, another man walked out the saloon door. He was wearing fancy Western clothes and wearing a large Stetson hat. A pistol was strapped around his waist. He looked at Slim, then at the man on the boardwalk.

"What the hell is going on out here, Ace?"

The man on the boardwalk started to get up. "This scarecrow hit me when I wasn't looking, Duce. He was harassing the girl."

Alf had been calmly watching the scene unfold, ready to back Slim up, but when he heard the name Duce, his senses perked up. It was the name of one of the men Willy James had confessed was with him that day they murdered his parents. Alf's eyes shifted to Duce's boots, and suddenly memories flashed in his mind of the fancy boots the four cowboys had worn as they rode past him and the rest of the children on that fateful day. He remembered the big red star on their boots, and this man named Duce had the same stitching on the boots he wore now. They couldn't be the same boots—these were newer—but they looked the same. Alf unhooked the latch string from his pistol's hammer.

"Hey, Duce Rangle, that's a nice pair of boots you got there."

Duce turned toward Alf and a puzzled look replaced his glare. "How do I know you?"

Alf tensed. The man seemed to accept the name. The anger he had suppressed for so long began to rise, but he had to be sure. "I've heard about you. You were in the war with Jude Brown and Willy James. You all had those fancy boots."

"What's your name, boy? Who told you about me and my friends? You look like Stinky. Is he your pa?"

Alf stared at Duce, everything and everybody around him forgotten. This man was one of the four who had raped his mother and then killed her. This man had turned his life upside down, and he wasn't going to walk away. "No, Duce. My pa was murdered ten years ago by you and your friends. Then you set our house on fire. I saw you that day. You came riding by me on the road, with my father's sword and all the other things you stole."

Slim and Billy, who had stood silently, now began moving away from him. Ace slowly stood and backed away too, pulling the woman with him. At first she resisted, but a worried look replaced the pain on her face and she willingly stepped back beside him. Other people on the boardwalk began to notice. Some of them stopped to listen, and then they too backed away. Duce glanced around before he spoke again.

"That wasn't me," Duce replied, but when he looked into Alf's eyes, his face turned ashen. "I don't know your pa and I don't know you. Whoever told you it was me is a damn liar."

Alf's heart was racing but his mind was clear. "Willy James told me as he lay dying in a pool of his own blood. He knew he was dying and he asked me and God to forgive him for what he'd done." Alf hesitated. "I couldn't forgive him and I can't forgive you, Duce Rangle, so you'd better ask God to forgive you quick because I'm going to shoot you down like the cowardly dog that you are."

As Alf spoke, he took a few steps back into the street. The crowd that had gathered around the two men quickly scrambled to get out of the line of fire. One woman screamed and another fainted.

Duce's nose flared and his face turned from pale to red. He leaned forward and grabbed for his pistol. When Alf saw Duce's hand move, he quickly went for his own gun.

Boom, boom, boom! Gun smoke billowed into the space between the two dueling men. Duce stood holding his gun, but it was pointing down. Slowly his legs folded and he sank to the ground. As he lay on his back, two blood-gushing holes were visible on his fancy shirt.

Alf watched him for a few minutes. He felt a small surge of satisfaction, but with it came guilt at what he'd done to achieve it. Would God forgive him? He thought of the Bible verse: "Vengeance is mine, sayeth the Lord."

Something touched his shoulder and he quickly turned, raising his gun. He stopped when he saw it was Billy's hand. Alf holstered his pistol as he glanced around at the crowd. Slim was beside him now too.

"Let's get out of here before the law comes," Alf said to his friends, almost in a whisper.

"Too late," Slim warned. "There's a policeman just walking up." The three men turned and faced the policeman as he walked over to the bleeding body lying on the boardwalk. He examined the body for a few minutes and cut his eyes to Ace, who was standing next to him.

"What happened here? Ace?"

Ace pointed at Alf. "That man shot Duce. He started the fight and then killed him."

The policeman addressed the woman beside Ace. "What did you see?"

"I didn't see nothing."

"Can anyone else tell me what happened?" the policeman asked the crowd.

"I can." A man stepped forward. "It was a fair fight. Duce pulled his gun first. The kid had to shoot him in self-defense."

"The kid was goading him," Ace shouted. "He called Duce a murderer!"

The policeman cocked his head at Ace and pursed his lips slightly. Ace paused and then blurted, "Ain't nobody ever proved Duce killed anybody."

The policeman walked over to Alf. "Did you shoot this man?"

"Yes, sir. He went for his gun and I had to go for mine to defend myself."

"Why did he go for his gun?"

Alf thought for a second. "It's a long story, sir, but the gist of it is I found out he was one of the men who killed my parents ten years ago, and as I called him on it, he went for his pistol."

The policeman started to speak but someone called his name. He turned as another policeman and a man in civilian clothes walked up.

"You got everything under control, Murphy?"

"Yes, Judge Turner, we just need to get all the facts straight," Murphy replied. "This man shot Duce Rangle, the man lying over there on the boardwalk, but he says it was self-defense. Ace Rangle says this man goaded him into drawing."

"Cuff him to that post over there until we get this all cleared up. I'll go see if I can pronounce Duce dead." Judge Turner knelt by the body and Murphy pulled out his handcuffs.

"Come on, boy, I got to cuff you to this post." He slapped one end of the cuffs onto Alf's arm.

"I understand, sir," Alf said as he followed Murphy. "I was a deputy sheriff back in Illinois."

"You were, huh? Well, I guess you know I need to take your gun," Murphy said. Then he noticed that Slim and Billy were following. "Are these men your friends?"

"Yes, sir. We work together down at the docks."

Murphy turned to Billy, who was closest to him. "Take his gun and put it in your belt, lad. It'll look better that way. You two just stay with him while I question some of the other witnesses."

Alf couldn't help but worry about how much trouble he had got himself into. He could see the two policemen talking to some of the onlookers, but he couldn't hear what they were saying. The judge came over once and asked him a few questions, but he didn't tell Alf anything. A funeral wagon came to pick up Duce's body. Ace got up by the driver and they left. A swamper came out of the saloon and cleaned up the blood. When he gathered up his bucket and rags, several customers followed him back inside. Finally the two policemen and Judge Turner walked over to Alf. Murphy took one of the handcuffs off Alf and cuffed it to one of his own hands.

"We're going down to the station to settle this." He turned to Slim and Billy. "You boys can come too."

A couple of blocks later, they arrived at the city hall. Judge Turner led the group into his office and asked Murphy to close the door. He sat down at his desk and looked at Alf.

"How old are you, son?"

"I'm twenty-one, sir."

"Where are you from?"

"Clark County, Illinois, sir."

"Tell me what happened to your parents."

Alf told the judge about the murder of his parents and the four cowboys from Texas.

"Did you see them do this?"

"No, sir."

"How do you know that these men did this to your parents?"

"One of the men was carrying a sword like the one my father got in the war. When we sifted through the ashes, the sword wasn't there. Also, all of our dishes and things made from silver were missing."

"That still doesn't prove that they did it. That might have been a different sword."

"Your Honor, I still wasn't sure myself so I decided to come down here and see if I could find the men."

"How did you know where to look?"

"That's another part of the story. On my way to Texas, I stopped in the town of Greenville, Illinois. I told my story to the local sheriff and his deputy. During the night I heard someone come into my room. I rolled out of bed just before he fired, and I shot him. Turns out it was the deputy, and he was one of the four men who killed my parents. When he heard me telling my story earlier that day, he panicked and decided to kill me. Afterward, as he lay dying on the floor, he asked me to forgive him. He told me the whole story. I know all their names and where they might be."

Judge Turner considered this. "Mr. Smith, can the sheriff verify your story?"

"Yes, sir, he heard the whole story."

Judge Turner paused for a few minutes and then wrote something on a sheet of paper on his desk. He looked at Alf. "I'm going to rule this shooting self-defense, Mr. Smith, but I want you out of my town. Galveston is a modern, growing city and we don't need vigilantes running around the streets. Usually one killing leads to another. I want you out of town before Ace decides to kill you or pay someone else to do it. If you're still in town tomorrow night, I'll have you arrested."

Alf smiled at first, and then frowned as he listened to the judge's ruling. He felt relieved that he wasn't going to jail, but he hated to lose his job and his friends. He would miss Galveston. "Thank you, Judge. I'll go pack my things." He looked sadly at his friends. "Come on, guys, let's get out of here."
They headed for the door but stopped when the judge called Alf's name.

"Alf, you seem like a smart young man. Don't let your anger rule your life. These men will get their punishment in hell."

Alf looked into the judge's eyes. "Yes, they will, sir. And I mean to put them there as quick as I can." He took a deep breath and walked out the door.

CHAPTER 11

High up on a rocky, cedar-covered hill, Jude Brown watched as his two brothers drove a small herd of scraggly longhorns out of the brush and into a small box canyon. Blinking from the sweat in his eyes, he pulled off his bandana and wiped his brow. Despite being December, a warm front had moved into central Texas and he was sweating like it was July. All the dust stirred up by the milling cattle didn't help matters. He looked at his sweat- and dirt-stained bandana with disgust and then tied it back around his neck. Spurring his mount, he urged him down a rocky trail to the bottom of the draw.

Jimbo was the first to see him coming out of the trees. His yellow teeth flashed in a grin as he glanced over at Bojack, who was helping him close the gap in the crudely built cedar fence.

"Well, look who found his way back," he said loudly enough for Jude to hear him. "We thought you might have gotten lost, big brother."

"Yeah, what'd you do, Jude, find you a pretty little calf to make love to?"

Jude stared at Bojack until he got off his horse. "I don't need calves like you do, Bojack. I have a wife." He looked at the cattle in the pen. "This all you could find?"

Jimbo spat. "Yeah, that's all. How about you? You find any on your side of the ridge?"

"No, just a few droppings about a month old." Jude leaned down and lifted his horse's hoof. "I went all the way to the Leon. Somebody built a cabin over there and done plowed up a field."

Bojack slapped at a fly on his face. "I think we need to move somewhere else. We done got about all the cows that were here." He looked at his hand and rubbed it on his britches.

Jude stared at his youngest brother. For once he agreed with him. The cedar brakes west of Waco were about played out. "Let's get these scrubs back to the ranch, boys. Maybe we need to go farther west—maybe farther on up the Leon."

The three brothers mounted their horses and opened the gate. Jude rode in and drove the longhorns out as Jimbo and Bojack waited to point them in the right direction. It was a good twenty miles to their ranch house and it would be dark when they arrived.

Boss, their Judas steer, headed for home and the scrub longhorns crowded in behind him. It wasn't hard for the men to herd them then. Boss had made the trip several times and knew where a bucket of corn was waiting. Jude stayed up front to make sure Boss didn't get curious about anything, and his brothers took the sides. The driving was a little rough at first, but when they come out of the cedar brakes into the prairie, the going got easier. The sun was just going down when they locked the small herd in a holding pen. Tomorrow they would brand them and geld the calves.

Jude left his brothers to finish up and went into the house to hear the latest news from town. They had been gone for three days and he wanted a bath and a change of clothes.

Martha, his wife, was waiting for him in the kitchen. She held a mason jar full of tea as he entered the gray clapboard ranch house. She was a tall, slim woman dressed in a dark brown dress and with her hair pulled back in a bun. Her face was pretty but sullen as she handed Jude his tea.

Jude pecked her cheek, took the tea, and sat down in one of the high-backed chairs at the table. He took a long drink of the strong dark liquid. "Anything happen since I've been gone?"

Martha picked up a pouch from the counter. "I got your tobacco." She placed the pouch on the table in front of him. "And you got a letter." She turned back to the counter and pulled an envelope from a shelf. She handed it to him, then stepped back and watched him open it.

Jude's eyebrows lifted as he took the letter. He stared at it for a moment, and then hastily opened it. He blinked as he read the scrawled words.

Jude,
A young man claiming to be the son of a farmer in in Illinois claims that you and Duce, Stinky, and Willy James killed his parents ten years ago and then burned their house. He claims he shot Willy James and Willy told him everything before he died. He outdrew Duce and killed him here in Galveston. He's headed your way, so be ready. He's young but he's fast. His name is Alf Smith.

Sincerely,
Ace Rangle

Jude rubbed his ear and read the letter again. He felt sweat bead on his brow as images of the killing and burning appeared in his mind. He furrowed his brow, remembering an image of the children he'd passed on the road that day. Suddenly his lip curled and he pounded the table with his fist. "That son of a bitch!" He looked up at Martha. "Has anyone been around here looking for me?"

Martha's eyes opened wide. "No. What's this all about?"

Jude's gaze drifted to a sword hanging over the fireplace. Something seemed caught in his throat and he swallowed. "A man is looking for me. He thinks I killed some of his family and he wants to kill me." Jude brought the jar to his lips and drank the last of his tea. He stood up and began pacing the floor. "If any strangers come around here, don't tell them anything."

"What are you going to do, Jude? Are you going to tell the sheriff?"

Jude's mind whirled with possible answers. "Pack me some clothes and food, Martha. Me and Jimbo are going to my brother's place in Tascosa."

CHAPTER 12

Alf opened his eyes Monday morning, tired from the nightmares that had invaded his sleep. Groggily he stumbled over to the coffeepot and filled a tin cup. He grimaced as he sipped the hot, bitter liquid and quickly added a little cream to it. After a few more gulps, he felt a little better and his thoughts turned to the new job Otto had found for him with a freight company.

Saturday night, when Alf had returned to the bunkhouse, Otto was still awake. Alf related to him what had happened and what the judge had told him. Otto said he was sorry to lose Alf, but leaving town was probably the best thing for him. He would talk to the judge and see if Alf could stay until Monday. In the meantime he would try to find a job for Alf on one of the freight outfits that worked out of their warehouse. The judge agreed to let Alf stay until Monday, but he would have to stay in the bunkhouse and not go to town. Otto talked to some of the freighters and found one who would give Alf a job. This morning Alf was leaving on a freight wagon heading east to Houston and beyond.

"Pour me a cup of that coffee, Alf."

Billy was slowly getting up from his bed. It was five o'clock and the crew had a ship to unload. Alf grabbed another cup and filled it.

"You want your usual four spoons of sugar?"

"Make it five. I need the energy." Billy stumbled over to the table and Alf handed him the sweetened coffee. "I'm going to miss you, Alf. Slim won't fix my coffee for me."

"Maybe if you sweet-talk him he might."

"No, I won't," Slim said drowsily from his bed. He pulled back his covers and swung his legs to the floor. "I hate Monday mornings." He picked up his overalls and slipped one leg in. As he stood, he attempted to stick his other leg in. Alf and Billie looked at one another and laughed. The night before, after Slim was asleep, Billy had put a knot in one of the pant legs, and now Slim was hopping around trying to get his leg in it.

"What the hell?" Slim fell on the floor. "Durn your hide, Billy, I know you did it!" He undid the knot and slipped his leg in. Billy and Alf were still laughing as Slim finished dressing, but Billy poured him a cup of coffee and handed it to him. Slim frowned and sipped it suspiciously. "This ain't going to work, Billy. I'll get you back."

The conversation ended when Otto came into the bunkhouse with a large pan of biscuits. "Time to eat, boys," he said, and set them on the table. Harrison followed with a platter of eggs and set them next to the biscuits. Billy grabbed a plate and a fork and hurried to the table, followed closely by Bear and Herman. Roberto, Slim, and Alf joined them as fast as they could, and soon all were busy feeding their faces.

"I'm going to be tagging along with you, Alf," Harrison said between a bite of biscuit and a drink of coffee.

"Are you going to work for the freight line too?"

"Just until we get to Belton. I'm going to help drive and I get a free ride home with meals."

"I thought you were going to take the train to Temple," Bear said with a mouth full of food.

"Hell, no, they wanted five dollars to ride that train. That's two days' pay!"

The men laughed, but as breakfast continued they settled down to quiet talk and finished eating. Soon it was time to go to work. Alf and Harrison, carrying all their belongings, trudged along with the others to the dock. When they got to the warehouse, several freight wagons were waiting in the yard to be loaded. Alf waved to his friends again as they went inside the warehouse to load up their gear. Alf had assured them he would see them again when the freight wagon came back to pick up another load, but he wasn't certain he would ever come back. He would miss his friends, but his desire for revenge was still strong in his mind and he would see it through. Maybe if he survived, he could settle down here.

Harrison nudged Alf and began walking toward to one of the freight wagons where a middle-aged man was talking to Smitty. He looked well fed, with a beer belly bulging from the front of his overalls. A trainman's hat covered his thin red hair, and a red mustache grew under his long, straight nose. Smitty turned when he saw them coming and said something to the man. They both waited for Alf and Harrison.

"Alf, Harrison," Smitty said, nodding toward the man. "This is the man you two will be working with. He'll show you what to do." He shook Harrison's hand, then Alf's. "Men, I hate to lose you, but I understand why you are leaving." He handed them each an envelope with their name on it. "Here's the pay you got coming. When you boys get ready, just come on back. I'll find a place for you." He turned to the man. "I'll see you when you get back, Mike." Smitty turned and headed for the ship, where his men were waiting for him.

Alf stuck out his hand to the driver. "I'm Alf Smith and this is Harrison Roberts. We're your new helpers. What do you want us to do?"

"Mike Talley," the man replied. He shook their hands and pointed at some wooden crates with "Remington" stenciled on the side. "Bring me those crates. Be careful, that's ammunition. When I get them stacked, bring the ten crates of canned goods next to them."

Alf and Harrison hurried over to the boxes and began bringing them to Mike, who had climbed into the wagon. He began stacking the boxes in the front of the wagon. Alf and Harrison quickly carried all the ammunition to the wagon, then began on the canned goods. Next they loaded the barrels of pickles and crackers. Last to go on were the wooden boxes of hardware. The wagon was huge and had high sideboards, but Mike was quick and knew how he wanted to place his load. An hour later the freight wagon was loaded and secured.

"Okay, men, put your things under the seat and let's go." Mike climbed into the driving seat. Alf and Harrison got in beside him and they headed toward the ferry.

As Alf gazed upon the island from the seat of the wagon, he wondered if he would ever see Galveston or the ocean again. He had grown used to the odor of the salty air and the sea gulls flying overhead. He enjoyed walking along the beach, looking for things that came from the sea.

"I'm going to miss this place, Harry."

"Not me. Too many people in one place. I need my space."

"I agree with you on that, but I like the ocean."

"I like the ocean too, but I wouldn't want to live here by it—too much noise from the waves." Harrison spat out a wad of tobacco. "And it's too flat. I like the hill country."

"There's the ferry," Mike interrupted.

Alf turned to see a large boat coming into the dock, carrying a wagon and several people. They waited for it to unload and then Mike urged the six mules onto the slowly rocking boat. Two other wagons and several people followed them on and they slowly made their way across the bay. Alf was glad it was a calm day. He had never had any trouble on the large riverboats, but the smaller ones sometimes made him sick if the waves were high. The trip seemed long but finally they docked and Mike drove the wagon into the main street in Texas City. The first stop was another warehouse, where they unloaded some of the goods and loaded others. Mike explained that they would be traveling west all the way to Belton, stopping at some of the small towns along the way to deliver orders from stores in those towns. It was noon when they left Texas City. Alf got a last look at the ocean as they topped a small hill a few miles from the coast. He wondered if he would ever see it again.

His thoughts were interrupted when Mike asked Harrison a question.

"Where're you from, Harrison, if you don't mind me asking? You have a peculiar way of talking."

Harrison laughed. "I come from Crab Orchard, Kentucky. I sold out my farm in seventy-eight and brought my family to Texas."

"Did you settle in Bell County?"

"No, I farmed for a while up above Fort Worth in Collin County." Harrison paused. "Buried my mother there. Later I bought some land in Bell County. How about you, Mike, where are you from?"

"I was born over in East Texas, but I got family in Bell County. They own a lot of land on the Leon River."

Harrison scratched his head. "I think I heard about some Talleys down on the river. My place is over by Cow House Creek."

Alf had been silently listening to the conversation, but he perked up when Mike mentioned the Leon River. That was one of the rivers on the map the old hostler had given him. "Mike, do you know a lot about the Leon River?" he asked.

"I guess I know a little. I know it joins the Lampasas and turns into the Little River."

Alf thought for a second. "Have you ever heard of any buried gold in that area?"

"I hear a lot of buried treasure stories, but not in that particular place. Most of them are about Jim Bowie's lost gold mine over in Llano and San Saba Counties."

Alf cocked his head to one side and chewed his lip. "Well, I heard a story, but the treasure was supposed to be in a place where three rivers meet." Alf narrowed his eyes. He didn't want to sound too interested.

"Three rivers, huh? Well, there's Salado Creek that comes in just a little ways above where the Leon and the Lampasas meet. It's a pretty big creek." He paused. "What story did you hear about the three rivers, Alf?"

Alf took a deep breath. "I heard that someone buried some gold down close to where the three rivers come together, but I don't see how anyone could find it without a map."

"Yeah, that's a big area to just start digging holes. But sometimes they leave a sign or something on a tree."

"I heard tell they would carve symbols on the tree to tell you where the treasure was and how far to dig to get it," Harrison added, then spat out of thc side of the wagon.

Alf thought about what the two men had said and remembered that the map mentioned a brass stake in a tree. Maybe someday he would go look for that brass spike. Right now he wished they would get to the next town.

It was late afternoon when they pulled into to the small bayou town of Houston. They unloaded a small order of horseshoes with the blacksmith and camped out at the town wagon yard. The weather had been pleasant during the day, but with night coming it was beginning to cool down. Alf wondered if Mike had brought plenty of blankets. The campsite had a fire pit with cordwood stored beside it. Harrison and Alf got a small fire started and unharnessed the mules while Mike cooked beans and potatoes for their supper. After they ate, Mike and Harrison decided to go over to the saloon for a beer. Alf was full and sleepy, so he laid his bedroll under the wagon and went to sleep.

The next morning, as soon as it was light enough to see, they were already on the road. Breakfast had been leftovers from the night before, plus two eggs apiece from the local store. They rolled into

Hempstead in the early afternoon and unloaded an order at the general store. Mike got some crackers, cheese, and sausage for their lunch, which they ate on their way to Brenham. It was almost dark when they arrived, but the mercantile was still open and they unloaded their order in the light of kerosene lanterns. The wagon yard was located behind the store, so they didn't have far to go to unhitch the mules. Harrison and Alf rubbed down the tired animals, penned them in the corral, and fed them. Mike built the fire and had supper going by the time Alf and Harrison were through. They sat around the fire and ate, and Mike brought up the subject of gold mines and lost treasure. He told them all the stories he had heard and asked them if they had heard any. Harrison told of a few he had heard in Kentucky, but he hadn't heard any in Texas. Alf didn't know of any buried treasure in Illinois, but he told them some of the stories about Jesse James. Finally he grew sleepy.

"I don't know about you men, but I'm tired. I'm going to get my bedroll and get some sleep."

"Yeah, me too," Harrison said as he got to his feet. "Five o'clock comes mighty early."

Mike laughed. "I bet both of you dream about buried treasure." He got his bedroll from the wagon and joined them.

The next morning there was a chill in the air as Harrison guided the mules onto the gravel road that would take them to Caldwell. It was over forty miles and would take a day to get there. Alf sat with Harrison on the driver's seat. Mike had made himself a pallet on top of the load and crawled back into it as soon as he was sure Harrison was doing his job. Alf looked back at Mike, and then closed the top button on his coat.

"I don't see how he can sleep back there with all this jerking and bouncing."

"I guess he's used to it. He's been doing this for a long time. I hope I get my chance to sleep back there later."

Alf crossed his arms and held them close to his body. "I just wish it would warm up some."

A half hour later the sun rose from behind the trees bordering the road and Alf began to warm up. He thought of how cold it got in Illinois around Christmas. Suddenly he remembered it was December.

"Harrison, do you know what the date is?"

"Yep, today is the December fifteenth."

"Dang. It'll be Christmas in ten days." Alf frowned. "I ain't never been away from home on Christmas."

"I was once, during the war," Harrison replied softly. He paused as if in deep thought. "I know how sad that can be. That's why I'm going home to be with my family."

Alf was quiet. Even with Jake, Christmas had been a special time. They usually went out to the Higgins's to eat Christmas dinner. Alf would buy gifts for Charley and his sisters, and they always had something for him. He was going to miss being there.

"I don't know where I'll be this Christmas," Alf said.

"You can come and have Christmas with us. We'd be glad to have you."

Suddenly their conversation was interrupted as a small, one-horse carriage passed them in a cloud of dust.

"Road hog!" shouted a small, pencil-thin man as he passed them. He spoke to a young girl sitting beside him, then popped his whip and pulled in front of the freight wagon just a few feet in front of the lead mules. Harrison looked at Alf and then at the carriage as it sped down the road ahead of them.

"Did you hear what he called me?"

"Yeah, he called you a road hog."

Both men laughed until Harrison almost choked on his wad of tobacco.

The rest of the day was uneventful, and at nightfall, Mike, who had taken over the driving after their noon meal in Somerville, pulled the team into the yard of the Caldwell general store. They unloaded several crates. Alf took care of the mules while Mike and Harrison went to the local saloon. Alf ate some cheese and crackers from the store for his supper and fixed his bedroll under the wagon. He was asleep when they returned, but he knew they must have stayed late because both of them were nursing headaches the next morning. After they hitched up the mules, Mike and Harrison crawled into the back and told Alf to take them to Cameron.

The weather stayed cool but the sun was shining and Alf enjoyed driving the wagon. The mules were well trained and traffic was sparse. Most of the countryside was wooded, with low hills and small streams. Farms were few and far between, mostly nestled close to a stream. Some of the cleared fields were fenced, but Alf saw huge unfenced fields too. He had asked Mike what they grew in those fields, and Mike explained to him about growing cotton. Once when they stopped, Alf walked to one such field where some of the cotton was still on the stalks. He examined one of the bolls and felt the seeds mixed in with the soft white fibers. He pulled one of the bolls and brought it to the wagon. Another time Mike showed him some pecan trees alongside the road and they stopped and gathered a bucket full of the tasty nuts. Alf found a hammer under the wagon seat, and he cracked and ate some of them as they traveled.

Alf also found out that there were a lot of strange plants and animals in Texas. The second day on the road, he saw an odd-looking critter with a hard shell covering its back. He asked Mike if it was a land turtle, and both Mike and Harrison laughed until they almost couldn't catch their breath. Finally they told him it was an armadillo. From then on, every time they saw one they would shout "land turtle," and both would laugh again. Another time a huge rabbit sat in the road looking at them. They were almost upon it before it took off down the road with speed Alf had never seen before in a rabbit. It was his first look at a Texas jackrabbit.

Alf was still in the driver's seat when they reached the small settlement of Milano. A couple of men sitting on the porch of the general store, smoking their pipes, and they waved when Alf directed the mules into the yard. Mike climbed out of the back with his order book in hand, checking to see which crates went to the store. Then Harrison and Alf carried them into the store. When they had the order unloaded, Mike bought stuff for lunch from the store. They moved the wagon out to the yard and parked it under a large oak. After they took care of the mules, they ate under the huge tree. They let the mules rest awhile longer and then hitched them back up to the wagon. With Mike driving, they headed west again.

There was still daylight left when they reached the Little River. An old wooden bridge that looked like it had seen better days spanned the muddy water. Mike stopped the wagon and all three men walked out on the bridge, testing the wooden planks every few feet. Satisfied, Mike got back in the wagon and started the mules across. Harrison and Alf walked ahead of it, looking for weak spots. Alf could feel the bridge shake as the heavy wagon rolled across the weathered planks. He was a little worried but he figured Mike knew what he was doing. Finally he reached the other side and waited for the wagon. They all breathed a sigh of relief as it cleared the bridge and rolled onto the solid bank. Harrison and Alf climbed back in and Mike started the mules.

A few miles later, Alf began to see small farms alongside the road, and then just houses with only enough room for a garden and some livestock. Soon they passed a blacksmith shop and a train station. Mike told Alf they only had one delivery to make in Cameron because a lot of the freight was carried by train now, and his company only served the outlying settlements far from the train routes. The Santa Fe Railroad had reached Cameron last year, and already a wholesaler was operating out of the growing town. Mike had never told them where the delivery was, so Alf was surprised when Mike stopped the team in front of the local funeral parlor.

Harrison frowned. "What the hell are you stopping here for?"

"Formaldehyde—they ordered a case of it. It's that big crate on the floor by the barrels."

Alf and Harrison followed Mike, carrying the big crate into the building. A man wearing a leather apron walked in from another room.

"Finally! I've been waiting for that." He motioned for them to follow him. "Bring it in here."

Alf felt his stomach churn as the smell in the room penetrated his nose. The body of a man lay on a metal bench. He almost gagged.

"Set it right here."

Alf could hardly wait to leave the room. He rushed outside with Harrison right behind him.

"Whew, what a smell! I thought I was going to throw up."

Harrison laughed. "That ain't nothing. During the war I was assigned to grave digging. You should've seen and smelled some of the bodies we had to bury. Some of them were days old and we had to pick 'em up with a blanket."

"How could you stand to do it?"

"It was hard but I got used to it after a while. But when my enlistment was up I went home."

"You didn't fight anymore?"

"No, I'd had enough of war. It's not as exciting as everyone thinks it is."

Alf thought about the people he had killed—the man who'd broken out of the jail, Billy James, Duce Randle. No, killing wasn't exciting, but his quest to find the men who killed his parents wasn't about excitement, it was about justice. It was something he had to do.

Mike was also gagging when he came out of the parlor. He quickly climbed onto the wagon and popped his whip to start the mules.

"I've got to have a whiskey to get this smell out of my nose," he said as he pulled up in front of a saloon. He handed the reins to Alf and climbed down. "The wagon yard is just down the road. You take care of the mules, then one of you can come get me and I'll round up some food for supper." He turned and went into the saloon.

They found the yard just a few blocks down the road. A young man met them at the gate. He was a tall, lanky kid around fourteen or fifteen years old. He motioned for them to drive on in, then walked up to the wagon on Alf's side.

"Where did you men come from?"

Alf grinned at the boy's question. "All the way from Galveston."

"Wow, I'd like to go to Galveston. That's where the ocean is, ain't it?"

"Yep, sure is." Alf looked around but didn't see anyone else. "Are you the yardmaster?"

"Yes, sir. Will Wiseman, at your service."

"Where can we park this wagon and camp for the night?"

"Pull over there by that tree. There's a fire pit and firewood already there."

Harrison pulled the wagon to the tree and Will showed them a small corral where they could put the mules. Alf filled the water trough while Will showed Harrison where to find some grain to feed them. When they finished, Harrison went to get Mike while Alf built a fire for cooking their meal. He had coffee made and some water on to boil by the time Mike and Harrison got back with the food.

"I got some news," Mike said when the meal was over and they were sitting around the fire. "The telegraph operator was in the saloon and he told me I had a telegram. He went to his office and got it. It said I won't be going back to Galveston. I'm going to operate out of Waco."

"Why are they changing your route?" Alf asked.

"Heidenheimer Brothers wholesalers built a new warehouse there. They get everything by train from Galveston, so I'm being transferred to Waco."

"Are we still going to Belton?"

"Yeah, we still have deliveries to Rogers and Belton. From there I go to Waco for another load. Are you going to stay with me, Alf?"

Alf thought a minute, then answered, "I guess so, Mike. For a while, anyway. I need to save some money."

"You got a job as long as you want it. You're a good hand."

"Thank you, Mike. I don't mind working. I'll stay with you as long as I can."

The next morning a cold north wind was blowing. It had rained sometime during the night but hardly enough to wet the ground. Alf wore his coat and had wrapped his scarf around his neck but the wind still cut into his body. Harrison was driving with a blanket wrapped around his legs to go along with his heavy sheepskin coat, but he too was feeling the cold. Mike had gone to the wagon bed again and was wrapped in all the extra blankets. Alf finally jumped down and walked alongside the wagon, hoping the exercise would help warm him up. They ate lunch in Buckholts at the store where they had to drop off a few small crates. They hung around, reluctant to leave, and Alf was able to rest by the big potbellied stove for a while, but eventually they had to go. When they pulled out again, he was driving; Harrison had gone to the back with Mike. It was late afternoon when they stopped at Rogers, and Mike arranged for them to eat supper at the store where they unloaded some of the crates. Mr. Hill, who owned the store, had a table over by the stove and he served them a bowl of hot chili and crackers. It was the first time Alf had eaten chili and he almost spat it out when he tasted the hot peppers in it. Mike laughed and handed him a glass of water. Alf gulped it down and wiped his lips.

"Wow, that stuff sure warms you up. I like the taste of it, though." Alf picked up his spoon and kept eating, but drank water after each bite. He finished his bowl and Mr. Hill offered him some more. "Thank you. This is pretty good stuff after you get past the heat."

Mr. Hill let them sleep in the store that night, then fed them breakfast the next morning. When they left Rogers, the wind wasn't blowing as hard and the temperature had risen. Mike was driving now and Alf was sitting with him. As they started down a hill just out of Rogers, Alf happened to notice some small hills off to the south.

"Those hills over there look out of place, Mike. What do they call them?"

"I don't know if they have a name. That's over close to Reed's Lake. A man named Reed settled over there on the Little River a long time ago."

Alf perked up at the mention of the Little River. "Is that close to where the three rivers come together to form the Little River?"

"No, the three rivers are about ten miles west. They call the place Three Forks."

Alf's heart began to beat faster as Mike spoke. The three rivers and the hills were right where the map showed them to be. The ten jack loads of gold were just sitting there waiting for someone to dig them up. He could see himself climbing the hill and digging up the gold that Steinheimer had buried on that fearful night. Then he would go to the river and find the rest of it. He would be rich! Anxiety gripped his heart. He was ready to jump off the wagon and race across the prairie to the hills, but he forced himself to calm down. The gold had been there for fifty years; it could wait a little longer.

He turned to Harrison, who had climbed into the back to lie down. "Harrison, do you know where I can buy a good horse? What would a good horse cost me?"

"You could get one down at the mule yard. All the traders gather there on Saturdays." He spat over the side of the wagon. "But you'd better know your horses if you want to buy one there. Them ol' boys will skin you if they can."

"I know some about horses. I had a good one when I left home, but he got stolen in Saint Louis."

"There's a man I know who's got a ranch west of my place. He's got some horses for sale. They might be a little green, but he's a God-fearing man—he won't cheat you."

"What will a good horse go for?"

"Anywhere from twenty to fifty dollars, I recollect." Harrison leaned over and spat again. "The green ones will be around twenty. If you can polish them out, that would be the way to go."

"I can do that. I trained Smokey to come when I whistled and to stand still when I dismounted."

"We can see about getting you a horse as soon as we get settled in back home."

"How long you been gone from home, Harrison?" Mike interrupted.

"I left right after harvest time last summer, about five months ago." Harrison turned back to Alf. "I got a saddle you can use until you can buy one."

"Thanks, Harrison, I appreciate it." Alf shifted his eyes to the hills in the distance once again. A few cattle grazed on the slopes. Just below them a hawk slowly circled a grassy field, looking for his next meal. Alf turned to Mike. "Does Mr. Reed still own all the land around here?"

"I think he does, but I could be wrong. I was told he runs cattle in the hills and farms the river valley."

The day was becoming warmer and Alf unbuttoned his coat as he scanned the hills, looking for more cattle. In his mind he could see himself riding his horse across the range and up the hill to where the gold was buried. Would Mr. Reed give him permission to look for the gold, or would he have to sneak in at night? Maybe he could get a job punching cattle for Reed. That way he could ride all over the place looking for the gold. When he found it, he would buy his own land and build a house and barn like his dad's. His chin began to tremble and his chest tightened as he thought of his mother and father. He turned his glistening eyes away from the hill to the road in front of him. He would wait before he looked for the buried treasure. He still had a score to settle, and he needed to keep working for Mike until he got settled in. Besides, he needed to ask around in Waco for Jude Brown, and working with Mike was the cheapest way to travel. The gold could wait.

CHAPTER 13

Jude paused just inside the saloon door and slowly looked around. A few of the patrons looked up at him but most went back to their drinking and poker playing. One of the men, his hat pulled down low over his eyes, slowly stood and walked toward him. Suddenly the room became quiet except for the ringing of the man's spurs and the rustling of his chaps. His hand hovered over a Colt hung low on his hips. Jude's hand inched down to his pistol, but he smiled when he recognized the man.

"Hello, Luke."

Luke grinned as he grabbed Jude around the shoulders. "We had 'em going there for a minute, didn't we?"

"Same old Luke. Always the joker."

"It's better than being a worrier like you." Luke cocked his head. "What brings you to Tascosa?"

"I'll tell you in a minute." Jude nodded toward an empty table in the corner. He had private business to discuss with his brother and he didn't want to be overheard. "First let's get a bottle and go over to that table where we can talk about it."

While Luke got the bottle, Jude claimed the table and sat down with his back to the wall. A few seconds later Luke arrived with a bottle and two glasses. He sat down and poured two shots of whiskey.

Jude downed his and turned his eyes to Luke. "I stopped by the ranch and the boys said you went to town to get supplies."

"Yeah. That, and to see if anyone is talking about missing cattle. I like to keep up on what the sheriff is doing."

Jude grinned. He knew what Luke was talking about. Luke had had to leave Waco when he found out the sheriff was coming to arrest him for rustling. "Are your cows still having all those twins and triplets?"

Luke shrugged. "I got good cows." He sipped his whiskey and raised his eyebrows as he studied Jude's face. "Now what brings you way out here? You in trouble again?"

Jude half grinned. "Kind of. I got a man gunning for me."

"I never saw you run from a fight." Luke frowned. "Why is he after you?"

Jude looked down at his glass. "He thinks I killed his folks somewhere in Illinois."

"Did you?"

"No. I ain't never heard of the man or his folks."

"Why are you running?"

Jude's face felt flushed as he looked up at Luke. "I ain't running. I just needed to get away from Waco for a while and I thought this would be a good time to do it. Pickings have gotten mighty slim back home."

Luke stared at Jude. "I could use some help. Me and my boys have been looking for cattle to increase my herd. I hope to make a drive to Dodge by spring. If you want to stay and help, I'll give you wages, plus you can have half the cows you bring in to sell for yourself."

"I got Jimbo with me. Same deal for him?"

Luke's eyes widened. "Sure. Where is he?"

"I left him back at your ranch. He was a little saddle sore and wanted to rest."

Luke laughed as he pulled a watch out of his pocket and looked at it. "It's getting late. Let's get out of here and head back to the ranch."

Jude followed Luke out of the saloon to the hitching post and they mounted their horses. As they rode down the street, Jude noticed Luke staring at a group of men in front of a hotel. He reined his horse closer to Luke's.

"You seem mighty interested in those men. Who are they?"

"That one in the white hat doing the talking is Goodnight. Him and Cornelia Adair own one of the biggest ranches around. The man he is talking to is the manager of the XIT, which is the biggest—some say it's the biggest in all of Texas."

Jude studied the men as they rode past. He had heard Goodnight was tough. He was one of the first ranchers to have settled in West Texas. He was out here when the Comanche Indians still owned the area. The XIT he didn't know much about. "Who owns the XIT?"

"A bunch of investors from back east, and maybe some from England. They hired a greenhorn to run the ranch." Luke grinned. "I find a lot of my stray calves over on their range." He kicked his horse into a slow lope. Jude did the same but turned and took a last look at Goodnight. The old man didn't look very tough. Maybe Jude would steal some of his cows just for the hell of it.

When Jude and Luke arrived at the ranch, Jimbo was out by the corral watching a cowboy trying to ride a bucking horse. Hearing their horses, he turned and watched them ride up to a hitching rail just outside a huge barn. He slowly walked over to them. Luke was in the process of loosening the girt when he noticed him.

"Hello, Jimbo." Luke took a step toward his brother and stuck out his hand. They shook, and then grabbed each other's shoulders in a quick manly hug. "I see you are still thin as a rail. Don't they feed you?"

Jimbo grinned and started to speak, but Jude beat him to it. "Hell, he eats more than me and you put together. I think he has worms."

Jimbo narrowed his eyes. "Bullshit, I just work a lot harder than you and Bojack. You just sit on your ass and tell us what to do."

Luke patted Jimbo on the shoulder. "Well, as soon as we get these horses put up we can go in and eat. My cook makes a mean pot of beans, with plenty of beef and bread to go with it. You'd best eat all you want, because tomorrow we'll be out all day looking for cattle."

CHAPTER 14

Stinky Sholt woke up to the sound of his wife relieving herself in the slop jar they kept in the corner of their small bedroom. The smell of urine permeated the air, but Stinky's fuzzy mind didn't acknowledge the all-too-common smell of his small shack. He lay on his cornhusk mattress, wishing he could go back to sleep, but he knew the throbbing pain in his back wouldn't let him. Knowing the room would be cold; he reluctantly crawled out of his bed and staggered over to the now-vacant slop jar. After fumbling with the flap in his long johns, he directed a weak stream of urine toward the jar. For a few seconds most of it went onto the floor, finally finding its target as it slowed to a dribble. Impatiently Stinky leaned against the wall as he hovered over the jar, knowing that soon the dribble would stop and he would have to urge it to start again several times until he felt he was through. It had been like this for several years and he was used to it. Finally, after several stops, he felt it was over and he went back to the bed where his pants lay on the floor. He pulled them on over his husky but lean body, grabbed his boots, and hurried to the kitchen where he could warm up by the stove.

Ida, his wife, was slicing off pieces of sow belly and putting them into a large frying pan, where they sizzled and popped. She was a small, dumpy woman with graying hair hanging haphazardly around her head and a lined face that made her look years older than her real age of just past forty. She was wearing a long, faded, patched green dress tied at the waist with a sash, and her feet were stuck in rundown leather shoes that had seen better days.

Mazie, their only child still at home out of the three, who'd managed to live past infancy, was cutting biscuits from a rolled-out slab of flour dough on the small counter. She was twelve, with a child's eagerness to please but also the early signs of womanhood. She was barefoot and wearing a long, waist less, flour-sack dress. She sneaked a look at her father for a second, and then went back to her biscuit making.

Stinky sat in his chair at the kitchen table and began to pull on his patched and rundown boots. He half smiled as he rubbed his hand across the faded red star on the leather. He was proud of his boots. The happiest he had been in his life was when he had worn the boots in the war. Memories from those days flashed in his mind. It had been exciting fighting with the Texas brigade, but when he joined with Quantrill, it had gotten even better. He had liked the screams and confusion of the Yankees when they ambushed them, but most of all he had loved raiding northern towns full of unaware civilians. Killing the men and raping the women had given him a thrill he would never forget. He felt a stirring in his groin just thinking about it. He looked up at his wife and felt disgust. She wasn't fit for wifely duties in the bed anymore, with all her female trouble of cramps and pain. He turned and looked at Mazie. He could see the small breasts and wider hips outlined on her dress. The feeling in his groin increased and a twisted desire slithered into his mind.

"Mazie, bring me some coffee."

Mazie looked at her father, her eyes wide. "Yes, sir." She hurriedly found his cup and waited as her mother filled it from the big pot on the stove. Carefully she carried it to the table and set it in front of her father. She turned to leave.

"Wait a minute, Mazie." Stinky reached up and ran his hand across her breast. She tried to push his hand away, but she stopped when he snarled, "You'd best be still or I'll give you a beating."

Mazie's face turned ashen. "Mother?" she whimpered.

Ida trembled as she took a few steps toward her husband. "Why don't you leave her alone? She's too young for what you want."

Stinky narrowed his eyes at his wife. "You stay out of this. You're useless. A man has needs that need taken care of."

Ida's eyes filled with tears. "You did that to Bessie and look what happened. She ran away and now she's in Waco working in the red light district."

"Bessie is there because she had bad blood from the start," Stinky sneered. "Remember? I found you there."

Ida's face flushed red and she gritted her teeth. "I never wanted to be there. It was only because I was an orphan and had no other choice. I thought when I married you I'd be free from all of that." She paused. "Let's go to the bedroom. I'll take care of your needs."

Stinky raised his eyebrows and cocked his head to one side. "The way I like it?"

Ida lowered her eyes. "Yes."

Stinky slowly rose from his chair. He rubbed his hand across Mazie's breast once more, and then slapped her on her rump. "Go finish cooking breakfast." He went into the small bedroom with Ida obediently following. She closed the curtain they used as a door as he pulled his pants down and lay back onto the bed. She started to remove her dress.

Stinky grinned and nodded toward his groin. "You don't need to get undressed."

Twenty minutes later Ida, her face pale, hurried out of the bedroom to the back porch, where she vomited several times. She waited a minute after the last time, then went to the water pail and dipped a cup into it. She gargled several times, gagging almost to the point of throwing up, then swished water in her mouth and spat. Stinky watched her for a minute and then turned to the table where Mazie had put his breakfast of meat, biscuits, and gravy. Her lips and chin were trembling as she refilled his coffee.

"It's something men and women like to do, Mazie, and I need to show you how it's done." Stinky turned as he heard Ida come back into the kitchen. "I'm going to town and sell my cedar post, then get me a few beers. When I get back tonight, have her ready. I'm going to give her some lessons on how to be a woman."

Tears came to Ida's eyes again. "Please don't do it. I can take care of—"

Stinky jumped from his chair and knocked Ida to the ground. He stood over her, shaking his fist. "You do what I say, woman, or I'll kick your ass out on the street and you can dig in the garbage for your food. As long as you stay under my roof, you do as I say." Stinky sat back down and finished his breakfast as Ida whimpered and slowly got to her feet. She clutched her chest as she looked tearfully at Mazie. With trembling lips Mazie ran to her mother and threw her arms around her. They stayed together for a minute. Then Ida, her head lowered, pushed her away and went to the stove. With tightened lips she carried the pot of coffee to Stinky and filled his cup.

CHAPTER 15

The freight wagon made good time after it left Rogers. The road was well kept and wooden bridges covered the few muddy creeks along their way. Alf begin to see more wagons and riders on the road as they drew closer to Belton, and when they arrived at the Leon River, they had to wait for another wagon to cross before they took their turn on the creaky wooden bridge.

Alf had noticed a gradual change of the landscape as they drew closer to the river, but when they reached the other side, the change was almost instant. The smooth, rolling hills of forest and prairie they had traveled through since leaving Galveston changed to a rugged, hilly land covered with bushy evergreen trees. Rocky white banks lined the river and the water was a deep green.

Alf waited until they had crossed the bridge and then pointed to the evergreens. "What kind of trees are those, Harrison?"

"Cedars. They stay green all year, like pine trees."

Alf studied one of the stunted, bushy trees as they drove by it. "What are they good for, firewood?"

"They burn hot but they pop a lot in a fireplace. They're okay for a potbelly." Harrison leaned out and spat tobacco on the ground, then slapped the reins on the mules' rumps. "They don't rot like other trees so they make real good post for stringing bob wire. There's good money cutting cedar post. Most of the ranchers let you come in and cut them for free just to get them off their cow pastures."

"You ever cut post?"

"Yep, me and the boys cut every chance we get. I even have me a little post yard out by the road in front of my house." Harrison slapped the mules' rumps again, and then reined them over to the side to make room for an approaching wagon. They were on the outskirts of Belton now and more people were on the road. As they began their descent into a valley, Alf turned his attention to the main part of town he could see in the distance. A large building dominated the landscape, with smaller buildings surrounding it. Past the buildings Alf could see houses lining the streets that fanned out from the center of town. Belton was nestled on the banks of a small river, and most of the businesses were on the north side of it.

99

"What's the name of that river, Mike?"

"Ain't no river, it's Nolan Creek."

They followed the creek a few blocks until they came to the big wooden building in the middle of the town square. Stores and other businesses lined the streets that bordered the square.

"That there's the courthouse," Mike said. "It was built in 1859. Belton is the Bell County seat."

"I heard they were going to build another one next year," Harrison remarked, then spat on the street. "I might try to get a job with the builder."

Alf studied the courthouse for a few minutes and then noticed the buildings around it. He counted four saloons mixed in with a few law offices and cafés. A large meat market and grocery store occupied half of another block just east of the courthouse. Just up the street from it was a nice stone building with concrete sidewalks at the front sides. A sign on it read "First National Bank."

"Looks like an interesting town, Harrison."

Mike drove past the courthouse and turned east on Central Avenue. He drove past the bank to Penelope Street, turned right, and pulled the mules over next to a large general store.

"Get those three crates marked Potts and bring them in that door." Mike pointed to a side door toward the back, set the brake, and climbed down from the wagon. "I'll go find the owner."

It only took Alf and Harrison a few minutes to find the crates but they were huge and it took both to bring the heavy crates into the store. By the time they had the last one inside; the owner had already opened one of them and was holding up a pair of blue denim pants.

"These are the new style of Levi pants from California. They cost a little more but they're made better than all the other brands." He handed the pants to Mike. "See those rivets on the pockets? It makes them stronger."

Alf watched as Mike pulled at different places on the pants to test their strength. Alf had already bought the same kind of Levis in Galveston and wore them most of the time so he turned his attention to other merchandise in the store. The shelves and tables around him were piled high with pants and shirts. In another area of the store were shelves with shoes and boots. Belts and hats hung from the ceiling. Alf was trying on a black hat when Mike hollered he was ready to go. They piled into the wagon and Mike drove them a block down the street and turned to the right. He went another block and stopped at Smith's meat market and grocery store. Alf and Harrison unloaded the last of the crates and barrels at Smith's while Mike went to the telegraph office. By the time Mike returned, they were finished and waiting at the back of the store.

Mike was silent as he got into the driver's seat and didn't speak as he guided the mules two blocks to the local wagon yard. He directed the mules to an open spot and pulled on the brake.

"Well, I got word to go to Waco. I'm leaving in the morning." He looked over at Alf. "I'm going to take off for Christmas so I won't be needing you to go with me. When I get to Waco, I'm going to take the train back to Galveston to see my family. You can meet me in Waco on the twenty-seventh."

Alf quickly calculated the days in his head. He would be on his own for over a week. "Where do I meet you in Waco?"

"I'll be at Heidenheimer Wholesalers, loading for my next run. It's close to the train station. Just ask anybody there and they can point it out to you."

"Okay, Mike, I'll see you there then on the twenty-seventh."

It was late in the afternoon when Alf and Harrison unhitched the mules for the last time and put them in the wagon yard corral. Mike paid them the money they had coming and they said their good-byes. As Mike walked away, Alf turned his attention to his surroundings. The wagon yard was located next to a blacksmith shop, and behind it was Nolan Creek. Several horses were staked out on the grassy banks alongside camps, most with tents and campfires. People were sitting around the fires talking, and a few kids were fishing in the creek. On the other side of the yard was a huge town square where people were selling all kinds of things, mostly fruit and vegetables.

Harrison tapped Alf on the shoulder. "I forgot today was Saturday. It's traders' day. Let's walk a bit and look around. I might see someone I know who will give us a ride to my place." Harrison picked up his bag and started off toward the vendors.

Alf got his carpetbag and followed, but he still didn't know if he wanted to stay at Harrison's house. He had enough money to stay at a hotel for a few days. With his savings from Galveston, he had over a hundred dollars in his poke now. He patted his pocket where he kept his leather pouch and checked to make sure the drawstring was tied securely to one of his belt loops. When he looked back up, he noticed they were approaching some horses tied to a rope between two wagons.

Harrison noticed Alf eyeing the horses and he nudged him. "You don't want to buy anything from that man. He's been known to fib a little about his horses."

Alf nodded. "Thanks. I was looking at that black one. He looks a little like my horse that got stolen back in Saint Louis." Alf figured he would have to buy a horse and saddle eventually, but first he needed a place to keep them, and stables were expensive. "Harrison, do you have a place I can keep a horse out at your place?"

Harrison scratched his head and turned and spat. "Sure, I got a shed and some fenced pasture I keep my mules in." He nodded toward the string of horses. "But I'd be real careful with ol' Keg Karl there."

"I'm just going to look at them. I'd like to hear his pitch." Alf strolled up to the black horse and rubbed his neck. His coat was shiny, but Alf felt oil on his hand. Several cuts on the horse's flesh had been covered with something black to match his hair. Alf opened the animal's mouth. The teeth were worn smooth.

"He's got a little age, but he's still got a lot of years in him."

Alf turned and found that the short, chunky owner of the horses had walked up to him. He was middle-aged, with graying hair sticking out from his stained, slouchy hat. His overalls looked like they had never been washed, and the red union suit he wore under them had faded to a dirty pink. Tobacco stains ran down his chin.

"I don't think he's what I'm looking for, Mr. Karl," Alf said, looking back at Keg. "Nope, don't see any I like."

"What about that pinto? He's only four years old and rides good." Keg blinked at the horse as he spoke. "I can let him go for fifty."

Alf studied the pinto. Jake Boone had been a horse trader before he became sheriff, and he had taught Alf a lot about horses. The first thing Alf looked at was the legs, and he noticed swollen ankles right away. The horse's hooves were worn and split, and there were saddle galls someone had tried to hide. Alf figured the horse had been ridden hard and was wind-broke from the way he was breathing. Harrison was right; the man was a tricky horse trader. Alf thought about telling the man what he thought of his trickery but decided to be nice. Maybe he knew Stinky Sholt.

"No, I don't think he will do. I'm looking for something bigger and wider in the chest." Alf paused. "You don't happen to know Stinky Sholt, do you?

Keg's shoulders slumped and he let out a deep sigh. He licked his lips and scratched his right butt cheek. "He was here this morning selling some firewood. I think he sold out. If he did you'll find him in one of the saloons." Keg didn't offer any more information but turned from Alf to another man who was looking at his horses.

Alf didn't move as he thought of Stinky Sholt being only a few blocks away. His eyes narrowed as the memories of a thousand nightmares flooded through his mind. He clenched his teeth as he remembered Willy James lying on the floor, confessing with his dying breath how they'd all raped his mother after Jude Brown had killed his father. Alf felt his rage building and he trembled. He had to calm down. He turned and looked for Harrison. Through the milling crowd he saw him talking to a man by a wagon loaded with canned fruits and vegetables. Alf hurried over and nudged him on the arm. "I'm going over to the saloons. I have to find somebody."

Harrison raised his eyebrows. "I didn't know you knew anybody around here."

"I don't know him, but I need to find him."

Harrison took Alf's arm and led him to the front of the wagon where no one could hear them. "Is this about that shooting you got into on the strand in Galveston? I heard Billy and Slim talking about it."

Alf looked into Harrison's face and saw only concern. "Yes, and one of the men I'm looking for is here in Belton. He's in one of the saloons."

Harrison quickly looked around to see if anyone was close enough to hear him. "What's his name?"

Alf narrowed his eyes. "Stinky Sholt."

Harrison raised his eyebrows. "I know him—I bought a few posts from him for my post yard." Harrison cocked his head. "What'd he do?"

Alf gritted his teeth. "He killed my parents ten years ago." He glanced toward the street where he had seen the saloons earlier. "I'll tell you the whole story later. Right now he's in one of the saloons, and I need to go find him." He looked into Harrison's eyes. "Are you going with me?"

Harrison laid his hand on Alf's shoulder. "I'm with you. Let's go." He led Alf through the crowd of vendors and buyers. They walked past Potts's store toward the courthouse, and then crossed the street to where the first saloon was squeezed between a lawyer's office and a drugstore. It was dark inside and they paused at the door to let their eyes adjust to the dim light. Harrison slowly walked around the room, then shook his head and led Alf out the door. The second saloon they tried was also void of Stinky, but Harrison talked to a friend and found out that the cedar-chopper always hung out at the Longhorn, a place over on Water Street. They hurried past the courthouse and off to the Longhorn. Alf grabbed Harrison's arm and stopped him at the door.

"If he's in here, point him out to me and get out of the way. I mean to call him out and kill him."

"What if he won't pull on you?"

Alf took a deep breath and the scent of apple blossoms tickled his nose. "I don't know. If he confesses I might wait and see him hang. If he doesn't, I'll kill him myself."

Harrison pressed his lips together and led them through the batwing doors. Even though the light was dim, Alf could see Harrison staring at someone standing at the bar. The man was backed up to the bar, holding a mug of beer and talking in a loud voice. No one seemed to be paying attention to him except a shabby-dressed man standing beside him. As Alf's eyes adjusted, he looked down at the man's scruffy, worn-out boots. The red star on them glared back at him as if the boots were shiny and new.

Stinky held up his mug. "Yeah, when I was riding with General Hood, we whipped them Yankees good." He finished off the beer and banged the mug on the bar. "Another round for me and my friend." When the bartender handed them the beer, Stinky nodded to his buddy and turned toward the crowded room. "We never lost a battle until Gettysburg, and we would've won that too if Lee hadn't decided to run away." Stinky paused to take another drink. "That's when I decided to join up with Major Quantrill. I wanted to fight with someone who wasn't afraid of the damn Yankees."

Alf had heard enough. He slid the leather thong off his pistol's hammer as he stepped closer. "How many women and kids did you kill when you fought with Quantrill?"

The room quieted as Alf's words were whispered to those who hadn't heard them.

Stinky narrowed his eyes at Alf. "We didn't kill any women and kids. Only Yankee soldiers."

Several men in the saloon voiced their disagreement, and then became quiet again. Alf took a step closer. With relief, he noticed Stinky had a pistol strapped to his waist. He just hoped Stinky had the guts to pull it. "I didn't come here to argue the point about the war. I came here to call you out for raping my mother and then killing her and my father."

Stinky looked around the room. "I didn't do anything like that. Who told you that?"

Alf kept his eyes on Stinky. "There were four of you. Jude Brown was the leader. You, Duce Rangle, and Willy James were the followers." Alf clenched his fist. "Ten years ago the four of you came to our farm and Jude killed my father. Then all of you raped my mother before you killed her. You ransacked the house and then set it afire, trying to hide what you did."

Stinky's eyes raced around the room. "I didn't do it. Where's your proof?"

Alf took a deep breath. "One of your partners got religion right after he tried to kill me a few months ago." He paused as the scenes whirled in his mind. "Back in Illinois, when your partner Willy James found out I was looking for the men who killed my parents, he panicked and tried to kill me. He missed and I shot him in the gut. As he lay dying he confessed to everything in front of me and the sheriff."

Stinky slumped. Everyone was looking at him. He looked toward the batwing door. Two men quickly stepped in front of it. He cut his eyes to the back door, but a lanky cowboy now blocked it too. Stinky grabbed a whiskey bottle from the bar, took a long swig, and turned back to Alf. He grinned as he set the bottle back on the bar. He took a step, then slowly reached down and pulled the leather fastener from his pistol's hammer. "Yankee boy, you need to take your lies back up north where you belong. When you get to be a man, come on back down here and we Southerners will show you what we do with Yankee liars."

Alf calmly backed up a step. His heart began to race, but it wasn't because he was afraid. He wanted to punish Stinky for what he'd done, and he didn't want to wait for a hanging. "Why don't you show me now, you cowardly son-of-a-bitching woman-killer."

Stinky blinked and went for his gun. Alf saw him reaching and his hand flashed down to his pistol. Two shots rang out. Bottles rattled on the shelves as gun smoke filled the space between Alf and Stinky.

Stinky fell back against the bar, and then slid slowly to the floor. Two holes in his dirty shirt blossomed red with blood. Pain racked his body. He felt like he had an anvil sitting on his chest. Suddenly he realized he was going to die. He remembered his boyhood pastor preaching about hell and he became afraid. He looked up at the people around him. "I don't want to go to hell. Somebody get me a preacher."

"Confess your sins, Stinky," one of the men said quietly. "You have to confess and ask forgiveness."

"I did it." Stinky shifted his eyes to Alf. "We did it just like you said." He gasped for breath. "Can you forgive me?"

Alf shook his head. "Ask God, not me. I won't forgive you. I hope you rot in hell."

Tears came to Stinky's eyes as he tried to speak, but slowly his eyes closed and he was gone.

Alf scanned the room. When he saw no threats, he lowered his pistol. His muscles relaxed and he let out his breath as he looked back at Stinky's body. He closed his eyes and pictured his mother and father. *One more to go,* he thought. The images slowly faded and he opened his eyes. The room was abuzz now with everyone talking about the gunfight. Some of them gathered around Stinky's body, pointing at the bloody wounds. Alf slowly pushed the spent shells from his gun and replaced them with good ones from his belt. He holstered it and turned to Harrison. "What now? Do we wait for the sheriff?"

"I think that would be a good idea, son. I think everyone knows that Stinky went for his gun first." Harrison moved over to a table a few feet away. "Let's sit down and wait."

Alf looked at Stinky's body for a few seconds and then joined Harrison at the table. They sat in silence for a few minutes until people who knew Harrison came over to their table. A tall, hefty cowboy was the first to speak. "Hello, Harry. I haven't seen you in a while."

Harrison looked up at the man and smiled. "Hello, John, good to see you. Yeah, I've been in Galveston working on the docks." He spat on the sawdust floor and nodded at Alf. "We just got back into Belton about two hours ago."

John turned to Alf and stuck out his hand. "My name's John Bowles. I have a ranch west of here."

Alf studied the man for a second and then shook hands. "Glad to meet you, John. My name's Alf Smith. Have a seat."

"Don't mind if I do." John pulled out the chair and sat down. "I'll even buy you boys a beer." He looked toward the bar and held up three fingers. The bartender, who had been eyeing Alf every so often, spotted John and nodded. A few minutes later he brought three cold mugs of beer and set them on the table.

"It's good and cold, John. I started getting ice from Brunet last year. Now everyone wants cold beer."

John laid four bits on the table. "Still ten cents a mug, Walter?"

The bartender dug into a pocket on his apron and pulled out two dimes. "Yes, sir, still ten cents."

As Walter walked away, Alf picked up his mug and took a sip. He didn't really like beer that much. He'd had his first one in Galveston when Slim and Billy made fun of him for drinking sarsaparilla, and he hadn't liked the taste of it. He set the mug down. "I wish the sheriff would hurry up. I want to get this over with."

John cut his eyes at Alf. "He'll be here in a minute." He paused. "I saw the whole thing, Alf, and I don't blame you for killing the man, but Sheriff Bigham may put you in jail until he can have a hearing."

Alf started to say something, but suddenly a huge, hefty man with a badge on his white shirt and a Colt in his hand burst through the door. The saloon became quiet as the sheriff scanned the room. Seeing Stinky lying on the floor, he walked over to him. He studied the body for a few seconds and then scanned the room again.

"Who shot this man?"

No one said a word but most of them pointed at Alf. Alf felt his face turn red as he raised his hand.

"I shot him, sir, in self-defense."

Sheriff Bigham glared at Alf. "A judge and jury will decide if it was self-defense." He walked over and pointed his pistol at Alf. "Stand up, unbuckle your gun belt, and hand it to me."

Alf looked at Harrison as he slid the chair back and removed his gun and holster rig. He handed it to the sheriff, who put it on his shoulder. "Are you going to put me in jail, Sheriff?"

The sheriff's eyes narrowed. "What's your name and where do you live?"

"I'm Alf Smith and I just got into town. I work for Mike Tally hauling freight. We just got into town a couple of hours ago."

One of Bigham's deputies had come in and was standing a few feet behind him. "Deputy Miller, stand by the door and take names and statements from these witnesses as they leave the saloon." The sheriff addressed the room in a loud voice. "Okay, everyone will have to leave. File out the door, give your name, and tell the deputy what you saw."

The patrons, who had listened quietly, began to stir. Some of them hurried to the door to give their statements while others lagged behind, their eyes on Alf and the sheriff.

Sheriff Bigham turned back to the table where Harrison and John still sat. "You boys wait here." He shifted his eyes to Alf. "Now tell me your side of the story."

Alf tried to think of a way to tell his story. Finally he decided to just start from the beginning. He told him about his parents' death, the fire, and the four men in the red-star boots carrying loot from his house. He told of living with Sheriff Boone and eventually becoming one of his deputies. Then he told about his journey from Illinois and how he had stumbled across Willy James. The sheriff frowned when Alf related how he'd shot Duce Rangle in Galveston and how the judge had told him to leave town. Alf studied the sheriff's face. "When I walked into the saloon, I heard this man talk about riding with Quantrill. When I saw his boots, I called him out for killing my folks. He went for his gun and I went for mine. I was a little faster."

Sheriff Bigham cocked his head to one side. "How did you know it was Stinky?"

"I told him," Harrison said. "I live around here. I know Stinky." He spat on the floor toward Stinky's body. "I never did like the son of a bitch. I once saw him beat his wife to the ground."

Sheriff Bigham narrowed his eyes. "Did you call him on it?"

"I pulled him off of her and slapped him a few times." Harrison placed his hands together. "He tried to pull his gun on me, but I took it away from him and pitched it into the rain barrel."

Sheriff Bigham rubbed one side of his face, looked toward the door, then turned back to John. "You're John Bowles, aren't you? What did you see?"

John sat up straight and cocked his head at the sheriff. "Stinky was blabbing as usual about riding with Quantrill when Alf and Harrison walked in. Alf called him on killing his folks and Stinky went for his gun. The man had to defend himself."

"Did you intend to kill Stinky when you were told it was him?" Bigham asked Alf. "Did you goad him into this fight?"

Alf thought for a few seconds and took a deep breath. "Sheriff, I wanted to see him punished for what he did and I told Harrison I was willing to let the law handle it, but Stinky didn't give me a chance to make a citizen's arrest."

Sheriff Bigham rubbed his chin. "Son, I'm sorry for your loss and I understand your anger, but I can't have revenge killings in my county. I'm going to have to lock you up until I get a hold of the judge and set up a hearing." He turned to Harrison. "If you boys want to give your testimony, go over to the courthouse and wait."

Harrison frowned. "Look, Sheriff, Stinky confessed to the rape and killing before he died. Does Alf have to be put in jail?"

Sheriff Bigham pursed his lips. "The law is the law, and we have to have a hearing."

"How long is this going to take? I ain't been home in six months."

"If the judge is at the courthouse, we can get it over with now. If not, it will be in the morning." Sheriff Bigham turned to Alf. "Come with me." He turned and headed for the door.

Alf shrugged at Harrison, and then followed the sheriff to the batwing door at the front of the saloon. The sheriff paused to give his deputy some instructions and then pushed through the swinging doors. Looking back to make sure Alf was following, he turned right and followed the boardwalk west toward the creek. They passed the courthouse and turned right onto a street that ran parallel to a small cliff that rose above the creek. They walked a few yards to a small building with bars on the windows and an iron-enforced door. The sheriff opened the door and then motioned for Alf to enter. A large cell at one side of the large room took up almost all the space inside the building. On the other side of the room in the back corner was a small closet. The rest of the open area contained a desk and chairs. Shelves lined the wall behind the desk, and a gun rack full of rifles leaned up against the side wall. Sheriff Bigham grabbed a ring of keys from the desk and ambled to the barred door. For the first time Alf noticed two men in the cell. They stepped back when the sheriff opened the door for Alf.

Alf stepped in and looked at the sheriff. "How long do you think this will take, Sheriff?"

Sheriff Bigham didn't reply as he closed the door with a loud bang and locked it. He pulled out his pocket watch. "The judge is supposed to hold court for these two at four o'clock. I'll see if he can squeeze you in." He tossed the keys on the desk and left.

Alf looked around the cell and went to the window. The two men sat on a cot and watched him, never saying a word. They were both slim and looked alike in the face, but one had black hair and the other's was the color of straw. Their blue denims were almost faded white and their shirts were store-bought cotton. Both wore spurs buckled on their well-worn boots, and their wide-brimmed hats were pushed down on their heads. Alf wondered if they were brothers. He stepped away from the window.

"My name's Alf Smith. What are you boys in for?"

The two young men hesitated as they looked at each other. Finally one said, "My name's Marty Lynch, and this is my brother, Silas. We're in here for public drunkenness."

"We wasn't really drunk in public, we was in the saloon," Silas blurted as he rose from the cot. He stepped up to Alf and stuck out his hand. "Glad to meet you, Alf."

Marty rose and did the same and then put his hands in his pockets. "We were just passing through and stopped for a few drinks, and this deputy Miller come in and arrested us for nothing."

Alf studied the brothers as Marty spoke. They seemed like likeable fellows, but he was a little wary of them still. "Glad to meet you men. If you boys don't live here, where are you from?"

"We were raised down close to Round Rock," Marty replied as he sat back down on the cot. "Our folks have a place down on the creek where they farm and raise a few cattle."

"But we ain't been home in a year," Silas added as he strolled over to the window and looked out. He turned back to Alf. "We've been working for Mr. Goodnight on his ranch out west and we were going home to visit."

Marty puffed out his chest. "We just got back from a trail drive to Dodge City, Kansas."

Alf rubbed his chin. "I thought the cattle drives were mostly over because of the railroad being in Texas now."

Silas cocked his head to one side and grinned. "Not up in the panhandle. It's closer to Dodge City than to Fort Worth."

"What's Dodge City like? Is it as wild as they say?"

Silas and Marty grinned at each other. They began to talk at once about the debauchery they had committed in the cow town. Then they took turns telling Alf about the whores they'd poked and how much beer they'd drunk. They told of fights in the saloons and horse races in the streets.

Alf smiled. This was the stuff he had read about in the dime novels. He felt a yearning to see the town for himself. "When are you guys going back out there?"

"We're going home for Christmas when we get out of this jail," Marty said. "Mr. Goodnight said we needed to be back by the middle of February when they begin the spring roundup. Then about the first of April we start another drive to Dodge."

Silas added, "Mr. Goodnight told us he needed some more hands for the drive, and if we knew anybody who wanted a job to bring them back with us." He paused. "Are you looking for a job?"

Alf almost told them yes. He would have loved to go back with them. Being a cowboy was what he'd dreamed about when he was younger, and pretending to be on a cattle drive had been his favorite game. But he thought of Jude Brown and knew he couldn't stray from his quest until he had found the last man who'd murdered his parents. He turned to the window and gazed at the clear, cold water flowing down the creek. Then he faced the brothers. "I would like to go with you, but I have an obligation to take care of first."

Silas and Marty both frowned. "What do you need to do, Alf?" Silas asked. "We could help."

"Yeah, we'll help you. But we do need to be home for Christmas," Marty added.

Alf's chest felt light and tingly. He had already decided he liked the brothers, and now he felt he could trust them too. He decided to tell them his story, ending with his meeting with Stinky Sholt.

"I called him out and he went for his gun but he was too slow. I killed him, and now I'm in jail with you two."

Silas and Marty had sat on the cot as they listened to Alf's story. Now their faces were masked with concern.

Marty was the first to speak. "I don't know if I could kill anyone who wasn't trying to kill me, Alf, but I'll sure 'nuff help you look for him."

Silas quickly added. "Me too. Where do you think he's at?"

Alf studied the two men. "He has a ranch close to Waco. I thought I would wait 'til after Christmas, then go up there and see if I can find him."

An eager look came over Marty's face. "You could come to our place for Christmas."

"Yeah!" Silas chimed in. "We have a sister who ain't married."

Marty elbowed Silas in the ribs. "He ain't interested in no girl. He's got things to do."

Alf smiled. He liked Silas and Marty and wanted to accept their offer, but he had told Harrison he would go to his place. He took off his hat and smoothed back his hair. "Thanks for the offer, guys, but I told my working buddy I would spend Christmas at his place. Maybe after Christmas I could come down and visit." He swept his eyes around the cell. "Hell, we may all be spending Christmas right here. I think the sheriff has forgotten us."

They all laughed, and then Marty told Alf how to get to their place in Round Rock. When he seemed sure Alf could find it, he asked if Alf had any family back in Illinois. Alf told them about Charley, Jenny, and Cordie, then he asked Silas and Marty about their family. He found out that their mother had died years ago and their father was remarried to a twenty-two-year-old woman who had been the girlfriend of their brother.

"All of my older brothers and sisters have married and moved out," Marty explained. "Our stepsister, Mary Francis, lives in a small house at the farm and takes care of our younger sister, Mattie, and our brothers Ed and Elias."

Alf pondered Marty and Silas's situation. "Where does your father live?" he asked Marty, who seemed to be the older of the two.

"He lives in the big house."

"Is Mary Francis married?"

"She was, but her husband died mysteriously."

"She has a three-year-old little girl," Silas added.

"She is your stepsister?"

"Yeah. The story is that Mother was married before she married Father, but I heard stories that she got pregnant by one of the hired hands at her father's farm."

"Everybody thinks she is part Indian," Silas blurted.

Marty frowned at his brother. "Do you have to tell everyone our family secrets?"

A crimson glow spread across Silas's face. "Well, it's true." Silas rose and walked to the window as Marty glowered at him.

Alf thought it was funny the way Marty and Silas bickered; it reminded him of his brother, Charley. He was half smiling when Marty cut his eyes at him. He shrugged. "I don't have anything against Indians."

There was not much talk about family after that. The three young men chatted about horses, guns, and women until an hour later when finally the sheriff returned.

"Okay, men, get your stuff. We're going to see the judge."

CHAPTER 16

Mary Francis froze when she heard her three-year-old daughter, Nancy, scream. Heart racing, she quickly moved from behind clothesline to get a better view of the backyard where Nancy had been playing with her puppy. She saw Nancy running toward then away from the dog, and she screamed again as the puppy turned and ran at her. Mary's heart slowed and she smiled as she realized there was no danger; her daughter was only playing. She was glad Nancy was playing today, having spent all yesterday in bed with a fever.

Mary looked across the large yard for her sister, Mattie, who was seven. She spied her at the barn, playing in the dirt with Elias, who was six. She shook her head as she went back to hanging up a pair of Ed's long johns. School was out for the holidays and Ed was off with his father doing something with the small herd of cattle her stepfather, Martin, kept. Mary sighed as she reached in her basket and pulled out one of Mattie's dresses. She was grateful for this little house Martin had provided for her. She shuddered as she thought of what she might have had to do if she were on her own. When her mother died three years ago, she'd been terrified that Martin would throw her and little Nancy out. She knew Martin didn't treat her like his other children. Mary Francis wasn't his blood, for one thing, and she was half Indian. Her mother had kept the real story of her father from Mary Francis for years. When she would ask about him, her mother would say she had married a man named Kendrick who got sick and died, and then later she married Martin. Finally, when she was lying on her deathbed, she called Mary to her and told her the real story.

"I was twenty-one years old and I had never kissed a boy when I first saw George Kendrick working on our farm. He was dark and exciting and I fell in love with him. The first time I talked with him in the barn, I could see by the look on his face that he loved me too. I told him I would meet him down at the river and we would talk. The first time we met, he told me that he was a Cherokee and that had been watching me for a long time but was afraid to approach me. The next night we met again and he kissed me. After that we met at the river many times, and soon our kisses led to more and more until one day I found myself pregnant with you. We ran away to the Cherokee land and a preacher from his tribe married us. We lived in on the reservation in a hut and George went to work for the Indian police. Even with living conditions I wasn't used to, I was happy living with George. He was gentle with me and eager for you to be born. He loved you even then. Then one day a man knocked on my door and told me my husband was dead. He had been killed in an ambush while out looking for a thief. At seven months pregnant, I went to his funeral and then back to Arkansas. Father took me in and you were born two months later. You and I lived a quiet life for a year until one day Father brought Martin to the house. A few days later he came back and asked if he could court me. Out of desperation I agreed. I grew to like Martin, but I always knew I would never love another man like I did George. Eventually I agreed to marry Martin, but I told him he would have to accept you along with me. He said he would treat you like his own daughter, and so we married. I found out later that my father had offered to give him a team and wagon along with money to buy land in Texas if he married me. I think my father thought you would be better off in a place where people didn't know you were a half-breed."

Mary Francis shook off her thoughts, pulled another dress out of her basket, and hung it up. She bent down for another but paused as she noticed Nancy running toward Ed and Elias. It was strange how her life mirrored her mother's. She had fallen in love with Nancy's father, Frank Mason, and married him, but he too had died violently in a gun battle, the victim of a robbery of the stagecoach he was driving. Mary Francis had moved back home, but no suitors had come around to court her. A half-breed with a child…she didn't expect to ever marry again.

She reached down to the basket, but seeing it empty she picked it up and started back to the wash pot. She set the basket down and looked for Nancy.

"Nancy, come with me to the house. I need to start supper."

"Mommy, I want to play with Elias."

Mary glanced at the wash pot. "No, you come in with me. I know if I leave you out here, you will get burned again."

Mary watched as Nancy reluctantly shuffled toward her. She was worried about her daughter. For two weeks she had had frequent bouts of fever and she complained that her back was hurting. When she took her to the doctor, he said it was an infection along with growing pains, but Mary wasn't so sure. Nancy's back seemed to be curving more than normal and she was having headaches frequently.

Mary took her hand and started toward the house. "How do you feel, dear?"

"My back is hurting, Mommy."

Mary wondered if she should find another doctor for her baby girl. Whatever sickness she had wasn't going away.

CHAPTER 17

Judge Tyler seemed impatient when he rushed into the courtroom and motioned for the bailiff to bring his first case. Alf's hearing was first on the list and didn't last long. After Wally Thornton, the bartender, and John Bowles gave their version, the judge made a ruling of self-defense.

Marty and Silas's trial was a little different in that they pled guilty of public intoxication. The judge fined them two dollars each and jail time served. Reluctantly the boys paid their fines, and the judge hammered his gavel and closed the court. A few minutes later, Alf and his friends were in front of the courthouse and the judge was driving away in his buggy. Sheriff Bigham was the last person to leave the courtroom and locked up. Seeing Alf, he walked over to him.

"Alf, let me give you some advice. Don't shoot anybody else in my town. If you have a problem with somebody, come to me and I'll handle it." Sheriff Bigham rubbed his chin. "Having said that, let me ask you a question."

Alf nodded. "Sure, Sheriff."

"You said you were a deputy under Sheriff Boone in Clark County, Illinois."

"Yes, sir. He took me in to live with him when I was twelve. When I was nineteen, he made me a deputy."

Sheriff Bigham cocked his head. "How old are you now?"

"I'm twenty-one, sir."

"Nineteen is pretty young to be a deputy sheriff."

"I learn fast and I had a good teacher."

The sheriff rubbed his chin again. "Well, if you want to get back into the deputy business, come by my office and we can talk about it."

Alf frowned. He wouldn't mind being a deputy again—it would be a good-paying job—but he still had one more murderer to find and he couldn't settle down anywhere until he finished what he'd started. "Let me think about it, Sheriff. I have some obligations to take care of first."

The sheriff nodded. "Okay. Look me up when you can." He turned and walked away.

Alf turned to Harrison. "You got us a ride to your place yet?"

"Yeah, John said he would drop us off. I already picked up some things to bring home."

John Bowles patted Alf on the shoulder. "If you boys are ready to go, I'm ready. I'd like to get home before dark."

Alf turned to Marty and Silas. "So long, boys. I'll see you sometime after Christmas."

"We'll be looking for you."

They all shook hands, then Marty and Silas mounted their horses and headed south to Round Rock. Alf watched them for a minute, kind of wishing he was riding with them, but he had already promised Harrison he would stay with him, so he grabbed his bag and followed him and John back to the square where John had left his wagon. Harrison climbed up beside John, and Alf found a box to sit on in the back. John popped his whip and started his mules down Main Street. He drove north for a few blocks, and then turned left on a gravel road. A signpost read "Sparta" with an arrow pointing west, the direction they were traveling. Off to the right, Alf noticed men working on something. When they got closer, he saw that they were clearing some kind of road.

"Mr. Bowles, what are those men doing?"

"They're getting the roadbed ready to lay tracks on next year."

"Is that the same railroad line as the one in Rogers?"

John spat a wad of tobacco toward the workers. "Yeah, sons of bitches were supposed to put the tracks right through Belton but instead they put them way out here." He pointed to a small building next to the tracks. "That's the depot."

"I heard that the Katy was coming to Belton too." Harrison spat toward the tracks too. "Whatever come of that, John?"

"They're coming. They already got the roadbed ready to Temple. When they get to Belton, they're going to build a depot just two blocks from the courthouse. Building a bridge over the Leon will hold them up for a while, but they're supposed to be up and running next year." John nudged Harrison as the road crossed the roadbed, and then pointed farther down to where men were cutting brush and trees. "See that? They're going to run the Gulf and Santa Fe on down to Lampasas sometime in the future."

Harrison chewed a few times and then spat out his chaw. He pulled a plug from his overalls pocket and bit off a fair-sized piece. He held the plug out to John.

"No, thanks, mine is still good." John popped his whip at his mules, then leaned back and propped his boot on the footboard. "I guess in a few more years you'll be able to get on a train and go anywhere in Texas."

Alf smiled as the two men talked about the railroads. He had yet to ride a train, but he figured he would someday. Maybe he would ride one to Waco.

"Mr. Bowles, where would I catch a train to Waco?"

"Well, you could take the train from Tanglefoot Station. I don't know what their schedule is, though."

"Where's Tanglefoot?"

"That's the town the railroad built just east of here." John spat again toward the tracks that were still visible to their left. "I would crawl to Waco before I would ride their damn train. They screwed Belton good. I donated twenty dollars for that bunch of crooks to lay tracks to downtown Belton and then they put them way out here." John popped the mules again. "Some of them railroad people bought a bunch of land from John Moore out at Birdsdale and then put the main construction site and depot there. Back in June they threw a big party and auctioned off a bunch of lots. They call it Temple now, named after some bigwig who works for the railroad."

Alf leaned back on the sideboard and closed his eyes. It had been a long day and he was tired. He pushed Harrison and John's conversation into background clutter as he let the events of the day run through his mind. The meet-up with Stinky was foremost; he took a deep breath then sighed deeply. Memories of his mother and father popped into his mind and he trembled as he held his breath. They were just memories now. Killing Stinky, Duce, and Willy couldn't bring them back, but he couldn't let any of them live either. He had one more man left to kill, and then he could rest. Maybe he would stay here in Bell County when his journey of vengeance was over. There was an addictive excitement to the continuous building and construction he had witnessed in this frontier part of Texas, and he wanted to be a part of it. His mind drifted to railroads and cattle drives, and then slowly he went to sleep.

"Wake up, Alf, we're home."

Alf was in the middle of roping a cow when someone began shaking his shoulder. The dream disappeared as he opened his eyes and realized it was dark. As Alf sat up, he saw the wagon had stopped in front of a house, and a woman holding a lantern was peering at them from a large front porch. Alf grabbed his bags and climbed out of the wagon. He set them down and helped Harrison unload the supplies he had bought in town.

Harrison looked up at John, who was up on the driver's seat. "I think I got everything, John. Thanks for the ride."

Alf stepped back from the wagon bed. "Thanks, John. Glad I met you."

John let off the brake as he cut his eyes to Harrison and Alf. "Glad to help. I'm going to hurry on home. Merry Christmas," John popped his whip and the team of mules leaned against their collars and pulled the wagon back onto the dirt road.

"Merry Christmas to you too, John," Harrison and Alf yelled almost at the same time. Then they turned toward the house where the woman still waited, but now several children surrounded her, along with another woman and an older man.

Alf held back when he saw the porch full of people. He thought he might have made a mistake in taking up Harrison's offer to stay with him. The house didn't look very big, and if all the people on the porch lived there, where was he going to sleep? He spied some buildings behind the house. Maybe they had a place for him to sleep in the barn.

Harrison stepped up on the porch, and immediately children rushed to him and threw their arms around him. One of the women waded through the children and grabbed him in a big hug around his body, then kissed him on the lips. Harrison returned her kiss and hugged her tight until one of the small girls yelled that she was getting squashed. Harrison picked her up and held her in his arms. "Lizzy, you're growing like a weed."

Lizzy stared at her hairy-faced daddy and then put her arms around his neck. The other children backed up as the man, with a wide smile on his face, stuck out his hand. "Hello, Harry. Good to see you home." He stepped back after they shook hands. The other woman moved closer and hugged Harrison.

"I'm g-glad you-you're back, Harry," she stuttered.

"I'm glad to be home." Harrison handed Lizzy to his wife, and then put his hand on Alf's shoulder. "Alf, this is my wife, Suzy. Suzy, this is my friend Alf Smith. He's going to stay with us until after Christmas."

Alf stepped closer to the porch and Harrison's family quieted down as they studied him. Slowly they stepped forward and Alf shook hands with all of them, including the children, as Harrison named them off. The oldest was fourteen-year-old William, whose eyes kept straying to Alf's Colt pistol. Twelve-year-old Becky was next, then Whitten, who was ten, and Mattie, who was eight. Ida Sue, the six-year-old, was shy and only touched his hand before moving back. Four-year-old Lizzy just looked at him, and then hid her face in her mama's bosom. The man and the woman were next.

"Alf, this is my brother Squire and my sister Martha."

Squire smiled as he shook Alf's hand. "Good to meet you, Alf." Martha shook his hand too, and then stepped back without saying anything.

Alf cleared his throat. "You have quite a family, Harrison. Are you sure you have room for me to stay?"

"Why sure, Alf, we got three bedrooms and a kitchen. You can sleep in the bedroom with Squire and the older boys. The girls sleep in the other room with Martha, and Suzy and I have our room."

"I don't want to put anybody out."

Harrison patted Alf on the back. "Don't worry about it, Alf." He nodded toward the door. "Come on, let's all go in and get something to eat." He turned to Suzy. "Have y'all ate supper yet?"

"No, we were just putting it on the table," Suzy replied as she set Lizzy down on the porch. "Set two more places at the table, Martha."

The two women went in first, followed by Bill and Whitten carrying Harrison's bags and the supplies. Harrison went in next, the children close behind him. Only Becky had hung back with Alf, but as soon as the door was clear she grabbed one of Alf's bags and carried it in for him. She led him to one of the bedrooms and set the bag on one of the beds. With wide eyes and a slight smile, she gazed at Alf.

"I'll be thirteen next month. How old are you, Alf?"

Alf was unprepared for that question. He studied Becky for a few seconds. She was tall for her age and already showing wide hips and small breasts under her long, straight dress. Her hair was long and slightly curly. Her face was pretty and smooth.

"I'll be twenty-two in March."

Becky cocked her head slightly. "Do you have a wife?"

Alf was saved from answering by Harrison calling out that supper was ready. Alf gestured to Becky to go first, and then followed her out the door.

"You sit over here, Alf." Harrison pulled out a chair at the head of a long table. Alf quickly sat down and Harrison sat next to him on the end. Suzy sat on the opposite side of the table. Martha and Squire sat at the other end of the long table, and the children all sat in between. When everyone was seated, Harrison held up his hands and everyone bowed their heads.

"Heavenly Father, bless this food we are about to receive. Thank You for all the blessing You have bestowed upon us and forgive us of our sins. I ask this in Jesus name, Amen."

The first few minutes after the blessing were chaotic with everyone passing plates and dishes, but then they all settled down to eating with only the adults talking. Harrison told his story of working on the docks first, and then the questions began to come to Alf. He told them he was born in Illinois, but when they asked about his parents he just told them they'd died in a fire. They asked how he'd gotten to Texas and he told them of his journey. They were all impressed that he had worked on a steamboat on the Mississippi River. Bill and Whitten forgot they were supposed to be seen and not heard and talked excitedly about the adventures of Tom Sawyer and Huckleberry Finn. Alf smiled and told them about meeting Mark Twain. The adults were impressed now and asked a lot of questions about the famous author.

When everyone was through eating, the women and Becky began putting up the food. Harrison took Alf to his room where his bags were and told him he could sleep on the bed by himself and the boys could sleep out in the kitchen. Squire would be in the other bed. Harrison showed him the girls' bedroom, which was larger and had three beds, and then his bedroom, which was smaller, with one big bed and a small bed off to the side.

Alf nodded toward the baby bed. "Does the little one sleep here?"

Harrison shook his head. "Not anymore. We keep it in here for the next one. It should be here in about five months."

Alf quickly figured in his head, then lifted his finger and started to say something.

Harrison interrupted with a wide grin. "I came home on the train for a week about four months ago."

Alf smiled and shook his head. Harrison nodded toward the door. "Come on, I'll show you the outhouse."

Alf woke the next morning to the smell of frying sausage and the sound of chattering children. It was still dark outside, but someone had left a candle burning in the room, probably Squire, who was already up and gone. Alf lay in bed for a while as he listened to the voices of the children eating in the kitchen. All of this was strange to him and he was reluctant to get up and dress. He felt he was intruding by taking up someone else's bed, plus he had never stayed in a house with so many children. He knew they would all be staring at him when he entered the kitchen. He had never liked a lot of attention.

Becky pushed aside the curtains that covered the door. "Time to get up, Alf!" For a few seconds she stared at Alf, who had thrown off his covers and was lying there in his long johns. "Breakfast is ready."

Alf was speechless at first as he lay looking up at Becky. His face flushed as he realized he had been scratching his butt. He quickly grabbed the heavy quilt and pulled it back over him. "I'll be up in a moment."

Becky smiled and a twinkle appeared in her eyes. "I don't think anyone's in the outhouse if you need to go."

Alf could feel the blood flowing to his face. "Thanks," he said as he sat up. With the quilt covering him, he turned and lowered his feet to the floor. He sat waiting for Becky to leave but she lingered until *whack!*—she jumped.

"Becky, get back over to the table and leave that boy alone." Suzy had come up behind Becky and spanked her on the butt.

Becky's face turned beet red as she lowered her head and hurried back to the kitchen.

Suzy glanced at Alf. "Sorry Alf, these pesky kids will drive you crazy if you let 'em." She closed the curtain and Alf could hear her as she walked away. "You kids finish eating and go outside. Don't be bothering Alf with a bunch of silly questions."

Alf quickly pulled on his pants and boots. He needed to relieve himself so he cautiously pulled back the curtain and walked toward the back door. All the kids noticed him and stopped what they were doing to stare. Alf cleared his throat. "Good morning, everyone."

All of the kids but Lizzy told Alf good morning back and then went back to their eating. Harrison, who was sitting at the head of the table, waited until the kids had said their greeting and then said, "Good morning! Are you ready for breakfast? How do you like your eggs?"

"I'm just about ready." Alf nodded toward the back door. "I got to go out back first."

"Sure, go ahead. There's water in a pan out back where you can wash up."

Alf started out the back door and then turned and looked at Suzy. "I like my eggs over easy, if you please."

Suzy smiled and was reaching for the eggs as Alf closed the door behind him. He hurried and relieved himself, then washed up from a blue wash pan. When he got back to the kitchen, most of the kids were gone, except Becky, who was washing dishes. A plate of eggs and sausage sat on the table next to Harrison.

Harrison pointed at the plate. "Sit here. Suzy got 'em all ready for you."

Alf sat and began cutting up his eggs as Harrison went back to eating. Suzy brought him a cup of coffee and asked if there was anything else he needed.

"I would like some salt and pepper if you have it, ma'am."

Suzy took two shakers from a shelf and set them in front of Alf. "I have to keep them away from the children or they will waste it." She paused, and then added, "Alf, you can call me Suzy like everyone else."

"Okay, ma'am—oops, I mean Suzy."

Suzy smiled and went back to clearing dishes from the table. Alf took a drink of his coffee and said to Harrison, "I'm not used to being around a bunch of kids. Before my parents died, I lived with my sisters and brother, but when I moved in with Sheriff Boone and Martha, I became an only child."

Harrison chuckled. "I grew up with four brothers and three sisters and I was the next-to-youngest, so this all seems natural to me. I was really getting lonesome for my kids back in Galveston. I don't know if I'll go back."

"Maybe you can find work around here. Surely with all the new construction you could find something." Alf thought for a second. "I don't think I'll work for Mike anymore. You might get a job with him."

"Why won't you work for Mike?"

Alf finished chewing his sausage. "I don't need to be tied down to a job right now. I have one more man to find." He pressed his lips together as he reached for his coffee.

"Can't you put that off for a while?"

"No. I can't rest until I find the last murderer of my parents. It's been in my mind for five years and I'm ready to put it behind me."

Harrison looked into Alf's eyes. "Have you ever thought that maybe it will be you who gets killed?"

Alf pondered the question. "I have thought about it, but it doesn't matter. It is in my mind and I can't relax or do anything else until I settle this one way or another. If I get killed, I guess it will be God's will."

"I guess you have to do what you have to do, Alf. You're welcome to stay here as long as you want."

"I appreciate that. If it's all right, I'd like to stay until I can get a horse, and I might need to work with him some to finish him out."

Harrison locked eyes with Alf. "Look, son, it ain't no problem you staying here. Christmas Eve is tomorrow and we can't get much done, but after Christmas we'll find you a horse and you can work with him here as long as you like. If you want that old saddle of mine, you can start working it into shape."

"I'm much obliged, Harrison, and I'll do that. But as soon as you think I have overstayed my welcome, you let me know."

"You'll be tired of us before we get tired of you, Alf."

Alf shook his head and smiled. "Okay. By the way, I need to go into town and pick up a few things today. You got something I can ride?"

Harrison shook his head. "I got to pick up some stuff in town today too. We'll hook up my mules in a minute and you can ride in with me and Suzy."

When Alf was through with breakfast, he went with Harrison to the barn and they hitched up the mules to the wagon. While they were waiting on Suzy, Alf went back to the barn to look at the old saddle Harrison was going to lend him. It wasn't bad but it needed some new skirts and some stitching. He decided it would be better to bring it to the saddle shop in town, so he threw it into the wagon. A few minutes later, Suzy came out of the house in her best dress, still giving instructions to Martha, who had followed her out the door. Alf helped her into the wagon while Harrison made sure the mules stood still. He climbed in beside her and they headed toward Belton.

The road followed the river part of the way and Harrison stopped once to let Alf walk along its banks. Alf enjoyed the stroll, but Harrison had told him it was a two-hour trip to town so he didn't tarry long. It was midmorning when they pulled into Belton and parked at the wagon yard. Alf carried the saddle to the leather shop while Harrison and Suzy went to Smith's store. The saddle maker told Alf he would fix Harrison's old saddle for two dollars, but Alf would have to leave it for a few days. Alf agreed and began walking around the town. He saw some pocketknives in Potts's window and went inside to look at them. He decided that most men could always use a new knife, so he bought four of them—two nice big ones for Harrison and Squire, and smaller ones for Bill and Whitten. That left the girls, but he didn't know what to buy them. He decided to find Suzy and give her money for the girls' presents. And he would slip some money to Harrison to get a present for Suzy. Alf hurried to Smith's and found them still there. Suzy agreed to help Alf find presents for the girls, so she pointed out things she thought they would like and Alf bought them. He frowned when she told him Becky would like some perfume, but he bought it for her anyhow. While they were looking for the girls' gifts, Suzy stopped and looked at a dainty lace-covered hat. Alf could see in her face that she wanted it, and when she tried it on it fit her, but when she looked at the price she frowned and put it back. Later, when he had paid for all the girls' gifts, he pulled Harrison aside and showed him the hat, then asked him what he thought.

Harrison rubbed his chin. "She looks at hats every time she comes into town but she never buys one—says we can't afford it. They want three dollars for that one, and that would buy a lot of food."

Alf looked at the hat again. "I'm going to buy it for her. Or we can buy it together if you want."

Harrison rubbed his chin again as he thought about Alf's proposition. "Okay, let's go halves and we'll tell her it's from both of us."

Alf took the hat to the counter and paid for it while Harrison kept Suzy busy out front where a lot of the bigger items were displayed on the boardwalk. The clerk wrapped the hat up and Alf put it in a burlap bag with his other stuff. When they were finished shopping, they took the packages back to the wagon and started home. They stopped by the river again and snacked on crackers and cheese while the mules rested. Alf liked this rough, rocky country with its huge oak trees in the valleys and the cedar-covered hills. It was all so different from the fertile woodland he had grown up in. Every few minutes he would see some animal or plant he had never seen before. Even the river was different, with its big pecan and cottonwood trees growing along its banks. Alf almost hated to leave its quiet, relaxing beauty, but Harrison and Suzy wanted to get home before dark, so they loaded up and journeyed home.

The next day Squire and the boys went out to the woods to look for a Christmas tree. Alf thought it was strange when they came back with a six-foot cedar. All the Christmas trees he had ever known were pine or spruce trees. Harrison built a stand for it out of wood scraps he had saved from some of his other projects, and the boys set it up in the large room that served as the kitchen and living room. The girls made popcorn and all the children strung the kernels on thread and looped it around the tree. The older kids cut stars out of colored paper and helped the younger ones hang them on the tree. When they were finished, they all stepped back and admired their work.

Mattie looked up to the top of the tree and frowned. "We don't have anything on top, Mommy."

Suzy smiled as she reached up on a shelf and took down a package. She undid the paper and held something up for all of them to see. "I have been saving this for last. I bought it in town yesterday."

"It's an angel!" Mattie exclaimed.

All of the children crowded around to see the angel. The body and the robes were made of metal and painted white and tan. Fastened to the body were silver silk wings. Over its head was a golden halo held up by a metal rod.

"It's beautiful!" Ida shouted.

"It bee-u-full," Lizzy repeated quietly.

Alf and the rest of the family laughed. Lizzy ran to her mother and hid behind her skirt.

Harrison secured the angel to the top of the tree. They all backed up to look at it and agreed it was the best part of the tree. Eventually the girls, whispering behind their hands, went to their room and closed the curtains. The boys did the same. Suzy and Martha began fixing supper.

Harrison nodded to Alf. "Let's go outside and I'll show you my place."

With Harrison leading the way, they walked around the farm. The fields were empty because it was way past harvest time, but there were still some vegetables in the garden. Alf had never seen okra before and couldn't wait to taste it. Turnip and collard greens were flourishing also. Next Harrison showed him the peach and plum orchard, which was dormant for the winter, and then they looked over the still-green pastures. The mules and two milk cows were in a small pasture by the barn. A half-dozen hogs were in a wooden pen past the barn. Alf thought it was a pretty nice farm except for the rocks that seemed to be everywhere, even in the fields. Harrison told him the rocks made plowing a nuisance, but his crops did pretty well.

"The only thing that doesn't grow very well around here is tobacco. I grow some, but it ain't near as good as what I growed in Kentucky." Harrison nodded toward a small shed by the barn.

"Come on to the curing shed and I'll show you." He led Alf to the shed and showed him the brown leaves hanging from racks close to the ceiling. He pulled some down and handed it to Alf.

"I've never seen the plants in Illinois," Alf said. "Looks like tobacco, though." He carefully pinched off a piece and tasted it. "Tastes like tobacco." He spat it on the ground. "I never did like to chew it. I smoke it every once in a while, but not much."

Harrison hung the plant back up. "I chew a lot and smoke too. When I was in the Confederate Army, tobacco was what kept us going. We would chew it to keep our minds off of being hungry."

Alf recalled stories his father had told him of the skinny, ragged Rebel soldiers who'd fought so hard. He wondered if his father had fought on some battlefield against Harrison. "Did you ever kill any Yankees during the war, Harrison?"

Harrison didn't answer at first. He closed his eyes and pressed his lips together. "I hope not, Alf. I shot at some but I don't know if I hit 'em." He paused. His mind seemed to be somewhere else. Finally he said, "My brother and me both lived in Illinois when the war started. I packed up and went back to Kentucky and joined the Confederates. I didn't know if my brother Granville joined the Yankees or not, but it got to whenever I shot at a Yankee; I could almost see Granville's face on him. I finally asked my captain to put me in something besides infantry. He sent me to the graves unit. From then on until my enlistment was up, I dug graves and buried soldiers, both ours and theirs." Harrison paused and again his mind seemed to be elsewhere. "When my enlistment was up, I went back home to Crab Orchard, Kentucky, and stayed there."

Alf waited to see if Harrison would say anything else, but after a few seconds he figured he didn't want to talk about it anymore. He decided to change the subject. "When did you come to Texas?"

Harrison's face changed as he let out a deep breath. He stepped out of the shed and into the yard. Alf followed. He didn't know if Harrison was going to answer or not. Finally Harrison said, "My pa died in 1870 and us kids divided up the farm. I tried to make a go of it, but after a few years, Momma, Martha, Squire, and I sold out our part and come to Texas. We settled up in Colin County for a while but it was rough going. We buried Momma up there in seventy-eight." Harrison lowered his head. "I heard from one of my cousins that there was cheap land down here, so I sold out, came down here and bought this place."

Alf glanced around. "I like it, Harrison, it's a nice place."

Harrison smiled and patted Alf on the shoulder. "Come on, I'll show you my post yard."

They started toward the front of the house where Alf had seen stacks of cedar posts, but Bill came out on the porch and called them to supper.

"Come on, Alf, let's wash up," Harrison said. They went to the back door, washed up, then stepped into the house. Most everyone was seated but impatiently waiting for Harrison and Alf. Harrison went to his place at the head of the table and motioned for Alf to sit by him.

Suzy quickly sat at the other end of the table and put her finger to her lips. "Father, would you say the blessing?"

Harrison spread out his arms toward Alf and Squire, who was sitting opposite Alf. Everyone held hands and Harrison bowed his head. "Dear God, thank You for all the blessings You have bestowed upon us, and thank You for watching over us and keeping us from harm. We ask, Father God, that You bless this food we are about to receive. We also ask that You bless each and every one of this family and also Alf, who is a long way from home. I ask You, Father God, to forgive us of our sins, the ones we know of and the ones we don't. Father God, watch over us and keep us safe. I ask this in the name of my Lord and Savior, Jesus Christ, amen."

Everyone began eating and passing plates. The children were excited about Christmas and chattered about the things they hoped would be under the tree for them. Alf smiled as he listened. It reminded him of Christmases at home before his parents were killed. He wondered what his brother and sisters were doing now. He felt thankful that the girls had moved in with the Higgins's; they were good people. The girls would have a nice Christmas.

After supper, when the dishes were washed and the food put up, they all gathered around the tree and sang Christmas songs. Alf got into the spirit as they sang a lot of his favorites. He especially liked "Silent Night" and "Away in a Manger" and called for them several times. Finally the children got sleepy and went to bed. The adults stayed up and talked, mostly about Christmases when they were children. Alf told them of his Christmases back in Illinois and how a lot of times there was snow on the ground. Harrison told him that in Kentucky it snowed a lot and his family sometimes had white Christmases too, but he'd never seen a white Christmas since he'd moved to Texas. In fact, he said, he hadn't seen snow since living here. Old-timers in the area told him it snowed sometimes, but it was rare. Alf didn't know if he would miss snow or not. He didn't like the cold, so maybe he would like Texas if it didn't get any colder than what he had already experienced.

Finally Alf started getting sleepy. He asked Harrison when they put presents under the tree for the kids. Harrison pulled out his watch.

"We will put them out in a little bit. Go on to bed if you want. The kids will get up about four and want to open gifts."

Alf rose from his chair. "I have some presents for the kids too. Should I get them now or give them out in the morning?"

"Why don't you just wait until sometime in the morning? Maybe after breakfast. That way it will be more of a surprise and they will enjoy it more."

"Okay, I'll do that. I'm going to bed now. Merry Christmas."

Harrison and Suzy smiled as they replied in unison, "Merry Christmas, Alf."

The next morning was chaos. Alf woke up to the sounds of the children cooing over the tree, and then a few minutes later Bill peeped into the room.

"Daddy said to get you up so we can open our presents."

Alf slipped his pants on and went into the living room. Presents wrapped in colored paper were scattered under the tree, along with bowls of candy and nuts. A box full of large orange and yellow ball-shaped objects caught his eye. He turned and looked at Harrison. "What are those things?"

"Those are oranges and grapefruit. They grow them down South. The Mexicans bring them up and sell them at the square in Belton."

Alf picked up one of the oranges. "I've heard of them but I never seen any. Where did you get these?"

"I bought these when you were in jail and I hid them in the wagon." Harrison began to peel one of the oranges. "You peel the skin off and then eat the inside." Harrison finished peeling the orange, then pulled it apart and handed half of it to Alf. "It's got seeds but you can just spit them out."

Alf watched as Harrison pulled off a slice of the orange and stuck it into his mouth. He pulled a slice from his own half and tried it. It was sweet but with a strange flavor he had never tasted before. As he spat the seeds into the fireplace, he decided he liked it and pulled off another slice. By now some of the children had grabbed an orange too. Bill held half of an orange to Alf.

"This is how I like to eat them." He picked out most of the seeds, bit into one of the halves, and pulled out the pulp with his teeth. As Alf watched Bill, Mattie and Ida Sue hurried over and showed him how they were eating their oranges too. They had cut a hole in one end and were sucking out the juice. Alf smiled as he watched them, and then finished his orange as he stood among the happy children.

Harrison looked at Suzy and she nodded. He walked to the Christmas tree and began giving out the presents to the children. Squeals of joy filled the room as the children opened their gift. The little girls got dolls and Becky got a necklace with a cross pendant. Whitten opened a menagerie of carved animals and immediately began to play with them on the floor. Bill whooped when he opened his gift and held up a skinning knife and scabbard for everyone to see. Martha and Squire were happy with clothes, and Suzy liked the new sewing kit and teapot Harrison had gotten for her in Galveston.

Finally everyone had opened their presents and settled down, and Suzy cooked breakfast. When they had eaten, Alf got out the presents he had bought and handed them to the kids. Harrison, Squire, and the boys were thrilled with their pocketknives. Mattie, Ida Sue, and Lizzy squealed happily when they opened their gifts. Becky slowly opened hers, and then sheepishly smiled as she cut her eyes at Alf. When Alf smiled back, her face turned crimson and she hurried to her room. Alf watched her for a second, and then walked over to Harrison and Suzy while pulling his last gift out of the bag.

"Suzy, Harrison and I went in together to buy you this gift because we thought you deserved it." Aft handed the gift to Harrison. "You give it to her." Harrison took it and handed it to Suzy. She slowly opened the paper and pulled out the hat. She was silent for a second as she stared at it, and tears came to her eyes.

"It's so beautiful." She looked at Harrison, then at Alf. "You shouldn't have, but thank you, both of you, thank you. I love it." She set the hat upon her head, wiped her eyes, and turned to the rest of her family, who were watching in silence. "How do I look?"

Everyone told her how much they liked the hat. The girls wanted to try it on, but Suzy told them maybe later she would let them. She put it back in the box and took it to her room.

The rest of the morning the men played dominos and checkers while the women prepared the Christmas dinner. The three little girls played with their dolls while Whitten built pens for his wooden animals. Bill sharpened his knives when he wasn't doing something for Suzy or Martha. Becky helped in the kitchen too, but a few times she came to watch the men at their games. Alf noticed that she would usually stand beside him. She would comment about the game, and once she put her hand on his shoulder and pointed out a domino he could play. It was this time that Alf caught the smell of the perfume he had given her. He frowned as he became aware that she was attracted to him. He felt flattered at first, but after thinking about it, he was bothered. There were ten years' difference in their ages, and he saw her as still a child. He was fond of her, but he hoped her infatuation with him wasn't too serious. He put it in the back of his mind and returned his attention to the game. He would be gone in a few days, maybe never to see Harrison and his family again.

The games continued until noon, when Suzy called for everyone to get ready for dinner. Alf and the rest of the men washed up in the back while the girls used a wash pan in the kitchen. After Alf washed up, he made his way to the kitchen. He stopped and stared. He hadn't paid close attention earlier, but now his eyes opened wide at the amount of food on the table. A golden-brown turkey in a pan of dressing sat in the center of the table. Next to it were two platters of roast chicken. A huge bowl of mashed potatoes balanced the table, along with a smaller bowl of white gravy. Other smaller bowls contained green beans, corn, and peas. A platter of sliced bread completed the spread, but smaller saucers and cups containing butter and spices were scattered around the table.

Everyone took their usual seats except for Suzy and Martha, who were fussing with a cake they were icing. Finally they wiped their hands and sat down. Harrison grasped Suzy's hand and reached out for Alf's. A warm, peaceful feeling came over Alf as he clasped hands with Harrison and Becky, who was now sitting beside him. He liked being with Harrison's family. Harrison bowed his head and said the blessing. Immediately after he said amen, the room erupted in conversation and the passing of food. Seconds later Alf was swamped with platters and bowls of food. Quickly he took what he wanted and passed the food to the next person. Finally the commotion stopped as one by one they began to eat. Alf too dug into his food and was quiet as he savored the taste and smells. He felt closer to Harrison and his family as he realized he had been accepted into the man's home during a sacred time of year, a time when family was most important. He smiled at Harrison and held up a chicken leg.

"This is the best chicken I have ever tasted, and these sweet potatoes are so good. I have never tasted anything like this."

Harrison grinned and touched Suzy's shoulder. "We call them yams. Suzy is a good cook, and so is Martha." He nodded toward the counter. "Wait until you taste that peach cobbler. It's better than what my mama used to make."

Alf glanced at the large dish of cobbler and shook his head. "I'll try to save some room for it." He turned back to his plate and forked his last lump of sauce-covered yams. After he shoved it into his mouth, he felt a touch on his arm. He turned to see Becky holding the bowl of yams. She didn't say anything as she held them out toward him, but Alf noticed a puppy-dog look in her eyes. He wondered how she had beat Bill out of his regular seat at the table.

Alf took the bowl, dipped out a few more of the yams, and passed it to Harrison. As he began eating again, he glanced at Becky. She was pretty, but she was just a child. Maybe in a few years he would be ready to settle down with some girl. But not now.

CHAPTER 18

Bojack Brown, wearing his best pants and shirt, stepped out of the bunkhouse, untied his pinto, and climbed into the saddle. The day was warm for January and only a brisk breeze from the south kept it from being perfect. Feeling the wind, Bojack pushed his hat tighter on his head, pulled its rawhide string, and tightened it under his chin. He checked the latchstring on his Colt and then turned the pinto, spurring him into a slow lope toward a small herd of cattle and two drivers slowly moving east on the road to Waco. One of the men noticed him coming and called out to him.

"You sure are slicked up, Bojack. You got a girl in town?"

"I got a lot of girls, Jesse, over on the reservation." Bojack slowed the pinto and reined him alongside Jesse. "I'm going to have me a good time over there without having to marry one of 'em."

Jesse glanced at Bojack. "I know what you mean. If you marry some woman then you have to get 'em a house and buy 'em things all the time. Before you know it you've spent all your money on them and you don't have any for yourself."

"Jesse, you already spend all your money on women and beer. Look at you! You've been wearing those same clothes for as long as I can remember."

Jesse looked down at his pants and shirt. Dust and grime had turned them to a greasy gray color. Awkwardly patched holes on the knees and elbows showed equally dirty skin. Jesse furrowed his brow as he lifted up his arm. "Can't say I remember what color this shirt was when I bought it a few years ago. I guess I could buy me some new clothes when we get to Waco—if you hold my money until I do."

Bojack glared at Jesse. "I will, and whatever you say, I ain't giving it to you like I did last time. You need to take a bath too."

"I will, Bojack, I will." Jesse popped his bullwhip and reined his horse behind a steer that had stopped to graze on a clump of prairie grass. He expertly nipped the steer on the rump and rode behind as it hurried to catch up with the herd.

Bojack watched for a few seconds, then turned the pinto and loped him up alongside the other herder, an older man with gray whiskers and hair. A streak of brown tobacco stain ran from the corner of his mouth down his chin. His clothes were in better shape than Jesse's but still well worn. His pistol was on his left side, butt forward.

"How's it going, Rusty?"

Rusty glanced over at Bojack. "It's going okay. I think that steer with the hurt leg will make it to Waco in good shape."

Bojack grinned. "As long as he makes it, I don't care. The butcher doesn't care if he has a bum leg. He'll just cut around it."

Rusty rolled his wad to one side, then spat. "You hear from Jude?"

"Yeah, they made it to Luke's ranch. They're gathering cattle to drive to Dodge City."

Rusty rolled his wad of tobacco to the other side of his mouth. "You hear anything else about that man who was looking for Jude?"

"Naw, I figure Ace embellished the story some. Luke should've stayed around and took care of the Yankee when he showed up. Now I have to do it."

"You gonna face him in the street?"

Bojack grinned. "I could, but why take chances? I'll just bushwhack him."

Rusty spat again, tobacco juice dripping off his chin. "How you going to find him?"

"If he asks around, people will tell him the location of the ranch. He's looking for Jude, not me. I'll just set him up and then pop a cap on his ass."

Rusty shook his head and took off after a straying steer. BoJack watched him for a minute, and then moved up to the front of the herd. They were only a few miles from the cattle pens and he had to get the steers used to following him.

A couple of hours later the cattle pens were in sight. The three men drove the cattle into an empty pen and then Bojack went to the office to arrange a sale. Thirty minutes later he returned with a buyer, and after haggling for a few minutes, they shook hands on the deal. They walked back to the office and a few minutes later Bojack came back holding a bank draft.

"Let's go cash this check and I'll give you boys your pay for the month."

Bojack cashed the bank draft and met the three men at a table in the lobby. Bojack carefully counted out Rusty's pay and handed it to him. Then he turned to Jesse.

"Come on, me and you are going to the store to get you some clothes and then to the bathhouse."

Rusty laughed as he headed for the door. "I'll meet you at Cora's dance hall, boys. I heard she has some new dancers."

Bojack grinned. "Okay, see you there later. Let's go, Jesse."

He started out the door with Jesse following. When they got to the street, Jesse touched Bojack softly on the shoulder. "I thought you was joking, Bojack. Give me my money; I can do this by myself."

Bojack stopped. He did want to go see one of the girls at Cora's place, and he didn't want Rusty to beat him there. "All right, I'm going to give you half of it. If you don't do like I said, I'm going to keep the rest of your money until you do."

Jesse glanced at his boss then dropped his gaze to the boardwalk. "Sure, Bojack, sure, you know me. I know I need new clothes and a bath. I'll go right to the clothing store."

Bojack counted out thirty dollars. "Here, this will get your clothes and a bath and a little to spend."

Jesse stuck the money in his pocket and headed toward Waco's commercial district. Bojack watched him for a minute, then turned and headed toward the reservation.

Jesse had every intention of following Bojack's orders, but his route to the clothing store chanced to pass a saloon. He paused when he saw the swinging doors. He brought up his hand and wiped his mouth. He was mighty thirsty. One drink would satisfy him and then he would go on to the store. He walked in and let his eyes adjust to the darkened room first and then he went up to the bar.

CHAPTER 19

The day after Christmas, Harrison and Alf hitched up the wagon to drive over to Rufus Light's place to look at some horses. First Bill and then Becky asked to go with them and Harrison agreed, so they all piled in the wagon. Bill climbed into the back but Becky squeezed herself in between Alf and her father. They had barely gotten started when Becky glanced over at Alf.

"I can tell you all the names of the trees and things on the way over." She scooted closer against him. "Do they have cedar trees in Illinois?"

Alf took a deep breath as he felt the heat from her body. The scent of the lilac perfume tickled his nose. "No, but we have a lot of pine and hemlock."

"What is a hemlock?"

Alf felt her leg push against his. He tried to move over but he was against the side rail already. "It's something like a pine." He felt her leg move against his again and could see it outlined under her long dress. "Uh, Becky…uh, do you go to school? What grade are you in?"

"I'm finished going to school." She smiled, and then pouted her lips.

Harrison, not seeming to notice Becky's flirting, said, "The school here in the valley only goes to six grades and she's already finished them." He smiled at Becky. "She's smart. I ought to send her to school in Belton but I can't afford it."

"Daddy, I'm through with school. I can read and write and I can do arithmetic." She looked at Alf again. "What else do I need to know except how to be a wife?"

Alf felt a chill in his stomach. He swallowed as he slowly inched his leg away from hers. He wet his lips and glanced sideways at her. "Have you read *Tom Sawyer*?"

Alf breathed a sigh of relief when Harrison finally pulled the wagon up to the front of the Light house. He noticed a man out by the corrals, so when he climbed down out of the wagon, he turned to walk over to him.

"Alf, will you help me down?"

Becky was still sitting. Alf knew that men were supposed to help ladies out of wagons, but he had seen Becky climbing in and out of that wagon several times without any help. He sighed as he stepped up closer and reached out his hand. She took it, and then jumped off the wagon into his arms. Alf was taken by surprise and grabbed her waist to keep her from falling. She grabbed him back tightly and looked up into his eyes.

"Thank you, Alf. I thought I was going to fall."

Alf froze when he felt her body next to his. She was warm and her perfume smelled so sweet. But a voice in his head roared at him, *"She is only twelve years old!"* He panicked and tried to push her away, but she clung to him.

"Turn me loose, Becky. You're okay now and I have to talk to John."

Becky released him and stepped back. Alf hurried to catch up with Harrison, who was halfway to the corral and oblivious to what was going on back at the wagon.

The man at the corral, who had seen them drive up, waited for them to get closer and then called out, "Howdy, neighbors! Harrison, this must be Alf, the man you said was looking for a horse." He stepped up to Alf and stuck out his hand.

Alf had been studying the man. He seemed to be in his early thirties, about Alf's size but with lighter hair. He had a mustache but was otherwise clean-shaven. Alf took his outstretched hand. "Glad to meet you. You must be Rufus."

"Yes, Rufus Light, at your service. Glad to meet you, Alf." He nodded toward the corral. "This is what I got to sell. Look 'em over." He turned back to Harrison. "Brought some of the young'uns, I see."

While the rest of them talked about Christmas and the latest gossip, Alf walked up to the corral fence and looked at the horses. They were all young and full of spirit, but one of them caught his eye, a stocky black horse with a wide chest and a short body.

Rufus and Harrison walked up beside him. "What do you think about them, Alf?"

"I like the looks of that black. He looks like he got some Morgan in him, but crossed with something else."

Rufus smiled. "You know your horses. He's half Morgan. I have a Morgan stud I breed with my mustangs. These colts make a hell of a cow horse. They're quick and they can turn on a dime."

"How old are they?"

"They'll be three in the spring, just right to start breaking. I already got 'em halter-broke."

"How much do you want for 'em, Rufus?" Harrison asked.

'Well, going rate is about twenty dollars." He turned to Alf. "You want to look at that black?"

"Yeah, let's catch him. I want to see him up close."

Rufus turned to a young cowboy who had walked up behind them. He was about Alf's age and was standing beside Bill at the corral fence. "Jack, go in there and put your rope on that black."

Jack scrambled over the fence and the horses turned and looked at him. Some started to move away, but the black and a line back dun stood their ground. Jack, talking in a soothing voice, slowly walked up to the black and slipped the rope over his head. He tugged gently on the rope and began walking toward the gate, and the black obediently followed. When they got to the gate, Rufus took a leather halter that was hanging on the fence and buckled it on the horse. Jack tied the rope to the halter and led the black out the gate.

As Alf went toward the black horse, he already felt he wanted it. He rubbed the black's cheeks and ran his hand down to its nose. Jake had taught him to always let a horse see and smell you first before you did anything else. Alf rubbed the black's silky nose and stroked his forehead. Then he ran his hands to the horse's shoulder and rubbed in a circular motion. Jake had told him the shoulder rubbing would calm a horse down and help it accept you as part of the herd. Alf rubbed for a few minutes, then moved his hand down the animal's back and to its hips. He ran his hand down its leg, and then carefully walked around its back to the other side. Still rubbing, he checked the back leg, then moved to the shoulder and rubbed some more. After a few seconds, he ran his hand down the black's front legs and then his neck. Finally he stepped back and looked over at Rufus.

"Have you put a saddle on him?"

Rufus shook his head. "No, but my hand here has been on him bareback." He looked over at Jack and nodded toward the black. "Show him."

Jack quickly jumped up on the black's back. The horse's only reaction was to turn his head to look at the boy. Jack leaned forward and rubbed the horse's neck. "I call him Blackjack. He's my favorite."

Alf trembled slightly as he watched Jack on the horse. His desire for Blackjack was growing and he was slightly jealous of Jack for sitting on him. He took a few short breaths and turned to Rufus. "I like him. I'll take him." He reached into his pocket and pulled out his wallet. "You said twenty, right?"

Rufus rubbed his chin. "Yeah, and I'll even throw in the halter. I know you'll need it to get him back to Harrisons."

Alf handed Rufus a twenty-dollar brown-back, then put his wallet back into his pocket. "Thanks, Rufus, I can use the halter. The only one Harrison has needs some mending. I did bring a rope, though." Alf turned to get the rope he had brought, but Bill was already tying it to Blackjack's halter. He handed the end to Alf. Alf led Blackjack to the wagon and began rubbing and petting him.

Becky, who had been watching the whole time, came over beside Alf. She rubbed Blackjack's neck, and then looked at Alf. "I like him. May I ride him?"

Alf smiled and shook his head. "I got to break him to ride first."

Becky cocked her head. "I saw Jack on him."

"He was just sitting on him." Alf run his hand down Blackjack's back. "Blackjack's gentle but he ain't ready to ride." Watching Bill and Jack come toward them, he had an idea. "Why don't you go ask Jack if you can ride one of their horses?"

Becky looked over at Jack. "You have a horse?"

Jack's face turned red. He looked in her eyes and then quickly away. "Yeah, I got a sorrel with four white feet. I call him Boots."

Becky smiled, and then cocked her head to one side. "May I ride him?"

Jack stared at her for a second, blinked rapidly, and answered, "Yeah, I'll go get him." He turned and raced off toward their barn.

Alf took a step away from Becky. "I think he likes you."

Becky frowned. "I see him at church sometimes but he never talks to me. Besides, he acts like he's Bill age."

Bill, who was standing beside her petting Blackjack, said, "He's a lot older than I am."

Becky tilted her head back and sniffed. "Well, girls mature faster than boys. Nancy Pruitt got married when she was thirteen and now she has a baby."

Bill shook his head. "I heard she had to get married *because* she was going to have a baby. Now Bobby Moore and her are living with her folks in that little house."

Becky pouted and glanced at Alf. "I'm going to marry a man who knows how to do something besides farm and cut cedar post."

Alf felt like a noose was tightening around his neck and he couldn't think of anything to say. Becky seemed determined to put a halter on him. He sighed with relief when Jack came riding up. When she crawled up on the horse behind Jack and put her arms around his waist, Alf felt a little hope that maybe she would turn her affections to him. He watched them for a few seconds and then walked back to Harrison and Rufus.

"I think you made a good choice, Alf," Rufus said. "I was telling Harrison here that the black was the best one I had."

"Yeah, I think he will make me a good horse. I hope to be riding him in a few days." Alf turned to Harrison. "I was wondering if I could use your wagon to go to town. I need to pick up the saddle and send a telegram to Mike telling him I'm not coming to work for him."

Harrison squinted. "Well, I was planning on moving some post over to John Bowles's place, but I guess we can move them tomorrow."

"I have a saddle horse you can use," Rufus offered. "It would be a lot quicker."

"Thanks, I appreciate it. The saddle is not that important, but Mike will be looking for me tomorrow if I don't let him know something. I almost forgot about him until something Becky said a while ago made me think of it."

Harrison patted Alf on the shoulder. "You know you're more than welcome to stay with me for a while, Alf. You can help us cut cedar post. John Bowles wants five hundred of 'em to fence off part of his place."

"Thanks, Harrison, you're a good friend. I'd like to stay long enough to finish up Blackjack."

Alf looked at the black horse. He was already thinking how he would train him. Blackjack would make a great horse, and when he was ready, Alf would ride him to Waco to look for the last murderer.

CHAPTER 20

The morning was still waiting for the sun to appear when Alf led Blackjack from the barn to the front of the house. Slowly and almost reluctantly he picked up his belongings from the porch and tied them behind his saddle. An unexpected gust of wind from the south tugged at his hat and he pushed it down tighter down on his head. Suddenly he felt lonely and he glanced toward the illuminated kitchen window where Harrison's family would soon be gathering for breakfast. Memories of living with the family crossed his mind and he smiled. It had been a happy time for him. They had welcomed him into their home and treated him like part of the family. He had grown attached to all of them, and a part of him didn't want to leave. As he stared at the window, he tried to think of a reason to stay, but then other, less-happy memories flashed in his mind. Slowly he turned away; it was time to move on.

He stuck his foot into the stirrup, grabbed the saddle horn, and pulled himself into the saddle. He took a deep breath, and then urged Blackjack toward the road. He glanced at the window again and his heart leaped into his throat. Becky was standing there with tears flowing from her pleading eyes. For a second Alf wanted to stop and run to her as he looked at her beautiful face, but his common sense kicked in and he knew he had to ride on. He had faced this same dilemma the night before when he'd gone to the barn to put Blackjack up for the night. Becky had been waiting for him to beg him not to leave. She told him she loved him and would do anything if he would stay. Alf was tempted, but he knew it was wrong and he knew he couldn't stay. He tried to explain but she ran from the barn crying. He hadn't seen her again until now. He studied her face for a few seconds more. Then, with his heart aching, he reluctantly raised his hand and waved good-bye. She turned from the window and he spurred Blackjack into the darkness.

The sun was up when Alf trotted up to Smith's in Belton. Not wanting to waste any time, he hurriedly gathered some food, a blanket, and a new rain slicker. Minutes later he was on the road to Temple. He could have ridden cross-country, but he knew there would be a few fences in the way and he didn't want any confrontations with angry farmers or ranchers. Besides, he wanted to see the town of Temple, or Tanglefoot, as the Belton people called it.

It was still early morning when he rode into Temple, but the growing town was already astir with wagons and people hurrying one way or another. Alf frowned when he saw all the dust they were raising, but then realized the streets were still just unpaved prairie dirt. Deep ruts from recent rains marked the streets with tiny gullies, and a few mud holes existed where the water had been deep. As Alf guided Blackjack closer to the center of town, he passed many empty lots, most of them with for-sale signs between the houses and businesses. Farther on he came to the railroad station. A well-traveled road led off to the north and Alf was sure it was the Waco road. He stopped at a store where two men were sitting on the porch, and they confirmed that it was the road to Waco. After Alf thanked them, he continued north until the road crossed the railroad tracks. Here several saloons lined the road, and even though it was early in the morning, most of them were open and going strong. Alf had just ridden past the batwing doors of one of them when a grubby-looking man staggered out into the street. Alf pulled back on the reins and watched as the apparently intoxicated man charged across the street, trying to navigate the ruts. It was comical and Alf thought maybe this was why they called it Tanglefoot. He waited until the drunk had weaved his way to the other side, and then urged Blackjack on out of town.

Alf took his time the thirty miles to Waco, so it was late in the afternoon when he arrived at the outskirts of the large town. Unlike Temple, here older, well-built homes lined gravel streets in the residential area. Farther into the older part of town, he came upon businesses and the train station fronted by brick-paved streets. A sign on the station told him it was the Missouri, Kansas, and Texas Railroad, or the Katy, as most people liked to call it. Alf stopped at the station. Seeing the clerk wasn't busy, he inquired about a livery stable. The man was very friendly. After he told Alf where to find the nearest one, he proceeded to explain all about how the MKT ran out of Kansas City to the Dallas–Fort Worth area and then to Waco. He told Alf the line was building toward Temple and would have a station in Belton. Alf was fascinated with railroads and listened patiently, but eventually a customer arrived wanting a ticket. Quickly thanking the clerk, Alf rode west down the tracks to the cattle pens. The blacksmith shop and livery was just across the street. Alf could hear someone hammering iron as he tied Blackjack to the hitching rail. When he entered the shop, he found a man, his barrel chest covered in sweat and his leather apron covered in grime, pounding on a cherry-red-hot horseshoe. He worked on the horseshoe for a few minutes, and then stuck it into a bed of hot coals. He nodded to a young man, who grabbed a bellows and began to pump air onto the coals. As the coals began glowing redder, the blacksmith turned to Alf.

"What can I do for you, son?"

"I need shoes on my horse and a place to sleep tonight."

"Let me see the horse," the blacksmith grunted as he headed toward Blackjack. He circled around the horse, lifting up his legs and looking at his hooves. "This the first time you've had him shod?"

"Yes, sir. I bought him about a month ago. I just rode in from Belton."

"His hooves are in pretty good shape. If he ain't no trouble, I get two dollars for the new shoes and twenty-five cents a night including hay. Oats is ten cents extra. You can sleep in the barn, but no smoking around the hay."

Alf pulled out his wallet and searched through his bills and coins. "He won't be any trouble. Here's for one night and the shoes and another dime for the oats."

The blacksmith counted and put up the money. "Go ahead and unsaddle him and put him in that first stall."

Alf led Blackjack to the stall, removed his saddle, and hung it on the fence. He gave him a good brushing, and when he was through he returned to the blacksmith, who was working on another horseshoe. Alf waited until he laid the shoe back into the hot coals.

"Do you know a rancher around here by the name of Jude Brown?"

The blacksmith turned to Alf. "Yeah, he's got a ranch west of here."

Alf felt his heart quicken and he took a deep breath. "Have you seen him lately?"

The blacksmith walked back to his forge and picked up the horseshoe he had been shaping. "No, but I saw his brother Bojack today. I'm shoeing his horse right now." He laid the glowing horseshoe on the anvil, pounded it a few times, and thrust it into a tub of water.

Alf waited until the horseshoe had stopped boiling the water. "Did Bojack say where he was going?"

The blacksmith walked over to a pinto, picked up its front hoof, and laid the horseshoe on it. "No, but I imagine he's at the reservation."

Alf frowned as he visualized a bunch of Indians sitting around their teepees. "There's Indians around here?"

The blacksmith hesitated for a second and then laughed so hard the pinto tried to move away from him. Finally he calmed to only an occasional chuckle and turned to Alf. "Where are you from, mister?"

The man pumping the bellows, who had also been laughing, added, "I thought everyone knew about the reservation."

Alf had stood watching them with his eyes half closed and his nose wrinkled. Now he said, "I'm from Illinois, so I don't know what reservation you're talking about."

The blacksmith grabbed a larger rasp and picked up the pinto's hoof. "You tell him, Louis. I got work to do."

Louis grinned as he came over. "The reservation is what we call the red night district. It's a city law—all the whores have to stay over around Third Street in what they call the gravel-bed district. We just call it the reservation."

Alf knew about prostitute districts. In Galveston it was on Post Office Street, the street where he'd run into Duce Rangle. Alf rubbed his chin. Maybe if he found Bojack, he could talk to him and find out where to find Jude. "Bojack didn't say which place he was going, did he?"

Louis thought for a second. "He didn't say, but I know he likes to go to Cora's dance hall. He might be there."

"How can I get to this reservation?"

Louis nodded for Alf to follow him and they walked outside the shop. He pointed to the street running north from the train station. "Take that street to Main Street, then turn left and go until you get to Third Street. Turn right and in about three or four blocks you will be in the reservation. Cora's dance hall is right on Third."

Alf looked at the street where Louis was pointing. "Thanks, I guess I'll go see if I can find him."

Louis grinned and nodded. "If I had some money, I'd go with you, but I guess I'd better go back to work." He turned and went back to the forge.

Alf grabbed his coat from his saddle and headed toward the street Louis had indicated. A few minutes later as he entered the business district, the smell of hay and manure from the cattle pens slowly faded and the odors from the various stores began to seep into his nose. Even though it was getting dark, a lot of the stores in the downtown area were still open and doing a robust business. Alf was in no hurry, so he entered some to see what they were selling. He bought a bandana and socks at one of the clothing stores and a lariat from a tack store. He had just left a gun shop when the aroma from a restaurant reminded him he was hungry.

It was full dark and cold when Alf stepped back out onto the boardwalk. He paused to button up his coat and then proceeded to Third Street and turned west. In a few blocks, the red lights plainly announced that it was the red-light district, and as he drew closer, he began to hear the music coming from the dance halls and the saloons.

It was like a different world as Alf slowly walked out of the dark and into the glow of a thousand lights. Traffic on the street increased immediately, with horses and buggies coming from all directions, some letting people out and others loading them up. On the boardwalks men laughed and talked as they made their way from one brightly lit place to another. Some of the buildings were just houses with a red lantern hanging on the porch, but among them were saloons emitting the sounds of clinking glass and tinny pianos accompanied by laughter and squeals. Stopping at one of the saloons, Alf studied the interior from the batwing doors. It looked like a typical saloon but there were a lot more women circulating around the floor. As he observed couples going up the stairs he felt a faint longing in his groin, but he remembered what Jake had told him about whores having diseases. He turned away and continued along the boardwalk. Farther up the street he could hear more music that seemed to be played by more than one piano.

The sign above the door told Alf he was at Cora's dance hall. He entered and looked around. A large dance floor took up most of the room, with tables and chairs lining the walls. A small bar crowded with customers was against the back wall with a staircase leading up to a second floor. He studied the men at the bar to see if there were any cowboys among them. He saw one man wearing a wide-brimmed hat and spurs and Alf shouldered his way beside him. He bought a beer and turned to face the dancers. Then he leaned toward the cowboy and said, "There's some good-looking ladies out there on that dance floor."

The cowboy glanced at Alf. "Yeah, sure are. I like that one in the yellow dress with the orange scarf."

"She's okay, but I kind of like the redhead in the green dress."

The cowboy studied the redhead. "I tried her one time and that was enough. She's got a temper on her."

"Thanks for the tip." Alf stuck out his hand. "By the way, my name's Alf Smith. I just rode in from Belton."

"My name's Rusty. Glad to meet you. You say you're from Belton?"

"I was in Belton for a while. Before that I lived in Galveston."

Rusty finished his beer and held up his mug to the bartender. "You just drifting, looking for work?"

"Yeah, I work here and there. I worked for a freight outfit out of Galveston. We brought a load up to Belton and then my boss took off for Christmas and I haven't seen him since."

"That's too bad. You should find something here in Waco, though."

Alf took a drink of his beer before he spoke again. "I don't like town living very much. A man in Belton told me that Jude Brown might need some hands out on his ranch."

Rusty narrowed his eyes at Alf. "Who told you that?"

"An older man I met down at the square. He went by the name of Stinky."

Rusty frowned. "I know Stinky, but that man don't know shit. I work for Jude, and right now him and his brother Jimbo are at their brother Luke's ranch up in the panhandle."

Alf pressed his lips together as he slumped against the bar. He was so close, and now it turned out Jude was hundreds of miles away. "I always wanted to see that country. Do you think he needs any hands out there?"

Rusty frowned as he studied Alf's face. "I don't know. They went to help their brother Luke gather up cattle to drive to Dodge City."

Alf had heard all he wanted to hear, but the man could be lying. "How could I find Luke's place if I rode out there?"

"Just ask anyone in Tascosa. They can tell you where Luke's ranch is." Just then the music stopped. "Got to go, this is my chance." He went up to the girl in the yellow dress and talked to her for a few minutes. The redhead joined them briefly, and then Rusty and the yellowed-dress girl walked toward the bar. Rusty grinned. "Red is waiting on you, Alf."

Alf shook his head. "I think I'll pass this time. I'm going back to the livery and get some sleep."

Rusty and the girl both laughed and went toward the stairs. Alf cut his eyes around the dance floor and saw the redhead arm in arm with a duded-up man in a suit. Alf watched them for a minute as he finished his beer, and then made his way back to the street. It was a long way back to Belton and he was tired.

CHAPTER 21

Rusty scanned the room for Bojack as he descended the dance hall stairs. A thought had come to him while he was upstairs with April, and it was something Bojack would want to know right away. Finally he located him at the bar and shoved in beside him.

"Bojack, I talked to a guy a while ago who asked about a job at the ranch. I didn't think about it then, but maybe he's the one looking for Jude."

Bojack frowned. "What did this cowboy look like?"

"He was young, slim, and dark headed. He didn't look like no cowboy."

Bojack rubbed his chin. "Yeah, could be him. Did he talk funny, like a Yankee?"

Rusty's eyes narrowed. "He sure did, but I didn't think anything about it at the time."

"What did you tell him?"

Rusty bit his bottom lip as he remembered the conversation. "I told him Jude wasn't around, that he had gone to Luke's place."

Bojack grimaced. "Damn, Rusty, did you tell him your life story? What did he say then?"

Rusty looked away. "He asked me how to get to Luke's, and I told him anybody in Tascosa could tell him."

Bojack slammed his fist down on the bar. "Son of a bitch!" He grabbed Rusty by the shoulder. "Look around and see if he's still here."

Rusty hurried around the dance floor, looking at every man until he was sure Alf wasn't there. He peered into every upstairs room too. Alf wasn't in the dance hall. Then he remembered that Alf had said he was going back to the livery to get some rest. He hurried back to Bojack and pulled him aside.

"He's not here, but I know where he's at. He told me he was going back to the livery to get some sleep."

Bojack's eyes narrowed. "Which livery?"

Rusty thought for a few seconds. "He said he rode in from Belton, so it has to be the one by the stock pens."

"Yeah, it's on the road to Belton." Bojack cut his eyes around the room and then back to Rusty. "Come on, we're going to that livery and take care of that asshole once and for all."

Rusty followed Bojack out to the street and toward the livery. They walked in silence at first, but as they neared the livery, Bojack spoke. "When we get there, you point him out to me and I'll offer him a job at the ranch. When we ride to the ranch, I'll get behind him and shoot him in the back. That way we can put his body out in the brush and nobody will ever find him."

Rusty was listening, but his mind was also sorting through the reasons why he was involved in this family matter. He had done a few things that the law frowned upon, but this was plain murder. He was getting too old to go to prison and he sure didn't want to be hung. "What if he's just some saddle bum looking for work? How are you going to know if he's the one looking for Jude?"

Bojack stopped under one of Waco's gas streetlights. "You're right. We got to be sure." He pressed his lips together. "We'll trick him into telling us if he's from up north."

Rusty shook his head. "He could still be the wrong Yankee."

Bojack cocked his head and sneered, "I could just ask him if he is looking for Jude so he can kill him."

"No, no, I mean he might tell us if we coax it out of him."

Bojack scratched his chin. "Okay, just let me do the talking."

When they got closer to the tracks, they left the streetlights behind but a full moon helped light their way. When they reached the livery, they could see a lamp burning inside.

Bojack paused and nodded toward the corral. "You saddle the horses. I'll take care of the Yankee." Bojack carefully made his way to the lamp. He saw the form of a man covered with a blanket and lying on a pile of hay in the corner. A hat covered his head. Bojack grinned as he pulled out his pistol and pointed it at the sleeping man.

"Wake up, you Yankee son of a bitch! I'm going to kill you." He cocked his pistol and fired. Gun smoke filled the room.

Louis was still cleaning the stables when Alf returned from his long walk from town. He stopped his sweeping and grinned at Alf.

"It didn't take you long. You must have been quick on the trigger."

Alf shook his head and grinned. "I didn't go down there for that. I was only looking for information."

Louis smirked. "Yeah, right; okay, did you find Bojack?"

"No, but I talked to Rusty. He told me Jude went to Tascosa. I never saw Bojack."

"You might be glad you didn't. Bojack is a mean bastard. He might shoot you just for asking about his brother."

Alf frowned as he remembered his conversation with Rusty. He had told him where he was staying the night; that might have been a mistake. "Bojack and Rusty left their horses here, right? Did they say when they were coming back to pick them up?"

"No, but probably anytime from about midnight to late in the morning; just depends on when they need to get back to the ranch." Louis made a sweep with his broom. "By the way, your horse is in the corral. I fed him his oats. Get your sleeping gear and I'll show you where to bed down. I'm fixing to lock up the blacksmith shop and go home. George will come in at about four in the morning to open up."

Alf got his things from the corral and followed Louis out to a small barn behind the shop. It had a few small one-horse stalls on one side and larger open pens on the other side.

Louis held up his lantern. "Find yourself a clean spot and have a nice night. I'm going home." He hung the lantern on a wire coming down from a rafter. "I'll leave the light on for you." He turned and walked back toward the blacksmith shop. A few minutes later Alf saw him heading toward town.

Alf was still thinking about Bojack and Rusty as he piled a layer of loose hay by the fence and laid his bedroll on it. He sure didn't want to be bushwhacked in his sleep. He remembered seeing a bench out front of the barn. He would sit and smoke his pipe while he thought about what he should do.

He had just lit his pipe when he heard Blackjack nicker. He laid his pipe down and slowly walked to the corral. The black horse quickly came to him when he walked up to the fence. Alf talked to him for a while, then crawled inside the pen and rubbed his shoulder and neck. He lifted the horse's feet and felt the new shoes. This was Blackjack's first set of shoes and he seemed to be taking to them in stride. Alf rubbed him a little more before he crawled back through the fence. He heard a train whistle and looked toward the train tracks. A long line of cattle cars was rumbling out town heading east. He watched it until it was gone and then returned to the bench. He smoked his pipe, thinking about what he should do, but his mind kept going back to what Louis had said about Bojack. If the man was really that mean, he might come looking for Alf when he came to get his horse. Maybe Alf should head back south tonight. He had already made up his mind to go to Georgetown and look up Marty and Silas.

Suddenly Alf looked toward the street. He thought he heard someone talking. Cocking his head, he listened and then heard it again. Maybe it was Bojack and Rusty. Alf went back into the barn and turned the lantern down to a dim light. He hurried back to where he had left his bedroll and lumped up enough hay to make it look like a man. He carefully covered it back up with his blanket, then rolled up his extra shirt, laid it at one end, and covered it with his hat. Glancing toward the road, he slowly backed into one of the small stalls and closed the gate. Then he hunched down in the shadows to wait.

He had only waited a few minutes when he saw a man creep slowly into the barn carrying a pistol. He walked up to the blanket, stopped, and cocked his pistol.

"Wake up, you Yankee son of a bitch! I'm going to kill you."

Boom, boom. Gun smoke filled the barn. Squawking chickens flew from their roosts in the rafters.

Seconds passed and Rusty sprinted into the barn, pistol in hand. "What the hell are you doing, Bojack?"

"I shot the bastard. Now we don't have to worry about him going to Tascosa." Bojack grinned at Rusty. "Get back out there and saddle them horses. We got to get out of here."

Rusty clumsily holstered his pistol as he hurried back outside. Bojack turned up the wick on the lantern first, then walked up to the blanket-covered form and kicked the blanket off. His face twisted in surprise and he straightened up as he stood over the pile of hay he'd thought was a man.

Alf slowly rose from behind the gate where he had watched the whole scene. "Looks like you missed me. You want to try it again looking into my face?"

In a single motion Bojack whirled, raised his gun, and pulled the trigger. Alf returned fire. Bojack's head snapped back as he was hurled into the fence. He collapsed to the floor, a forty-five-caliber hole between his eyes.

Sweat poured down Alf's face and he trembled as he realized he had made a mistake by not having his gun out when he spoke to Bojack. If Bojack hadn't missed, Alf would be the one lying in the hay.

"What are you doing in there, Bojack? You're going to wake everybody up."

Alf turned, his pistol up and cocked. He could see Rusty hurrying toward the barn, leading two horses. Rusty tied the horses' reins as he hurried into the barn. He froze when he saw Bojack lying on the floor and he swept his eyes around the barn.

"I'm over here."

Rusty jerked and turned toward Alf. "I thought you were dead."

"No, Bojack just killed a pile of hay." Alf walked up to Rusty and stuck the pistol in his gut. "Give me your pistol, butt first."

Rusty clenched his teeth as he handed Alf his gun. "I didn't know he was going to shoot at you. I thought he was only going to talk to you and find out if you were the one looking for Jude to kill him." He looked over at Bojack's body. "Did you have to kill him?"

Alf stuck Rusty's gun in his belt. "He shot at me first. I had to defend myself."

Suddenly a voice called out from the street, "Hey, what's going on in there?"

"A man is dead," Alf called back. "I need the sheriff."

"I'm a city policeman. I'm coming in." A man in a blue uniform walked into the light. "I'm Officer Kelly. Who did the killing?"

"I did, but I was defending myself. The one on the ground and this man saw my bedroll and thought I was sleeping in it. The dead one pumped a few bullets into the blanket and came over to see if I was still alive. When I called out to him from a stall, he turned and fired at me. He missed and I didn't."

Kelly looked at Rusty. "Is that what happened?"

Rusty looked at Alf and swallowed. "I didn't have anything to do with trying to kill this man. Bojack said he was only going to talk to him. When he shot into the blanket, I was surprised too."

Alf interrupted before Kelly could ask another question. "He may be telling the truth, officer. He was getting their horses when it happened, and he acted like he didn't know Bojack was going to do what he did."

"That's right. Like I said, Bojack told me he was just going to talk to him."

Kelly pulled out a notepad. "What is your name, and what's Bojack's last name?"

"I'm Rusty Jones and that's Bojack Brown. Him and his brothers have a ranch just west of here. I work for them."

Kelly wrote the information down and turned to Alf. "And what is your name?"

"I'm Alf Smith. I just rode into Waco today looking for work. When I ran into Rusty at a dance hall, he told me he worked on the Brown ranch. I asked him if they were hiring and he told me they wasn't, but he said Jude Brown was in West Texas and might need some hands up there. Then he told me how to find him."

Kelly turned back to Rusty. "Is that what happened?"

Rusty glanced at Alf and back at Kelly. "Yeah."

Kelly cocked his head. "What did Bojack Brown want to talk to this man about?"

Rusty scratched his neck. "Jude Brown got word that there was a man gunning for him, and Bojack thought it might be this man."

Kelly began to write but stopped and glanced toward some people who were approaching the barn. "You people stay back until this investigation is over."

Louis came up to them. "I work here, officer. What happened?"

"There's been a shooting. If you could get someone to get the JP, I would be grateful." Louis left and Kelly turned back to Alf. "I want to see your blanket and Bojack's gun."

Alf showed Kelly the two bullet holes in his blanket. Kelly checked Bojack's gun and found three bullets missing.

"You say he shot at you first?"

"Yes, sir. I don't know how he missed me." Alf showed Kelly where he had been standing.

Officer Kelly went over to Bojack's body and then looked toward the stall where Alf had been. He entered the stall and looked at the wall. "I don't see anything. Show me exactly where you were standing."

Alf positioned himself, thought for a minute, and pulled the gate closed. "I was standing right here."

Kelly hurried to the gate and looked on the other side of it. "Ha, here it is." He took out his pocketknife and dug out the bullet.

A cold chill went up Alf's spine as he studied the hole from which Kelly extracted the bullet. "This was right in front of where I was standing. If that gate wasn't there, he would have drilled me."

Louis returned then and came over to Alf. "I guess you were lucky. Looks like it would've hit you right in the gut."

Alf felt weak all of a sudden and he leaned back against the wall. With shaking hands he pulled off his bandana and wiped the sweat from his face. It was the first time he had felt like this after he had killed someone. Maybe because this time the man he'd killed wasn't one of the men he had been looking for, or maybe because this time he himself had almost been killed.

His thoughts were interrupted when a portly man in a black suit waddled into the barn.

"What's going on, Kelly? Where's the body?"

"He's right over here, Judge Johnson. It's Bojack Brown."

The judge examined the body and turned to Kelly. "What happened?"

Kelly told him what he knew about the shooting, and Alf told the judge everything that had happened that night. Alf didn't say he had been looking for Jude Brown to bring him to justice, though. When the judge was through with Alf, he asked if there were other witnesses. Kelly pointed out Rusty and Louis. Rusty told the same story he'd told Kelly, and then Louis told what he knew. Finally Judge Johnson turned to Alf.

"Young man, you were lucky tonight. You could have been killed. Bojack Brown has killed a few people in Waco but he has always gotten away with it by claiming self-defense. This time I'm ruling self-defense, but against him this time. You are free to go, and I would advise you to leave Waco. Bojack Brown has two brothers and some other cronies who might want revenge."

Alf thanked the judge and Officer Kelly, and then hung back as Bojack's body was removed. Finally the crowd left and Alf crawled into his makeshift bed and tried to sleep. He tossed and turned at first, and when he did doze off, he woke every time he heard a strange noise. Finally, at four a.m., he heard George the blacksmith arrive and begin working in the shop. Alf felt a little safer then. He dozed off and didn't wake until daylight.

CHAPTER 22

Alf was running through the barn trying to escape from Bojack, who was right behind him firing his pistol. The shots rang in his ears and he could feel the bullets hitting his back. Why wasn't he dead? Gradually the pistol shots changed to the banging of a hammer on an anvil and he awoke groggily. He lay there relieved that it was only a dream, but then he felt something hit his back for real. With visions of Bojack in his mind, he grabbed his Colt and jumped up from his bed in the hay. With flapping wings and squawks, a flock of chickens scattered in all directions. Louis, who was a few feet away, was doubled over with laughter. Alf looked on the ground and saw corn scattered around him on the ground. Alf stared back at Louis. "That's a good way to get shot, Louis."

Louis tried to straighten his face. "I just thought you wanted to get up early."

Alf shook his head as he stood up. It was one of the oldest tricks around a farm and he had been the butt of it a few times, but now wasn't the best time to pull it on him. He glared at Louis for a few seconds and then picked up his gear and went out to saddle Blackjack. He tied his bedroll and bag behind the saddle, and then went inside to tell the blacksmith and Louis good-bye. A few minutes later, Alf was on the road back to Belton.

The trip was uneventful and boring for Alf, but he used the time to think about his next move. After his close call with Bojack, Alf realized for the first time he could be the one to get killed when he confronted Jude. But after thinking about it most of the night, he decided it didn't matter. He had started this vendetta because he believed his parents deserved to be avenged, and the thought of the murderers getting away with it would haunt him forever if he didn't finish it.

He decided to stop in Belton for the night and then go on to Round Rock. If Marty and Si were going back to the Goodnight ranch, he wanted to go with them. He would be smarter this time. He would find Jude first and then pick the time and the place to settle it.

It was early afternoon when Alf arrived in Temple. It had rained sometime in the night and Main Street was knee deep with gooey mud. Blackjack struggled as he tried to make his way through the mud, so Alf turned him onto another street that had easier walking. They had only gone a few blocks when Alf realized he was getting hungry, and he began looking for a place to eat. A little café with blue flowers painted on it caught his eye, so he stopped Blackjack and went inside. The café was busy and Alf started to leave, but he noticed that the menu board behind the counter announced that the day's special was chicken-fried steak. Alf had never eaten much beef back in Illinois, usually only in a stew, but in Texas beef was plentiful and cheap. He'd tried a fried beefsteak back in Galveston and now he craved it, especially with thick white gravy.

Alf looked again for a table and spied two people getting up from one by the window. He hurried over to it and sat down. A few minutes later, the waiter came over to take his order and Alf ordered the chicken-fried steak. While he waited, he watched the people and horses trudge through the mud and goo in the street. He chuckled as one man fell down in the mud and someone had to help him out. He was watching a team of horses pulling a wagon full of beer barrels through the goo when the waiter brought his food. The sides of the steak hung over the sides of the plate and it was covered with white gravy. Another plate contained mashed potatoes and creamed corn. Alf hastily cut a piece. It was the best steak he had ever tasted. Alf scarfed down every last bite and ordered apple pie for dessert. Alf took a last swig from the mason jar of tea and went to the counter to pay the seventy-five-cent bill. He noticed some more of the blue flowers painted on the wall behind the counter.

"I've never seen flowers like those. Where do they grow?" Alf remarked as he handed the waiter a dollar.

"They only grow in Texas," the waiter replied as he handed Alf a quarter. "They bloom by the thousands starting in late winter and through the spring and then they're gone. They're the most beautiful flowers you will ever see."

"I hope I'm in Texas long enough to see them," Alf replied as he turned and headed out the door.

The wind was blowing from the north and the temperature was dropping when Alf rode into Belton. He stabled Blackjack and went to the closest hotel and paid for a room. After washing up, he strolled around Belton for a while, browsing in the stores. Most of general stores sold the same things—dry goods, provisions, drugs, and books—but other stores sold feed and seeds, furniture, and leather goods. A lumberyard with stacks of new boards was down Central Avenue past the square. A buggy shop was across the street from it.

After looking for a while, Alf passed a café and the smells coming from it reminded him it was time for supper. Even after eating that big steak for dinner, he was hungry again, so he strolled in and sat down at an empty table. In a few minutes, a middle-aged woman came over to his table. She raised her eyebrows when she first walked up but then smiled and greeted him.

"Hello, sir, thank you for coming in. Our special today is a plate of enchiladas with tortillas and a glass of tea for fifty cents."

Alf smiled. "That is just what I was wanting. I'll take it." The waitress left to get his order and Alf looked around the room. He noticed Sheriff Bigham at one of the tables with Judge Tyler. As Alf watched they scooted their chairs back and rose from the table. The sheriff put money on the table before they headed toward the door. When the sheriff got to Alf's table, he cocked his head to one side.

"Alf Smith! I didn't expect to see you around here."

"Hello, Sheriff." Alf turned to Judge Tyler. "Hello, sir."

Judge Tyler nodded. "Hello, Mr. Smith." He turned to the sheriff. "I'll see you later, John." He nodded to Alf and departed.

"I just rode in from Waco, Sheriff," Alf said.

"You come back to take me up on that job?"

Alf grinned and shook his head. "No. I'm staying the night, and then I'm heading for Georgetown first thing in the morning."

Sheriff Bigham glanced toward the waitress, who had come up behind them and was waiting for the sheriff to move so she could set Alf's food on the table. He stepped behind Alf and patted him on the shoulder. "Well, you stay out of trouble, son. See you next time. I need to get over to the office." He lumbered toward the door.

Alf watched him for a second before he turned to the waitress. "That looks good."

The waitress smiled. "Thank you, sir, I hope you enjoy it." She hesitated. "Did I hear the sheriff say your name was Alf Smith?"

Alf studied her face. "Yes, it is; do I know you?"

The waitress pressed her lips together and her eyes glistened. "No, you don't know me. My name is Ida Sholt and I want to thank you."

Alf stared at Ida and creased his brow. The name didn't register in his mind. "What are you thanking me for?"

Ida's face turned ugly. "You rid me of the sorriest, meanest, most low-down bastard in Texas, and for that I am much obliged."

"I don't understand."

"Stinky Sholt was my husband, and I put up with his abuse for a long time because I was afraid to leave him." Ida gritted her teeth and shook her head. "I didn't think my daughter and I could make it on our own. I sure couldn't leave Mazie there with him." Tears began to run down Ida's cheeks. "His dirty ways caused my oldest daughter, Bessie, to leave home, and lately he'd been trying to mess with my Mazie."

Alf began to understand what she was saying. "Ida, I called out Stinky because he helped kill my parents years ago in Illinois. I would have turned him over to Sheriff Bigham if he had given up. But I was hoping he wouldn't."

Ida looked into Alf's eyes. "I'm glad he didn't too."

"Are you going to make it now? I see you have a job."

Ida smiled as she tipped her head back. "I haven't been this happy in years. Jose gave me this job, and then I found out he needed a dishwasher too. That's Mazie over there."

Alf saw a pretty girl about Becky's age sweeping the floor. She seemed to sense them looking at her and she looked up at her mother, then at Alf. She smiled and went back to sweeping.

Ida smiled at her then turned back to Alf. "Pretty, ain't she? She'll make some man a good wife someday." Ida winked at Alf and glanced toward the kitchen. "I've got to go back to work now, Mr. Smith. Thank you again."

As Ida walked away, Alf shook his head and began eating. He was glad Ida was better off without Stinky. Killing Stinky hadn't bothered him much, but knowing Ida and Mazie wouldn't have to take his abuse anymore made him feel a little better. He finished his food and left a dollar tip on the table. As he left, he saw Ida pick up the money and glance his way. He nodded and went out the door. It was getting dark now and the wind was howling out of the north, but Alf wasn't ready to go back to the hotel so he decided to go to the Longhorn Saloon and get a beer. The saloon would be warm and maybe he would see someone he knew.

The large wooden door at the entrance to the Longhorn was closed but a sign on it read "open." Alf opened the door and stepped inside, then hurriedly closed it. A modest crowd of patrons all cut their eyes at Alf as he entered, but most of them went back to what they were doing. Alf scanned the room then walked over to the bar where Walter was wiping beer mugs. He glanced up at Alf.

"Hello, Alf, what can I get you?"

"Hello, Walter. Give me a beer."

Walter filled the mug he had just wiped from a large keg and set it in front of Alf. "Here you go." He pulled another mug from a tub of water and began wiping it. "How you been, Alf? You have a nice Christmas?"

Alf put down his mug and wiped his mouth. "Yeah, I did. I stayed out at Harrison's place. Being around all those kids made it a good Christmas."

"I'm glad it's over myself," Walter remarked as he turned to another customer who had walked up to the bar.

Alf took another sip of his beer and scanned the room again. There were a few card games going on, and over by the wall on a small raised stage, a man was playing a guitar. He was sitting in a chair and next to him was another chair with a banjo beside it. Alf sat down at a table close to the stage. The man was a good player, but he was playing a song Alf had never heard before. He finished the song and set down his guitar. Alf clapped a few times and nodded to a chair at his table. The man strolled over and sat down.

Alf stuck out his hand. "I'm Alf Smith. Let me buy you a beer."

The man shook hands with Alf. "I'm Freckles Morgan. Thanks, I was getting pretty thirsty." He waved at Walter. The bartender filled a mug and brought it to the table.

"Here you go, Freckles."

Alf handed Walter a dime and the bartender walked away. "You play pretty good," Alf said. "Do you play the banjo too?"

Freckles ran his hands over his lips. "Yep, but not as good as the guitar. A friend of mine, Buster Snow, usually plays with me, but he didn't show up tonight."

Alf looked over at the banjo and memories began to appear in his mind. Jake had taught him how to play the banjo and the guitar. Alf had found he had a knack for it and had gotten pretty good, or at least that was what Jake and a few others had told him. At one time he'd played at a lot of parties and weddings, but after Jake was killed, he quit playing. He'd sold his instruments before he left for Texas.

Alf turned to Freckles. "You mind if I play a few songs with you on your banjo?"

CHAPTER 23

The next morning Alf woke up with a splitting headache. With half-open eyes, he got up out of his warm bed and shuffled over to the slop jar. As he emptied his bladder, he vaguely remembered going to the Longhorn, but as his mind began to clear he remembered playing the banjo and singing songs with Freckles. The patrons had called out for song after song and kept them there until almost twelve o'clock. Alf put on his pants and sat down to pull on his boots. When he rose, a dizzy spell hit him and he sat back down. Walter must have brought him a lot of free beer. Alf sat there until his head cleared some, then got up and got a drink of water. He pulled out his pocket watch. It was four o'clock. Alf began to feel the coldness of the room; he looked at the warm bed and sighed. He wanted to crawl back in it, but he knew if he did he would sleep for hours. Clenching his teeth he finished dressing, gathered up his things, and headed out toward Jose's café. His head still ached and he needed some coffee.

Ida was wiping the counter when Alf came in and sat down at the table closest to the warm stove. She glanced at his face and half smiled, then quickly brought him a cup of coffee.

"Do you want something to eat?"

Alf grimaced as he felt his stomach trying to turn inside out. "No, just coffee for now." He took a cautious sip of the scalding liquid and held his hands around the cup. It was freezing outside and his hands were cold. After a few minutes, he sipped again, and then quickly took another sip. The coffee helped and his head began to feel better, but his stomach was still doing flip-flops. Alf warmed his hands around the cup for a few more seconds and then took another drink, almost emptying the cup. He looked around and saw Ida pouring coffee for another customer. He waited until she looked in his direction and then nodded toward his cup. She smiled and strolled toward him.

"I wondered if I would see you again," she said as she refilled his cup.

Alf looked up at her face. Was she flirting with him? She was old enough to be his mother. "I'm leaving as soon as I warm up some. I don't know if I will ever be back this way." He picked up his cup and sipped at the coffee.

"Oh," Ida said as she turned to walk away.

"Wait a minute."

Ida stopped and looked back. "Yes?"

"Would you fix me some of those breakfast tacos to take with me on my journey? I don't feel like eating right now, but after a while I'll be starving."

"Sure, I'll fix them right up."

A few moments later, Ida brought his food and warmed up his coffee. Alf paid her with a good tip included, then nursed his coffee as he thought of the long cold trip ahead of him. He was reluctant to leave the café but he needed to get going if he was going to be in Round Rock by sundown. He took a final drink of his coffee, grabbed his bag, and hurried to the livery. Blackjack nickered and pranced in his stall when he saw Alf come into the barn. He seemed anxious to go as Alf saddled him and tied his bedroll and bag to the saddle. With a last look to be sure he had everything, Alf mounted Blackjack and they rode out into the night.

It was still dark when he forded Nolan Creek and headed toward Salado, but the road was well kept and Blackjack had no trouble keeping on it. A few miles out of Belton, Alf came to the Lampasas River and it too was an easy crossing. Just past the river, Alf caught up with a freight wagon and rode behind it until it stopped in Salado. The Salado Creek crossing was next to a grist mill that was already grinding corn as Blackjack carried Alf through the shallow water. It was getting light now and Alf stopped for a few minutes to eat his tacos while he watched the mill make its cornmeal. A line of wagons waited for their turn at the wheel while their drivers huddled around a fire. Alf warmed himself up for a few minutes, then climbed back on Blackjack and returned to the road. The sun was peeping above the horizon now and Alf grew warmer as he basked in its rays. Past Salado the land began to change to prairie-like country with rolling hills and only small streams to cross. Alf rode past a small store with a sign out front that read "Prairie Dell." A few miles later, he passed the small community of Jerrel. It was past noon now, and as Alf drew closer to Georgetown, the land gradually changed to a more rocky terrain. It was midafternoon when Alf came to the north fork of the San Gabriel River. It was much like the Leon, with its limestone-lined banks and shallow rapids spaced between deeper pools of dark green water. Past the river between the north and south forks of the San Gabriel was Georgetown, a medium-sized town that reminded him of Belton. Georgetown was the county seat of Williamson County and had a nice big courthouse surrounded by stores.

Alf was feeling hungry again when he rode into town, and he stopped and ate another chicken-fried steak at a café across from the courthouse. After looking in some of the stores, he rode on toward Round Rock. An hour later he could see the town in the distance, and thirty minutes later he pulled Blackjack to a stop in front of the only general store in the small town.

A man wearing a long white apron over his large belly and a visor on his bald head came hurrying to the front as Alf entered the store. The clerk wasn't a tall man and his short steps made Alf think of a piglet hurrying to the trough.

"I'm Jerry. May I help you, sir?"

Alf glanced around the store. "I need a few things, but first I need some information. Do you know where the Lynch ranch is located?"

"Well, of course I do. Everybody around here knows where the Lynches live."

"I'm not from around here."

"Oh, I see. Well, sir, you keep going south on this road until you come to Round Rock Creek." Jerry walked to the door and pointed south. "It's just down the road. Turn west on the road that follows the creek and go until you come to a large house on the left. Beside it is a smaller house. That is where the Lynches live."

"Thank you, sir; I'm sure I can find it with those directions. Do you know the Lynches?'

"Oh, yeah, they come in here all the time."

"Do you know if Marty and Si are still around?"

"They were in here this morning—they picked up a twenty-pound bag of flour and some tobacco."

Alf thanked him, and after buying a few items, he mounted Blackjack and turned him into the road. He found the creek just a little ways from the store. It was a clear stream running over a gravel-and-rock bottom. In the middle of the rushing water, a large round rock the size of a small wagon extended from the creek bed, rising several feet above the water. Alf studied the rock as he paused to let Blackjack drink. It was an unusual formation, and he assumed it gave the creek and surrounding settlement their names. He waited until Blackjack finished drinking and then turned him down a well-used dirt-and-gravel road that led off to the west.

It was sundown and getting colder when Alf arrived at the Lynch place. He didn't see anyone outside so he tied Blackjack to a hitching post out in front of the big house, then walked up and knocked on the door. He waited a few minutes and knocked louder. He heard movement and then the door opened and Marty stood in front of him.

Alf grinned and stuck out his hand. "Hello, Marty, remember me?"

Marty paused and then a large smile plastered his face. "Alf Smith! I was wondering if you were going to come see us." He grabbed Alf's hand. "Come on in, we was just having supper."

Alf hesitated, and then stepped inside. "I don't want to interrupt your supper, Marty. I can wait out here until you are finished."

Marty put his hand on Alf's shoulder. "Naw, it ain't no trouble at all. We have plenty of room and food. Come on, I want to introduce you to my family."

Alf swallowed, and then followed Marty down a hall into a large dining room. An older man was sitting at the head of the table, and at the other end sat a young woman, obviously pregnant. On one side of the table a young woman sat by the highchair of a young girl, putting food on her plate. Two other children sat on that side of the table, a boy and a girl. On the other side of the table was Si and an empty chair. The man rose when Marty and Alf entered.

"Papa, this is my friend Alf; Si and I met him in Belton. Remember I told you about him?"

Mr. Lynch frowned. "So you're the man my boys met while they were in jail—the one who killed a man?"

Alf's face reddened. He didn't like the man's judgmental tone. "No, I didn't kill a man. I killed a piece of rotten scum. He could have surrendered but he chose to pull his gun." Alf was ready to tell Marty he was leaving and would meet them somewhere else, but Mr. Lynch interrupted him.

"I didn't mean to rile you up, young man." He stepped toward Alf and stuck out his hand. "I'm Martin Lynch. The boys told me the whole story. You're welcome in my house."

Alf hesitated, and then shook hands with Martin. "I'm Alf Smith. Thank you, Mr. Lynch."

"Come join us for supper. You can set over there by Silas." He looked toward the woman sitting by the small child. "Mary Francis, would you get Alf a place setting?"

Mary Francis went to the kitchen and soon returned with a plate and utensils. When Alf and Marty were seated, Martin, who was still standing, turned to Alf.

"Let me introduce my family. You know Marty and Si. The woman with child is my wife, Mary. My sons Ed and Elias, my daughter Mattie, and my stepdaughter, Mary Francis; the little one is her daughter, Nancy."

Alf nodded to each person as Martin introduced them. He assumed that the pregnant woman was Martin's second wife, since he'd introduced Mary Francis as a stepdaughter. He looked at Mary Francis again. She was a pretty woman with dark curly hair and light olive skin. Her face was pixie-like, with a small nose and brown eyes. Alf seemed drawn to her. Suddenly, as if she sensed his eyes on her, she raised her head and looked at him. His face flushed and he smiled sheepishly as he let his eyes turn down to his plate. He saw it was empty and Si was patiently holding a platter of bread out to him. He quickly took a piece. Marty handed him a platter of fried chicken and he took a breast from it, and then passed it to Si. Several minutes later everyone had the food they wanted and the dining room became quiet. Alf ate a few bites, and then glanced back to Mary Francis. She was helping Nancy with her drink, but like before, she cut her eyes to Alf. She smiled at him and went back to helping Nancy. Alf felt warmth in his chest along with a tingle. He went back to eating but didn't feel very hungry. He wanted to look at Mary Francis again but Martin began asking him questions about his home in Illinois and then his journey to Texas. Alf told him a short version of his story, leaving out his gunfights. Marty and Si wanted him to tell of them but he declined, saying he didn't want to speak of them in front of the children.

When the meal was over, the men went into the living room and sat in front of the fireplace. The fire was low and Edward carefully put another log on the glowing coals. Martin pulled out his tobacco pouch and filled his pipe, then offered it to Alf. Alf filled his pipe and Si and Marty rolled cigarettes using paper from an old catalog. Edward reached for the bag when Si was through with it.

"You're too young to smoke," Si said as he handed the bag back to his father. Edward scowled at his brother but didn't say anything.

"How was your Christmas, Alf?" Marty asked after he blew out his first puff of smoke.

"It was remarkable. Harrison has quite a large family." Alf puffed on his pipe. "How many children do you have, Mr. Lynch?"

"I have ten counting Mary Francis, and as you probably noticed, we have one on the way. My four oldest children—William, James, Jennie, and Margaret—have married and moved out on their own."

Si leaned forward on his chair, "how many kids in your family, Alf?"

"There are just four of us, me and my brother, Charley, and my two sisters, Cordie and Jennie."

Marty nudged Alf's arm. "How old were you when your parents died?"

Alf hesitated as his burning home flashed in his mind. For a few minutes, he relived the fear and the heartbreak he had felt that day when he realized his parents were dead. He closed his eyes and shivered. Slowly he opened his eyes and began telling them about that day. With his eyes glistening, he told them everything—the four horsemen, the funeral, going to live with Jake, his sisters and Charley going to live with the Higgins's. He told them of Jake's death and why he'd come to Texas.

"I came to Texas to look for the men who killed my parents. I had no clue what their names were or where they lived, just that they all wore those same Texas boots with the red star on them."

Martin tilted his head. "How did you find out their names?"

"I found one of them in Quincy, Illinois, or rather he found me. The local sheriff asked me where I was going. I told him and his deputy the whole story. Little did I know that the deputy was one of the four men I had been looking for. During the night he came to my room and tried to kill me. I heard him coming, and when he shot at me and missed, I shot him. I hit him in the gut and it took him a long time to die. He went religious and told me and the sheriff the names of his three accomplices and where they lived."

Marty, Si, and Edward sat silent. Martin raised his chin. "The boys told me about the gunfight with Stinky Sholt. Have you found any of the others?"

"I found Duce Rangle in Galveston. When I confronted him with what I knew, he went for his gun. I was a little faster."

Edward leaned forward, eyes wide. "Are you as fast as Wes Harden and Sam Bass?"

Alf shook his head and grinned. "I've heard of those men but I don't know how fast they were."

Marty waved his arm toward the front of the house. "Sam Bass and his gang rode by our house on his way to rob the bank in Round Rock, but the Texas Rangers were waiting for him."

Si nodded and pointed. "Yeah, they stopped and rested under that big old shade tree down the road. We saw 'em."

Alf furrowed his brow. "I heard about that. It was about four or five years ago."

Marty sat back in his chair. "A man we know, Soapy Smith, was there. He told me that Ranger George Herold shot Sam Bass first, and then Ranger Richard Ware shot him again. He got away, but later they found him in a field by the railroad tracks, barely alive. He died later."

Alf nodded. "Pulling your gun out first doesn't matter if you miss your target. I practiced a lot when Jake gave me my first pistol. He was the county sheriff and he knew how to handle a gun. He taught me a lot."

Martin pulled out his watch. "You boys need to finish your chores. It's getting late."

The three young men quickly stood up. Si looked at his father. "What about Alf?"

"What are your plans, Alf?" Marty asked. "You can bunk in with us for a while if you want to."

Alf looked toward Martin, "if it's all right with your father."

"Why of course, Alf. You can stay as long as you like."

"Let me get my horse, Marty, and then I'll help you do the chores."

It was dark when they stepped outside but Si and Edward had already lit lanterns by the time Alf and Marty got Blackjack. The four men made their way to the barn and Marty showed Alf where to put his horse. They put out feed for the four cows while Si and Edward squeezed milk from their udders. They gathered the eggs and fed the pigs. Alf was no stranger to farm chores and it felt good helping. It reminded him of back home at his parents' farm when he and Charley did their share of the work. He remembered his father showing him how to plow the fields and how they'd gathered the corn. A tear slipped from his eye and he sighed. It had been nine years but he still missed his mom and dad. Memories of the day they died swirled in his mind and the anger built again in his heart. He saw the four men on their horses, riding past them, grinning and gloating of the loot they had stolen. The image of their boots grew until all he saw was the big red star. Alf began to shake as he closed his eyes and clenched his fist.

"Come on, Alf; let's go back to the house."

Alf opened his eyes. His friend was looking at him strangely.

"What's wrong? Are you cold?"

"No, I was just thinking back to when I did chores on our farm when I was a kid. I didn't like them back then, but now I wish I was back there doing them again."

Marty pressed his lips together. "I think I know how you feel. It's good out here with Si and Edward. I missed my family when I went out to West Texas."

Alf clenched his teeth and looked out at the house. "You had a family to come back to, Marty."

About that time Si and Edward ran past them. Edward, who was in the lead, called, "Last one to the house is a rotten egg!"

Marty grinned at Alf. "Let's catch 'em."

Alf snapped out of his melancholy as he took out after the rest of the Lynch boys. It didn't matter that he was the last one there. Si was a fast runner and came in first, but it was all good-natured fun and Alf joined right in with them. They were still laughing as they walked into the living room. Mary Francis and Mattie were sitting at a table playing checkers while Martin read a newspaper in front of the fireplace. Mary sat in a stuffed chair beside him, knitting. Eli and Nancy were playing on the floor.

"Let's play dominos," Edward yelled as he hurried to another table where a box of dominos sat. The four men scrambled for chairs and yelled for partners. It ended up with Alf and Marty against Si and Edward. They played a few games and then changed partners. After a while Mary Francis went to the kitchen and brought back cookies and milk. She teased the boys that it was only for the little kids, but she gave Alf one because he was company. She let the other boys grumble a little longer before she gave them theirs. It was all in fun and Alf enjoyed every minute of it. He liked the Lynches and being with men his own age. Besides that, he thought Mary Francis was pretty and he wanted to get to know her better. An hour later he was playing checkers with her and Martin had taken his place at the domino table. Alf was shy with Mary Francis at first, but as they played and talked, he loosened up and they were soon gabbing like old friends. Mary Francis wasn't shy at all and she asked him a lot of questions about his life. When she mentioned his parents, he began to feel melancholy. She sympathized with him, then smiled and asked him to tell her about the happy times in his life.

Alf took a deep breath before he spoke. "I know my parents are in heaven because they were good people, so I shouldn't grieve for them that much. My brother and sisters went to a good home and I went to live with Jake and Martha. I got the best deal because I didn't have all those farm chores to do, even though I did have chores. Jake gave me a horse and taught me how to ride; he gave me a gun and taught me how to shoot. I would never have learned that on the farm."

"The boys said you were a gunfighter. They said you could draw and shoot real fast."

"Jake taught me, but he also taught me how to hit my target. That's what really counts."

Mary Francis smiled. "Tell me about your journey to Texas, Alf."

Alf smiled back. He had pushed his grief to the back of his mind again. He decided he liked this girl. She had a child and she was a few years older than he, but her smile was driving him mad.

The checkers were forgotten as Alf told her his story. He left out the gunfights but told her of meeting Mark Twain and working on the steamboat. She took his hand when he told her he'd seen New Orleans.

"Alf, you are so lucky! I would love to see New Orleans."

Alf felt like his heart was going to burst. "It was real pretty. Maybe you could go see it someday."

"Oh, I don't think so. I have a child to take care of, and besides, it's not easy for a woman to do those kinds of things, not like a man could."

Alf felt his heart melting. "It wasn't all good times. There were a few times when I wished I was back home."

Mary Francis smiled again. "Maybe I will marry again and my husband will take me places."

Alf felt a chill, then tightness in his chest. His emotions clashed as her words penetrated his mind. He had never thought of marriage, but his feelings for Mary Francis were strong. On the other hand, he wasn't ready for marriage, and he still had one more man to find. His quest for vengeance was the first thing in his heart, and he could never do anything else until it was finished. He felt at a loss for words as he turned his eyes back to Mary Francis. He was spared when she spoke first.

"Nancy has fallen asleep and I have to put her to bed. I have to stay with her, so good night and I'll see you tomorrow." She told the rest of the family good night as she picked up Nancy and carried her out of the room. Alf watched her leave. Then Eli took her chair and wanted to play checkers too. Alf played with him until the domino game broke up and everyone was ready for bed. After they had all said their good nights, Marty led Alf to a girlishly decorated room with one bed in it.

"This was my sister Margaret's room until she had got married last summer. You can wash up there at the night stand. If you need more water, just get it at the kitchen pump." Marty turned and headed down the hall. "See you in the morning."

Alf picked up his bag from by the door where Edward had set it earlier and went through his clothes to see what he would wear the next day. After laying out a fresh pair of Levis, he quickly undressed, washed up, and climbed under the heavy quilts. He was thinking of Mary Francis when he fell asleep, and he dreamed that they were married and had a house full of kids. He awoke in a cold sweat. The dream had seemed so real he wondered if he was destined to marry her. Alf shook his head as he got up to use the bed pot, but after he got a drink of water and went back to bed, he was still wondering.

The next day, after a huge breakfast, Alf rode with Marty and Si around their land, checking fences and seeing about the cattle. Marty told Alf he needed to practice with his lariat, but he soon found that Alf was no stranger to a rope when he felt it settle around his body.

"Where did you learn to rope like that?" Marty exclaimed as he pulled the rope off. "You all got cattle ranches in Illinois?"

"Most of the farmers back home keep a few cows for meat and to sell to the local butchers," Alf replied as he began gathering up his rope. "When Jake gave me my first horse, I was reading books about cattle drives in Texas. I wanted to be a cowboy so I got me a rope and practiced. Pretty soon I was helping drive cattle to the market for the local farmers. Made me a little spending money but mostly I just enjoyed doing it."

"Alf, you're full of surprises. What else can you do?"

"I can play a guitar a little. Banjo too."

Si grinned as he rode closer. "I have a guitar and can play a little. Maybe after supper we can play some songs."

"I'd be glad to, Si."

Marty motioned toward the fence. "Come on, we have to check this fence."

Alf heeled Blackjack, and with Si beside him they hurried to catch up to Marty, who had raced ahead. They galloped until they were just behind Marty, but suddenly he pulled up and stopped his horse.

"Got a broke wire," Marty called out as he dismounted. Alf and Si rode up to see the top strand of the fence broken and curled up in both directions. Si grabbed some wire from his saddlebag, and with Alf and Marty holding the two ends, he spliced it together. Marty pulled on the wire to test it. Satisfied, they resumed their inspection. Alf was enjoying the day so far. Marty and Si were good company.

As they rode, Marty and Si told about the things they had learned from the ranchers about driving cattle. Alf was surprised that a lot of the drivers used dogs to keep the stragglers in the herd, and some of the cowboys preferred bullwhips to control the cattle and keep them moving.

"Did you learn all of that out west?"

Marty slowed to let Alf catch up. "No, we worked on a few ranches around here before we ever went out west. There used to be a roundup and a drive to the rail yard in Waco every spring."

"What do they do now? Drive them to Belton or Temple?"

Si rode up on Alf's other side. "Around here they take them to the auction. There's one in Belton and a big one in Austin."

Alf suddenly had a thought. "You ever work for the Reed ranch over by Heidenheimer?"

Marty pushed his hat back. "Sure, we signed on with them a few times for their roundup. Why do you ask?"

Alf took off his hat and pushed his hair back. "You ever hear about any buried gold around that area?"

Marty stared at Alf as Si moved his horse closer. "No, what do you know?"

Alf pulled Blackjack to a stop. He looked back over his shoulder and back at Marty. "I like you guys and I want to cut you in on this because you know the country around here. But we have to keep this among ourselves. Can you boys keep a secret?"

"I can," Si exclaimed as he crossed his heart.

"I can too."

"I know where there is a jack load of gold bars buried in that area. You help me find them and I'll cut you in for a third."

"How do you know this?" Marty asked.

"Yeah, and why just a third? Are you keeping two-thirds?"

Alf shook his head. "No, there's someone else involved—the one who told me about the gold."

"How did he know where it was?" Si asked.

"He had a map."

Marty moved his horse closer but Blackjack didn't like it and he laid back his ears. Alf had to rub his neck to get him to settle down.

Marty moved his horse away a little. "We're in, Alf. What do you want to do?"

"Do both of you swear on a Bible that you won't tell anybody about the gold?"

"Yes," Marty and Si answered at the same time.

Alf paused, thinking. "We need to get onto the Reed place. How far is it from here?"

"It's about twenty-five miles as the crow flys," Marty said. "We could get there in half a day."

"Do you think Mr. Reed would let us look around?"

Marty shook his head. "I don't know. Maybe we could ask him for a job?"

Si frowned. "We could just tell him what we were doing."

Marty pulled off his hat and scratched his head. "Why don't we just get our bedrolls and supplies and ride over there in the morning? We can think of something on the way."

Si leaned back in the saddle. "We can't go tomorrow. It's Sunday and we got to go to church."

Marty rubbed his chin. "Well, Monday will be fine. We need to get together some tools to dig with."

Alf's face lit up. "I know, we can tell him we heard he was looking for somebody to dig postholes. He's bound to have some place he needs a fence."

Marty cocked his head. "Yeah, that's a good plan. Come on; let's finish up this fence-riding. I'm getting hungry."

The next day Alf went to church with the Lynches. Somehow or another he ended up sitting by Mary Francis. He didn't mind too much—he did like her and she smelled real good—but he was a little nervous about her intentions. He was sure she was husband hunting and he didn't want any part of that. He turned his attention to the pastor, who was waiting patiently at the pulpit for the people to settle down. When everyone was quiet, he started out the morning with a few announcements and then turned it over to the choir. They began singing "Rock of Ages" and Alf settled down to listen, but Nancy, who was sitting on the other side of her mother, became restless. Mary Francis scooted right up against Alf to give Nancy room to lie down in the pew. Alf froze when he felt her body next to his.

She turned and smiled. "This is cozy. I hope you don't mind."

Alf felt a stirring in his body. Hot flashes ran up his leg. Unexpectedly she turned toward Nancy to smooth her dress and her hips pushed into Alf's. Pleasant sensations radiated from her touch throughout his body. Alf was against the end of the pew and he couldn't move but he didn't care. He felt tightness in his groin; quickly he glanced at the front of his pants where an unusual bulge was growing. Mary Francis settled back down in her seat and mouthed the word "sorry" to him, then smiled again. Alf saw her eyes swing to his pants front before she quickly turned away. She pressed her lips together as if suppressing a chuckle. Alf could feel his face flush. He was torn between happiness and embarrassment, but he didn't want to change anything. He had never felt this way and it bothered him.

The singing finally ended, and thankfully for Alf, the congregation wasn't asked to stand and sing. The preacher gave a good sermon, and when they did stand for the final invitation, Alf's problem was gone. After the closing prayer, he followed Mary Francis out of the church and to Martin's buggy. Nancy was still fussy as they stood waiting for the rest of the family, and on an impulse Alf reached and picked her up. She settled into his arms and in a few minutes she was asleep. When Martin, Mary, and the rest of the young children arrived at the buggy ready to head home, Alf was almost reluctant to hand Nancy back to Mary Francis, who was already in the buggy. He had always liked kids and was beginning to feel an attachment to Nancy even though he had only known her for a short time.

The trip back to the farm was uneventful, and after a large lunch, Alf, Marty, and Si spent the rest of the afternoon getting ready to leave early the next morning. When suppertime arrived Alf was ready to see Mary Francis again and maybe afterward play checkers with her, but she wasn't at the table when he came into the dining room. Marty asked about her and Mary said that Nancy was feeling bad again and Mary Francis was staying home with her. After supper the family gathered in the living room, but after a few games of dominos Alf was feeling edgy and he asked Martin about Nancy.

"The doctor doesn't seem to know what is wrong with her," Martin explained. "She has had influenza symptoms periodically for a year now, and at other times her legs become so weak she can't walk."

Alf frowned, knowing they would be leaving early in the morning. He wouldn't see her again until he got back. He looked at

Marty. "I think I'm going to bed. Four o'clock will come mighty early."

CHAPTER 24

The morning was cold when Alf, Marty, and Si rode out, but the sun brought warmth and by midday they were shucking their coats. They had ridden south out of Round Rock toward Georgetown and then cut back east to Granger. They ate a late lunch in Holland and then crossed the Little River just east of the small farming town.

Alf pulled Blackjack up as a ranch house next to a small lake came into view. Corrals and a barn were behind the house. He didn't see anyone outside.

"That's the Reed place," Marty remarked as he and Si rode up beside Alf. "We worked the roundup here last year."

Alf nodded. "Lead the way, Marty. See if he needs any postholes dug. If not, just ask him if we can camp out up on those hills over there. Tell him we want to look for bear."

"Tell him we saw tracks up there last year," Si added.

Marty heeled his horse toward the house; Alf and Si fell in beside him. When they got closer, Marty called out, "Hello! It's the Lynch boys out of Round Rock. We helped with the roundup last year."

They rode closer and Marty called out again. A few seconds later the front door opened and an old man holding a Winchester stepped out the door.

"Ride on up slowly with your hands where I can see them. What did you say your names were?"

"I'm Marty Lynch and this is my brother Si. We helped on the roundup last year, Mr. Reed."

"Who's the other fellow?"

"He's Alf Smith, a friend of ours."

"Yeah, I remember you boys. What do you want?"

"We're trying to make some money so we can ride out to Tascosa. We have jobs out there with Charles Goodnight."

"I don't need anybody 'til spring roundup."

"We could dig some postholes if you need them."

Pop Reed paused for a minute, scratching his head. "I could use a few postholes dug, but I just need about a hundred. I'll pay ten dollars if you dig 'em and set the post." He tilted his head to one side. "I recall you boys are from down around Round Rock. I would think you could find more work around there than here."

Marty and Alf looked at each another. Alf nodded toward the hills. "Tell him about the bear, Marty."

"Well, sir, you're right, but we had another reason for coming here."

Reed began to raise his Winchester. "What was that?"

"My friend Alf here is from up north, and we got to telling him we saw bear tracks on your place up in them hills, and he said he had never seen a bear. We were hoping you would let us camp out up there and look for one to shoot."

Reed studied Marty before he spoke. "You boys come on in the house. We can talk later about them bears that have been getting my calves."

Later that afternoon, after a long talk with Pop Reed, the boys moved into the bunkhouse with old Charlie Utley, who was Reed's only full-time worker. After they got settled in, Pop showed them where he had staked out the holes he wanted dug for a catch pen. Charlie was already there digging but Reed told him to take a break and give the posthole digger to Marty. Si grabbed the crowbar and began loosening the dirt at the next stake. Alf found a shovel and began clearing the dirt around the holes. Reed and Charley sat back and watched until Marty finished the first hole and went to work on the next one. Charley walked over to a pile of cedar posts, selected one, and brought it back to the newly dug hole. When he stuck it into the hole, Alf came over and began filing the hole with dirt and rocks while Si tamped it down with the crowbar. When the hole was full, he tamped more rocks into the top of the hole until the post was nice and tight.

Charlie, who had stepped back out of the way when the boys took over, nodded his approval. "You boys must have done this before."

Si smiled as he began working at another hole. "We were raised on a farm and Alf was too; this ain't anything new to us. Matter of fact, this is easy digging compared to back home. Not near as many rocks."

Pop smiled and turned to Charlie. "Charlie, go on and take care of the animals. I think these boys can take care of this job."

After Charlie wandered off to do his chores, Pop watched them dig a few more holes, and then he too went back to the house. The boys dug holes and put in posts until Pop called them in to supper.

"How many holes did you boys get dug?" Pop asked after they had settled down to eating.

"We got fifteen posts in and a couple of holes almost ready, sir," Alf answered.

Pop finished chewing a bite of beef. "You boys ought to finish up in a couple of days, and then you can go hunting."

Alf smiled and reached for his tea glass. "We plan on finishing tomorrow night, Mr. Reed."

Pop nodded. "Suits me if you do a good job."

The next day the boys got up early and dug a dozen holes before Pop called them for breakfast. They each ate enough for two people and then went back to work. They worked quickly, and by sundown they were setting the last post and Alf's hands had raw blisters, even though he'd worn his gloves. When Pop called them to supper, they shuffled wearily into the kitchen and plopped down at the table. When they began to eat, they perked up some and began talking about hunting the next day. Pop thought they should hunt along the river, but Marty quickly reminded him of the bear tracks they had seen up in the hills. That was where they wanted to start. Pop Reed, who had killed a few bears on his place, just shook his head and smiled.

The next day they got up early, ate breakfast, and got their gear ready for the hunt. Marty made a show of cleaning his Winchester and stuck it in the saddle boot. Si had a Winchester too, but Alf carried a Sharps rifle that had been Jake's. It was a single shot but used a heavier bullet than the Winchester carbine and would carry farther.

They rode out just a few minutes after sunup, heading east toward the hills. They followed a trail along the lake, then across a plowed field divided by a swift creek. The land changed from rich black soil to rocky, sand-like dirt as they rode up to the base of the first hill. From a distance the hill had looked smooth, but now Alf could see there were gullies and rough drop-offs along the slopes. Luckily Marty and Si had been on the hill before, looking for cattle, and they knew the trails that the cattle traveled.

Marty turned to Alf. "Where do we look?"

Alf grimaced. The hill was huge and there were a thousand places to hide a load of gold. "I guess we go to the top. The story was that Steinheimer had fled up the biggest hill because the Indians were chasing him and that he found a place where he could defend himself. He buried the gold and then escaped in the night."

Marty nodded and turned his horse toward a clearing at the bottom of the hill. Alf and Si followed him across the clearing and onto a trail winding up the hill through the brush and trees. Marty led them up, calling out to warn them when he came to a low limb or a bad place on the trail. It seemed to Alf that the hill had turned into a mountain as each turn led to another and seemed to go on forever, but eventually they reached a place where the trail leveled off.

"This is as high as it goes, Alf," Marty said as he stopped at a wide place on the trail.

Alf stopped beside him and studied the terrain. To the east across a grassy valley was another hill, slightly lower than the one they were on, and to the south of it another. Brush and trees grew in scattered clumps in the grassy meadows and on the hillsides. Several longhorns raised their heads as they noticed the three men, and then slowly moved away into the trees.

Si frowned as he swiveled his head back and forth. "Where do we start looking, Alf?"

Alf didn't speak for a second as he scanned the area. "I guess we look for a place where a person could hold off the Indians. Maybe look for signs of something out of place or man-made."

Si cocked his head. "Like a fort?"

"Maybe some logs piled up, or a dugout."

Marty rubbed his chin. "He might have found a place to hide from the Indians."

"We can fan out and look around, but first let's make our base camp right here."

They selected four trees where they could string up the tarp, then cleared the brush and a few small trees out from under and around it. Si made a fire ring with rocks and gathered some dead limbs for firewood. With all their camping gear under the tarp, they were ready to look for the gold.

Marty and Si turned to Alf. "How you want to do this, Alf?"

Alf shrugged. "I guess the best way is to start walking around this hill and see what we find." He pointed toward the south. "I'll go this way. Si, you take the area to my left, and Marty can take the area to my right."

They spread out and started out walking. Alf was excited as he zigzagged down the hill, checking every dead tree or gorge for signs. He was about to cross a cattle trail when he spied a piece of metal sticking out of some dirt. His heart raced as he wrenched it out of the ground, but his face fell when he saw it was only a horseshoe some horse had lost. He started to throw it away but changed his mind and stuck it in his belt as he continued looking for signs. A large fallen tree caught his eye, but when he studied it, he decided it wasn't old enough to be from fifty years ago.

He searched for three hours but found nothing that would indicate the presence of a man fighting off Indians. Maybe Steinheimer had just hidden from them. Alf felt his stomach growling. It was close to noon so he decided to go back to camp and rustle up some grub.

Marty was already there with a roaring fire going when Alf arrived. He turned when he heard Alf and explained with a sheepish grin, "I thought I would get us a fire going and start cooking lunch. Did you find anything?"

"Yeah, I did." Alf pulled the horseshoe from his belt and pitched it toward Marty. "I found a golden horseshoe."

Marty stared at the rusted metal and frowned. "Dang it, Alf, you had me all excited for a second." He reached in his pocket and tossed something to Alf. "I found this cartridge shell. Looks like a thirty-thirty. Do you think this could be part of the Indian fight?"

"No, this all happened before they had bullets. Back then they only had muzzle-loaders."

Marty studied the shell and then tossed it in the fire. He turned in the direction Si had gone. "I wonder if Si found anything."

Alf heated up a can of beans and he and Marty shared them, along with slices of homemade bread Mrs. Reed had made for them. Si never showed up, even after they shouted for him. But Marty didn't seem worried. "He is probably too excited to eat. He likes to explore."

They cleaned up after they finished eating and then went back to their areas to search again. Alf hurried back to the place where he'd left off his search. He had only gone a little ways before he stepped into a ravine that cut deep in the hill. It was only a couple of feet deep where Alf was standing, but he could see that flood water had cut deeper in other places up the hill. He decided to walk it to the top of the hill and see if the water had cut through the buried gold. He proceeded make his way up, examining the sides and bottom as he walked. It was easy walking for a while but eventually he came to a jumble of dead trees blocking his way. He had started to climb over a large log when he spotted something embedded in it. Leaning closer, he discovered it was a piece of broken flint. Quickly he pulled out his hunting knife and dug out the flint. He wiped it off and examined it. A broken arrowhead lay in his hand. His heart was beating faster as he carefully placed it in his pocket. He pulled another log out of the pile, looking for more arrowheads, and then another. A half hour later he'd had no further success, so he continued to trudge up the gully to the top.

A small meadow came into view as Alf pushed through some low-hanging branches and crawled over a three-foot drop-off at the head of the ravine. He stood up and looked around. A small concave cliff bordered the meadow across from where the ravine started. The other two sides led down the hill and were steep and covered with brush. A few long-dead logs lay against the cliff. Alf walked toward them.

Suddenly a gust of cold wind shook the trees and sent a cold chill over Alf's body. He looked into the sky and shivered again. The sunny sky that had started their day was being invaded by a solid wave of dark blue clouds coming out of the northwest. Alf had never seen anything like it. He stared at the clouds, mesmerized by the constantly changing forms.

He was jolted out of his trance as a deluge of cold rain dropped from the sky. He ran for the cover of the trees to escape the chilling rain, but most of the trees were bare and he could find no refuge. He huddled next to a small cedar but the blowing rain continued to find him. Alf was miserable. He tried to burrow back under the cedar but the stickers bit into his back. He finally decided he couldn't get any wetter, so he stood and headed for the camp. He followed the gully for a while but the water in it was increasing and he had to climb out and try to follow beside it. A thick clump of brush forced him to move farther away until he couldn't see the gully at all. Figuring he was close to the bottom of it, he turned to the right in the direction he had approached it and started up the hill. The rain was still coming down in buckets as he reached the top of the hill, and Alf was shivering. Frantically he searched for the camp, pushing through the brush and running up and down the hilly terrain. It was getting darker now. The rain slowed but began to come down as ice. Alf was exhausted. Seeing a large cedar, he squeezed under it to catch his breath. The sky was completely dark now, and even though it was midafternoon, the day turned into night and the rain turned to sleet. Alf was shivering uncontrollably now. He knew he needed to get up and find the camp, but he was all turned around and didn't know which way to go.

Suddenly he heard a shot, but it sounded far away. He stood and faced the way he thought it had come from. Another shot rang out from the same direction. Alf headed toward it, crashing through the brush and trying to go in a straight line. Another shot and Alf adjusted his direction, hoping whoever was shooting wouldn't run out of bullets. Alf couldn't remember how many hills and valleys he crossed before he saw the faint light of the fire ahead of him. His energy seemed to increase as he hurried to its precious warmth. Si was ready to fire another shot when Alf stumbled out of the darkness and under the tarp. Si threw a blanket over Alf's shoulders and poured him a cup of coffee. Marty wasn't there. Alf knelt before the fire for a long time nursing the coffee before he felt warm enough to talk. Si had asked him questions about Marty, but Alf only shook his head. Finally he turned to Si and said, "How did you find the camp?"

Si squatted down by Alf. "As soon as I saw the blue norther coming, I hurried back to camp and covered all our stuff to keep it dry. I knew what was coming. I've seen this happen before." He stood up, pulled his pistol, and fired again. "I hope Marty hears the shots like you did."

Alf peered out into the darkness. "If he keeps moving he will." Alf shivered. "I need to get out of these wet clothes. Could you get me my bag?"

Si pulled Alf's bedroll from under his saddle and set it beside him. Alf quickly shucked his wet clothes down to his bare skin and put on dry ones. He donned his heavy coat and covered back up with his blanket. As he began to feel warmer, he looked around to see what he needed to do. Firewood was getting low under the tarp, but there were still a lot of downed trees and brush around the camp. Alf found his hatchet and dashed out to the brush pile to cut more firewood. Si peered back into the darkness and fired his pistol into the air again. The sleet was turning into snow now and getting heavy. Alf had just set a load of firewood under the tarp when a shot rang out from the darkness.

Si looked at Alf with relief that slowly changed to worry. "I'm going out there. Keep firing every five or ten minutes." He dashed out into the falling snow.

Alf huddled by the fire as he counted off the seconds. When he reached four hundred, he fired his pistol. He began counting again. Another shot rang out somewhere in the dark. Minutes passed and Alf fired again. Five times he fired until finally movement caught his eye, and Si came into view with Marty by his side. They staggered into camp and immediately Marty went to the fire, hovering over it until his clothes began to steam. Alf handed him a cup of coffee and he wrapped his hands around it for a few seconds, soaking in the warmth. Si brought him dry clothes, which he quickly changed into and then crouched by the fire again.

"I've never been so cold in my life," he managed to say through chattering teeth. "If Si hadn't found me, I think I would have frozen to death."

Alf squatted down beside him. "I feel the same way. I got turned around too, and if I hadn't heard Si's shots, I would still be wandering around out there."

Si joined them by the fire and filled his tin cup with coffee. "What do we do now?"

Alf gazed out at the falling snow. "We can't look for any signs in this stuff. What do you think, Marty?"

"Naw, we might as well go home. I didn't see anything anyhow."

Si shook his head. "I didn't either. I guess after fifty years, everything that would have been a sign has rotted down to nothing."

"Yeah," Alf agreed. "The only way to find the lost gold would be to dig in likely places, and I saw a lot of places where a man could hide. We could dig for years and not find it."

"I agree." Marty sipped his coffee. "There's too many places to dig."

Si glanced at the falling snow. "Could we make it back to Reed's place tonight?"

"No, it'd be too dangerous," Marty said as he filled his coffee cup. "Not in the dark. We can try it in the morning."

Alf stood up. "I'm going to cut more wood. Why don't we fix some food and eat? It might make us feel better."

Alf walked to the brush pile and began chopping. Si got out a pot, poured three cans of beans in it, and set it on the fire. Marty began to peel potatoes. After supper the three men sat around the fire talking. Alf learned a lot about Marty and Si, and he told them a lot about himself. Later the talk turned to working cattle for Goodnight in West Texas. Marty told him they would leave in a few days and Alf would have a job with them on the cattle drive.

The next morning the snow had stopped falling but it covered the ground. Alf had opened his eyes to a snow-covered mess but to Marty and Si it was a snow-covered wonderland. With wide eyes they climbed out of their blankets, babbling about how pretty the snow looked covering the ground and piled up on the tree limbs. As soon as they got their boots on, they rushed out into it, whooping and hollering as they threw snowballs at each other. Tired of that, they began to make snow angels and other shapes. Alf watched them for a few minutes, then crawled out of his warm blanket and pulled on his boots. Their campfire was down to only glowing coals so he threw more firewood on it until it was roaring again. He looked out at Marty and Si as they played in the snow and shook his head. He saw snow every winter. It didn't impress him, and even though he enjoyed being around Marty and Si, he wasn't going to get in it unless he had to.

Suddenly Si hollered real loud and Alf turned to look. Marty had dumped a handful of snow down his back. Alf shook his head and smiled. They were just as much fun to be around as Slim and Billy had been.

"Are you boys going to play in the snow all day or are we riding out of here?"

Si walked up to the fire, shaking the snow off his back. "I'm ready to eat something. Let's cook them eggs and eat first."

Marty agreed and grabbed the coffeepot and went out to find some clean snow. Alf went to get more wood. Si got out the frying pan and began cracking eggs.

After they ate they packed up and started back down the trail. Marty led the way, feeling out the trail as they slowly zigzagged down the hill. Finally they reached the bottom and the traveling was easier. The ride to the house was quick, and after putting their horses in the barn, they went to the house. Pop Reed and his wife greeted them warmly, seemingly glad to see them. They sat and talked for a while, drinking coffee and warming at the fire. Marty explained to Pop that they didn't have time to stay and wait for the snow to melt. They would be leaving soon for West Texas. Pop pulled some bills out of his pocket. He paid them five dollars each for working on the fence, and then offered to let them spend the night. They agreed, knowing Mrs. Reed would feed them well and the roads would be better for traveling in the morning. They passed the day getting things ready for the trip home and then playing dominos and cards with the Reeds and Charlie Utley. Mrs. Reed fixed them a nice lunch, and at supper she topped off the meal with hot apple pie. They played more games after they ate, but by eight o'clock everyone was ready for bed.

Alf was glad when he climbed into the bunk that night. He was tired and ready to get back to Round Rock. He had been thinking about Mary Francis and was anxious to see her again.

CHAPTER 25

The sun was shining and the roads were almost clear of snow when Alf saw the Lynch house come into view. His heart seemed to swell as he thought of seeing Mary Francis again. They took care of the horses first, and then hurried to the house. Martin greeted them at the back door and followed them into the living room where Mary, Mattie, and Eli were waiting. Marty and Si began telling the family about their adventures in the snowstorm. Alf tossed in a word or two, but mostly he was wondering where Mary Francis and Nancy were. Finally, when the conversation waned, Alf couldn't hold back his curiosity anymore.

"Martin, why isn't Mary Francis here?"

"She went to her grandmother's in Arkansas. She left two days after you and the boys took off to Reed's place."

"How long is she going to be gone?"

"She's going to live with them for a while. She said to tell you good-bye."

Alf felt like a hammer had struck him in the stomach. His shoulders slumped and he felt like he was going to cry. He thought she'd liked him, but to leave like that without telling him anything about it must mean she didn't care for him. He sat down in one of the chairs and stared at the fire. The conversation continued among the family but Alf didn't care. His heart was broken. A few minutes later he excused himself and went to his room. After he put up his things, he pulled off his boots and gun belt and lay down on the bed. Memories of Mary Francis swirled in his head. Tears welled in his eyes and he quickly wiped them off. He tried to think of something else but her smiling face kept appearing. Finally he went to sleep, but he dreamed of her, and when he awoke hours later, he sobbed. A few minutes later someone knocked on his door. Alf hurriedly wiped his eyes and opened the door. Marty was standing there with a worried look on his face.

"Time to wake up, sleepyhead. Supper is ready."

"I don't feel very good, Marty. I don't feel like eating."

Marty frowned. "Are you hurting or anything?"

"Yes, I'm aching all over. I must have caught something when I got so cold."

Marty shook his head. "Okay, just rest, you'll be all right in the morning."

Alf closed the door, then lay back down on the bed. He closed his eyes and instantly Mary Francis appeared in his mind. His face screwed up to cry but he held it back. He had to face the fact that she wasn't attracted to him and get on with his life. Besides, he wasn't ready to settle down, and she was looking for a husband and a father for Nancy. He gritted his teeth and tried to think about finding Jude Brown, but her face kept flashing in his thoughts. She was so pretty. His face screwed up again and he cried for a long time until he finally fell asleep.

The next morning Alf woke up in a somber mood. Sometime during the night, he had accepted his fate and was determined to put Mary Francis out of his mind. After breakfast he went out to the barn and fed Blackjack, then checked him for cuts and loose shoes. Later he and the boys rode the fences again, and practiced roping and herding the cattle. Marty was going to tell Goodnight that he was an experienced cowboy and Alf wanted to learn all he could so he wouldn't make a liar out of his friend.

A week went by and Alf figured he was getting pretty good with the cattle, but he also knew that half of the credit went to Blackjack. He was a smart horse and soon caught on to what Alf expected of him. When cutting a calf out of the herd, Alf didn't even have to rein him. He just showed him which calf he wanted, and if he roped the calf, Blackjack put just the right tension on the rope as Alf tied the calf. Marty and Si even remarked about what a good cow horse he had become.

Alf had just turned a calf loose and was rolling up his lariat when Marty rode up beside him. "I think it's time to go, Alf. We'll leave in the morning."

Alf relaxed a little. He had been ready to leave ever since he found out Mary Francis was gone, but Marty had kept putting it off. Alf had kept his mind on practicing to be cowboy, but foremost in his mind was finding Jude Brown and finishing his quest. "Okay by me. Most of my stuff's packed already." He pulled out his pocket watch. "It's four o'clock. You ready to ride in?"

"Yeah. We need to get everything ready tonight so we can leave early in the morning."

Alf mounted Blackjack and rode over to the fence where he had left his coat. It was late February and the day had been cold when they started that morning, but the sun was out and it had warmed up quickly. Edward rode up to the fence and waited as Alf picked up his coat. Edward had been riding with them this week, readying himself to taking care of the livestock alone. He had wanted to go with them but Martin wouldn't let him. Alf nodded and they both rode to the house in silence, lost in their own thoughts of the days ahead.

They left the next morning before daylight. It was another cold morning but the sky was clear, and by noon it would probably be warm enough to take off their coats. They followed a road that would take them to the small town of Lampasas, and by noon they were watering the horses in the river that shared the same name. They had brought food with them and ate as the horses rested and grazed. It took them the rest of the day to get to the county seat of Lampasas, known for its flowing springs. Lampasas was a thriving town, catering to the farms and ranches that had sprung up after the Comanche were finally put on the reservation. They camped that night in the wagon yard and ate the rest of the fresh food they had brought with them. The rest of the way it would be canned beans and smoked side meat. The next morning they were out of Lampasas before the sun rose, heading northwest toward the town of Goldwaite. The riding was easy and midday found them crossing into Mills County, according to a sign nailed to a tree. Midafternoon they arrived at the sleepy little village and stopped at the general store to stock up on supplies. They rode on, and that night they camped off the road by a small stream.

Stars were still glittering in the sky when they headed out the next morning. The wind was blowing hard out of the south. By midmorning they crossed into Brown County, and by noon they were in Brownwood, the county seat. They bought some corn for the horses and treated themselves to a meal at a local café while the horses rested. Later, when they rode out of town, clouds were beginning to build in the west and the wind from the south had lost some of its bluster. Two hours later dark clouds began to form and the wind began blowing out of the north. Alf slipped on his coat and slicker when it began to rain. It came slowly at first, but minutes later the bottom fell out and the boys hurriedly looked for cover. At first they crowded together under a large oak tree, but they had only been there a few minutes when a bolt of lightning hit a tree about a hundred yards away. They ran to a rocky ledge surrounded by stunted cedars and huddled against it. An hour later the storm had passed, but an ice-cold wind had taken its place. Despite wearing his slicker, Alf's clothes had gotten wet during the storm and he was shivering as he guided Blackjack back onto the road. They went on until they found a place to camp for the night out of the wind. First they gathered wood for a fire so they could warm up and change their clothes. Later, while Si cooked their beans and coffee, Alf and Marty took care of the horses and rustled up more firewood to last the night. After supper they cut cedar branches to use as cover on the wet ground where they put their bedrolls.

There was ice on the puddles when they headed out the next morning, but the sun was shining and by noon it was warm enough for them to consider taking off their coats. The countryside began to change as they rode farther west. The rolling hills became larger and more rugged, while the valleys were covered with cactus and stunted trees. The road they had followed all the way from Round Rock slowly changed to a lightly traveled trail the farther they rode west from Brownwood. They rode for two days, seeing only a few cattle and sheep, the occasional wild animal and a few scattered cabins.

As Alf studied the landscape, he felt he was seeing virgin land that people had yet to alter. The land had looked like this for thousands of years and would probably be the same for many years to come. He could think of no reason for people to settle here.

The sun was touching the horizon when they topped a hill and saw Abilene in the distance. With higher spirits they urged their horses faster and soon entered the outskirts of the bustling town. Alf wondered what had brought this many people to this desolate area, but he soon found out when they came to a small river surrounded by a fertile valley dotted with small farms. It was dark when they rode into the main part of town. They boarded their horses first and then found a bunkhouse where they could sleep for the night. After eating they found a general store, where they bought more supplies. They knew they wouldn't find many stores on the rest of their journey, and the ones they did find would have high prices.

Alf bought a few things at one store and found the prices as cheap as they were in Belton.

"If I might ask, sir, where do you get your merchandise?" Alf asked.

The clerk smiled. "I get it shipped in by railroad."

"There's a railroad here?"

"Yes, sir. The Texas and Pacific got here over a year ago and this place has been booming ever since. Settlers are coming in every day."

Alf paid for his things and met Marty and Si at the bunkhouse. They talked for a while and went to bed. They still had a long way to go and would be leaving again early in the morning.

The next morning they were five miles from Abilene before the sun came up, riding on a trail that had started out as a rough road. They followed it for a while, then turned onto a trail that followed the clear fork of the Brazos River. By noon on the second day they left the river and rode overland until nightfall. The next night they camped on the Double Mountain fork of the Brazos. They next day they crossed the river and rode north through barren country for two days until they came to another fork of the Brazos. Marty told Alf this was the Salt Fork and that they would follow it for a while.

They camped on the Salt Fork twice before they left the river and rode up a long, winding trail to a high mesa that that meandered in both directions. Marty and Si told him they were going up on the cap rock and Alf would see something at the top he wouldn't believe. They were right. A flat, level sea of brown grass stretched out from the edge of the cap rock as far as Alf could see. He pulled up Blackjack and stared. He had never imagined anything like this in his life and he wanted to take it all in, relishing the moment in his wonderment.

Marty watched him for a few minutes and then shook his head. "We can't stay here all day, Alf. Let's ride."

Si rode up beside Alf. "Ain't it something, Alf? Me and Marty did the same thing the first time we saw it. Mr. Goodnight told us this was the south end of the Great Plains, where the buffalo live, or used to live. Ain't many of 'em left now with the hide skinners killing them all."

Marty moved his horse closer to Alf. "Yeah, we came up on a place where there were about two hundred or more dead buffalo just sitting there rotting. We smelled them a half-day's ride away before we got to 'em."

Alf shook his head. "What do they get for the hides?"

Marty scratched his chin. "About a dollar, I think."

"It's a shame to waste all that meat for a one-dollar hide." He paused for a minute, scanning the plain. "Which way do we go from here?"

"We follow the cap rock for a few days, and then turn northwest."

The riding was easy now and they made good time. On the first evening, they camped next to a large area of bleached-out buffalo bones. It was a dry camp but they had full canteens to make coffee with and dried buffalo chips to fuel their fire. Alf screwed up his face in disgust when Marty and Si told him they were going to cook with buffalo poop. He told them he wasn't going to eat anything cooked on a shit fire, but he changed his mind when he saw that the fire didn't stink much and the beans seemed to be cooking just fine. When Si handed him his tin plate, he smelled the beans and cautiously took a small bite, chewed, then took a bigger bite. He swallowed and looked up at Marty and Si, who were snickering at him.

"You boys better never tell anybody I ate beans cooked over a buffalo-crap fire."

The next day was their thirteenth day on the trail. They rode all day and the scenery didn't change until finally at dark they came upon a small river. Marty said it was the Tule, and farther up it ran into a big canyon where MacKenzie had defeated the Comanche and killed all their horses. Alf had read about the battle in Palo Duro Canyon. Maybe he would see the canyon while he was up in this area. The next day he got his wish. They camped by the river that night, then crossed it the next morning and traveled north. By noon they came to the Red River and followed it northwest. Soon they were in Palo Duro Canyon and Alf was gawking at the beautiful cliffs and formations.

They rode into what looked like an old Indian camp. Fire pits were scattered around next to lodge poles and scraps of buffalo hide. A few broken arrows and spears littered the ground, along with empty brass shells. Alf realized this was the Comanche camp that Mackenzie had attacked. They camped that night farther down the canyon under a cloudless sky. Alf realized he liked this country. He might decide to stay here for the rest of his life.

On the second day they left the canyon and headed northwest. After their noon stop, they began to see a few cattle and sheep, and just before dark, they spotted a rider heading north. He seemed to be a cowboy; he wore leather chaps and carried two lariats and several pigging' strings on his saddle. The man stopped when he saw the Alf, Marty, and Si riding toward him. He moved his hand close to his pistol.

Marty rode up to him. "Mister, could you tell us where we're at? We just came across the plain."

The cowboy eyed them. "Sure, you're just a mile from Tascosa." He pointed north. "You're on the right trail. Just follow it on into town."

"Thanks, mister. I thought this was the right way, but this country up here can fool you."

The cowboy narrowed his eyes. "You've been up here before?"

Marty nodded toward Si. "Yeah, me and my brother ride for Goodnight. We went home to Round Rock for Christmas."

The cowboy seemed to relax. He moved his hand back to the reins. "My name's Jimbo Brown. I ride for the Brown Ranch."

"My name's Marty, and my brother is Si. That's Alf."

"Glad to meet you boys. I guess I'd better get going. I'll probably see you in town or during the roundup." He turned and rode west.

A cold chill run up Alf's back when he heard the man say his name. Jimbo Brown was Jude Brown's brother, the one who had gone with Jude to their brother's ranch.

CHAPTER 26

Tascosa was a lot different than the small, sleepy town Alf had envisioned would be in this empty land. He leaned back in his saddle as he gazed at a thriving town, complete with a stone courthouse surrounded by scores of businesses and stores. The boardwalks were crowded with people and wagons and cowboys on horseback and fancy buggies filled the streets. Past the courthouse on another street, Alf saw saloons and dance halls, their hitching racks lined with horses. A broad river flowed just yards past the last saloon.

Marty seemed to know where he was going as he led them to an empty hitching rack across from the courthouse. After they got off their horses, Marty nodded toward the sheriff's office.

"I'm going in here to see if Goodnight or his foreman is in town. You can come if you want to." He turned and sauntered into the door. Alf decided to wait outside with the horses. A few minutes later Marty returned.

"The foreman is down at the Equity Saloon. We can walk, it ain't far."

Alf followed Marty and Si to the saloon and then over to a table where a tall, broad-shouldered man in his thirties sat drinking whiskey with a woman. He looked up when they approached his table.

"We're back, boss. Picked up another hand too," Marty drawled as he nodded toward Alf.

"I was just thinking of you boys, wondering if you was going to make it back." He turned to Alf. "I'm Ed King."

Alf stuck out his hand. "I'm Alf Smith."

"Where have you been working, Alf?" Ed asked as they shook hands.

Alf paused. "Well, sir, I done some herding back home and some with Marty and Si at their dad's place." He paused again, and then added, "Worked a little on the Reed Ranch."

Ed looked Alf up and down. "Okay, you're hired." He turned to Marty. "You boys go on out to the ranch when you're ready. In case you haven't kept up, today's Saturday and most of the boys are down at the saloons spending what money they got left from payday. If you go down there, be careful. Been a little trouble lately."

Marty frowned. "What kind of trouble, boss?"

"Just the usual stuff—men fighting over a woman. This time it's Sally Emory down at the Hog Town dance hall. Bill Gibson was found dead in her room, shot in the back. She claimed she wasn't there when he was killed."

"Who do they think did it?"

"Sheriff East thinks it was the bartender, Johnny Maley, but he don't have no evidence."

Alf turned to Marty. "How far is it to the ranch?"

"It's about a three-hour ride. We can pick up a few things and ride on out there if you want."

Si nudged his brother. "Can't we go to one of the dance halls for a while?"

Marty looked at Alf. "What do you say?"

Alf rubbed his chin. "We could take the horses down to the blacksmith shop and get their shoes reset. While he's doing that we could look over the town, maybe get a beer."

Si looked at Marty. "Yeah, let's do that."

Marty grinned at his brother. "I know what you want." He turned to Alf. "You're right; we need to take care of the horses." He turned to Ed. "I guess we'll stay in town for a while and ride out later."

Ed nodded. "That's all right with me, Marty, just be ready to go to work Monday morning bright and early. We're going to start the roundup and you won't see town again until it's over."

The blacksmith was busy when they brought their horses but he said he would have them ready by five o'clock. That would give Alf and the boys four hours to see the town. They went to the general store first, where they picked up a few things they would need out at the ranch. After packing their purchases in their saddles, they walked down to one of the dance halls.

Alf's muscles tensed as he walked into the Tuscosa saloon and dance hall. Most of the men were young and seemed to be having a good time dancing with the girls, but a few rough-looking men turned and glared at them. Alf headed straight to the bar and ordered a beer while Marty and Si, with big smiles on their faces, gazed at the girls who were dancing around the dance floor to the sounds of a small band playing "Buffalo Gals." They watched for a while and joined Alf at the bar. They had just ordered their own beers when the dance ended and a couple of the girls strolled over. They were young, with fancy dresses and powdered faces, but they seemed tired and sweaty. One of them took Si's beer and downed half of it. She looked up at him, a pouty smile on her face.

"You boys want to dance? It's only ten cents a dance." She nodded toward the stairs. "Or we can go upstairs for a dollar."

Si grinned as he jammed his hand into his pocket and pulled out his wallet. He handed her a dollar. "I want to go upstairs."

She reached for his hand. "Come on, cowboy."

Alf watched as they walked away, and then turned to see Marty hand in hand with the other girl, going the same way. He felt a stirring in his loins as he watched them. He had been taught in church that poking a woman who wasn't his wife was a sin. He turned back to his beer and tried to suppress his feeling, but images kept coming back to his mind. He had succumbed to his urges before in a personal way, but he was still a virgin and he wanted to keep it that way.

Suddenly he felt a hand on his waist and he turned to see deep blue eyes gazing up at him from a pixie face framed in corn-silk hair.

"My name's Sally. You want to dance?" She looked down at the floor. "Or maybe we could go upstairs?"

Her name was Sally and she had picked him. Alf's mind melted and seeped down to his groin. He couldn't think of anything but those blue eyes and that beautiful face. He pulled his eyes from hers and glanced at the staircase. He looked back into her eyes and his only thought was going up those stairs with her. He put his arm around her, and without saying a word, they walked toward the stairs.

CHAPTER 27

The longhorn steer was determined he wasn't going to be roped. He dodged through the brush, twisting one way, then another, trying to escape the horse and rider chasing him. Turning right to avoid a boulder in his path, he emerged into a small meadow. Frantically he increased his speed and headed straight for the stunted trees on the other side. He was almost there when something grabbed his horns and began pulling on them. He raised his head to dislodge whatever had ahold of him, but it kept pulling until finally he turned to confront his attacker. As the horse and rider came into his view, he charged, the tips of his horns lowered to gore his foe. Suddenly another rope settled over his head and he was pulled from another direction. He turned to charge the new foe but now he was pulled from both sides, and he only went a little ways before he was stopped again. He struggled to move but was held fast. After a few minutes he stopped and hung his head, too tired to move.

Marty looked over at Alf. "This is a tough one. We may have to sew his eyelids." He looked back at the steer. "We'll try to lead him first. I'll take the front." Marty turned his horse and released some of the tension on his lariat. "Give him a little slack."

The steer's ropes loosened. He shook his head and stared at his antagonist. His quick breaths slowed as he took a step toward Marty, but again there was pressure on his neck and he stopped. The pressure increased from one direction and he stepped toward it, paused, and then took another step. He lowered his head to charge but then the pressure was back on both sides and he was held motionless again. The ropes loosened briefly. Then one of them tightened. Again he stepped toward it and it loosened, but then it tightened again, and he took another step toward it to allow it to loosen again. The action kept repeating until eventually the steer was following the horse. Every once in a while there was pressure from behind and he would slow down, but he was a quick learner and soon he was following like a trained pony.

The small valley where Goodnight kept his herd was a long way off now that they had been out on the range for a month. It had taken Alf and Marty half an hour to reach the three-thousand-cattle herd. Alf flipped his lariat off the steer and watched as it hurried to join the herd. He wiped his brow and rode over to the chuck wagon to fill his empty canteen. There were several cowboys standing around the water barrel when he rode up. He tied his horse to the wagon wheel and joined them.

"You boys leave me any water?"

Randy, one of the older cowboys, nodded toward the barrel. "Help yourself, Alf, plenty left." He took the dipper from its hook, dipped it into the barrel, and held it out. "Hold your canteen out and I'll fill it for you."

"Thanks, Randy. I'm as dry as this dust all over me."

Randy filled the canteen twice and handed it to Alf. Alf drank deep and hung the dipper up. Most of the cowboys had drifted off, but Randy was one of the roundup captains and had waited to talk to Alf.

"We're going to drive the other rancher's cattle to the sorting place and drive ours back here. I want you and the Lynch brothers to go."

"Are we through looking for cattle?"

"Yeah. As soon as we get the sorted cattle, we start moving the herd north."

"We going to take them to Dodge?"

"Yep." Randy nodded toward the herd. "Go on and start cutting out the odd brands, but look at them good to see if they've been changed. Goodnight thinks the rustlers are hitting us hard."

Alf remounted and headed for the herd. He found Marty and Si already there and he teamed up with them to separate the cattle. They worked the rest of the day, and by nightfall they had cut out all the other brands. Some of them had looked suspicious and Randy marked them with red paint. The roundup judges would decide if the brands had been changed or not back at the sorting place.

The last steer Alf cut out of the herd had a blurred-up brand. Alf got Marty to help rope it and called Randy over. "I got a bad one, Randy."

"It looks to me like the LB brand of Luke Brown, but it's not clean. It could be a JA changed to an LB." He marked the steer with red paint and nodded for Alf to release him.

As Marty chased the steer into the herd, Alf asked Randy, "Where are we going to take this herd?"

"The cattlemen's association decided to exchange the off-brand cattle at a holding pen on the river just west of Tascosa."

Alf leaned back and cocked his head. He had been thinking of Sally a lot and wanted to see her. "You think we'll be able to go to town?"

Randy smiled. "I think we can arrange it. We should be there a few days and the cowboys can take shifts guarding the herd. The ones not on herd duty can do what they want."

It was raining the next morning but the cowboys put on their slickers and started the herd of odd-branded cattle toward Tascosa. They made good time despite the rain, and at noon on the next day, they arrived at the holding pens. The sun was shining but a brisk north wind was cold when Randy reported to the roundup judges. When he returned he told his cowboys to herd the marked cattle into a special wired-in holding pen, and then push the rest of the cattle in with the main herd. Then they could start looking for cattle with the JA brand and herd them to an area he would select.

When Alf and the rest of the cowboys reached the main herd, cowboys from other ranches were already there cutting out their cattle and driving them to their own separate areas. The JA cowboys rode in and began to search the herd, calling out when one of them saw one of their brands. It was hectic at first with so many cowboys milling among the wide horns of the half-wild herd, but soon Alf and Blackjack got the hang of it. Alf was good at spotting brands and he soon had Marty and Si busy cutting the JA cattle out while he looked for them. They worked until the failing light made it too dangerous to ride through the herd and the herd master called it quits by ringing the supper bell. All the cowboys hurried to the chuck wagon to get in line for supper.

As Alf and the rest of the JA cowboys ate, Randy gave out night-watch assignments. Alf grinned when he was told that his watch was at midnight. He'd have time to go see Sally before his shift. He quickly finished eating and washed up, then put on a clean shirt. Si, whose shift was late too, joined him and they headed toward town. Alf didn't talk much as they rode, but Si rambled on about dancing and poking his favorite girl. Alf's only thoughts were of Sally. When he had made love to her that first time, he had fallen in love with her, and now he didn't know what to do about it. She was a whore, but she had told him she had been forced into prostitution when her parents died and her uncle forced himself on her. Her uncle was a freight driver on the Santa Fe Trail and she had slipped away from him at Dodge City. The only work she could find was in a saloon, and when her boss decided to move to Tascosa, she came with him. She told Alf she wanted to quit but she owed her boss a lot of money and had to pay him first.

Alf felt his pocket where he kept his wallet. He still had some money. He had to help her get out of that dance hall. Maybe he could get a job with the sheriff and they could get married and get their own house. He would talk to her about it when he saw her.

When they got to the dance hall, Alf searched for Sally but she wasn't on the floor. He ordered a beer and waited. He knew she was probably upstairs with someone and he was poking her. He gritted his teeth as pangs of jealousy filled his chest. He wanted to do something but didn't know what. He sighed, feeling helpless. He would have to accept what she was doing now and put it behind him. He would do what he must to free her from this hell.

It was thirty minutes and two beers later that Sally came down the stairs. As soon as Alf saw her, he rushed over and put his arm on her shoulder.

"Hello, Sally, remember me?"

Sally smiled. "Of course I do. It's been a while. I thought maybe you left town."

"No, I told you I would be back. I told you I love you, remember?"

Sally hesitated, and then pursed her lips. "A lot of cowboys tell me that. I don't know if they really mean it."

"But I meant it, Sally. I do love you." Alf glanced around the room. "Can we go upstairs?"

Sally smiled. "Sure, cowboy." She reached for his hand and led him up the stairs to her room. It was small, only big enough for a bed and a washstand. Sally pulled off her dress and undergarments and climbed into bed as Alf watched in amazement. He couldn't believe how lucky he was that she loved him. Quickly he pulled off all his clothes except his long johns and crawled into bed beside her.

"I love you, Sally." He turned toward her and they kissed. He had planned on talking to her first, but his body took over and they made love. Alf was still new at this and it was over quickly. He lay beside her for a few minutes, savoring his feelings, and then reached for her and they kissed. As soon as their lips parted, Sally rolled out of bed and began putting on her clothes.

Alf frowned. "I want to talk to you, Sally."

"What do you want to say, cowboy?"

Alf rose up in the bed. "I want to help you, Sally. You told me you wanted to quit but that you owed your boss money."

Sally stared at him for a minute and her eyes softened. "I'm ashamed, cowboy. I remember telling you that, but I don't remember your name. It's been a while."

"It's Alf, Alf Smith. I understand it's been a long time, but I've been working on the roundup and I just today got a chance to see you."

Sally smiled and sat back down on the bed. "I remember now, Alf. You said such sweet things but I didn't know if I could believe you. I do want to quit, but I owe my boss a hundred dollars and I have to work to pay him."

"If I give you the money, you could quit and we could get married."

Sally lowered her eyes. "Yes, Alf, we could, but do you have that kind of money?"

"I have over a hundred dollars I can give you right now. Then when I draw my pay from Goodnight, we can leave town and go somewhere else. I can get a job and we can get a house."

Sally's eyes widened as she listened. She held her hand up to his mouth. "Alf, that's wonderful. Give me the hundred and I'll pay him when you leave."

Alf quickly pulled out his wallet and handed her the money. "I don't have night watch until midnight. I can stay until about eleven."

Sally smiled as she put the money under the mattress and got back into bed. "I love you, Alf. We are going to be so happy."

It was just a few minutes past midnight when Alf arrived at the herd to ride his shift. He talked to Marty for a few minutes but he seemed anxious to leave for town and he didn't ask Alf how his night had gone. They exchanged a few words and then Marty spurred his horse toward Tascosa. Alf thought of Sally and his heartbeat quickened. He was the happiest he had ever been in his life. He slowly began circling the herd, softly singing and thinking of how great his life was going to be.

The next morning Alf woke up in a joyful mood. He was nice to everyone and didn't even gripe to the cook about the food. He threw himself into his job spotting and cutting cattle, and he even helped cut out cattle for other ranchers when he couldn't find any of the JA cattle. The small herds of off-brand cattle kept coming for the next three days, but on the fourth day, the last bunch came in and by noon they were finished. The marked cattle had all been studied and a few were definitely changed brands, but there was no real evidence of who had done it. After lunch Alf and the rest of the JA cowboys drove their cattle home.

The next day was payday and the cowboys were given one more day to go to Tascosa. Alf took Mr. Goodnight aside and told him he was quitting and getting married.

Goodnight frowned, and then sighed. "I hope you know what you are doing, Alf. I hope you have a happy life, but if things don't work out, your job will be waiting. We leave for Dodge City in three days."

Alf stuck out his hand. "I know it will work out, sir, but thank you."

When Alf got back to the bunkhouse, Marty and Si were waiting for him. "Alf, are you sure you're doing the right thing?" Marty asked. "This is awful sudden."

"I think I'm doing the right thing. I love Sally and she loves me. I want to be with her the rest of my life."

"What are you going to do after you get married?"

"I can get a job as a lawman, but not here. Too many people know Sally and I might have to shoot them if they insulted her. I'll take her to Belton or maybe Abilene. We're going to get a house and settle down."

Marty pressed his lips together. "Well, Alf, I wish you the best of luck."

"Thanks, Marty. I want you and Si to stand up with me at my wedding."

Marty and Si waited as Alf washed up and put on his best clothes, and then the three of them rode into town. It was midafternoon when they arrived in Tascosa, having ridden the last few miles at a gallop. Alf thoughts had been entirely on Sally as they rode—her face, her lips, and her naked body. He ached for her and couldn't wait to see her again.

When they got to dance hall, Alf jumped off Blackjack and hurried inside, rapidly scanning the room for a glimpse of her. He didn't see her and his heartbeat raced as he scanned the room a second time. His eyes settled on the staircase and it came to him that she might be in her room. He raced up the stairs and pushed in the door.

Alf froze in confusion. Sally was in her bed, naked, her head back and her mouth open as she moaned. A naked man lay on top of her, rapidly pumping his hips. Alf clenched his teeth, and then pounded the wall with his fist.

Sally's eyes flew open and she screamed, "Alf, what are you doing here?"

"What the hell?" The man looked around at Alf. "Get the hell out of here, cowboy, can't you see we're busy?"

Alf looked at Sally, trying to understand what was happening. "I came in so we could get married. Who is this man? Why are you doing this? I thought you loved me."

The man sneered as he shook his head. "You, marry her? She's my girl and she ain't getting married to nobody."

A flash of jealousy filled Alf's mind. "Tell me he's lying. Did he force you to do this?"

Sally shrugged, picked up a bottle of whiskey from the nightstand, and took a long drink. "No, he didn't force me. This is my husband, Johnny."

Tears welled up in Alf's eyes. "So what you told me was all a lie?"

Sally drank from the bottle again and licked her lips. "I told you what you wanted to hear. Hell, I'm a whore; I like this kind of life. I ain't going to marry some hick and raise his snot-nosed kids."

While she was talking, Johnny rose and slipped on his pants, then his gun belt. "I told you to get out of here, kid."

Alf looked at him and then turned back to Sally. He began to realize he had been suckered by her. He could feel his face flush and he gritted his teeth. "I want my hundred dollars back."

Sally glanced at Johnny and chirped, "You paid for all night and gave me a tip. I don't owe you anything."

Johnny's hand went for his pistol. Alf caught the action out of the corner of his eye. He drew his Colt and fired. Johnny's hand jerked back as shards of metal tore into his flesh. He looked at the blood on his hands and then at his holster. His pistol was shattered into pieces. Quickly he thrust his hands over his head. "Give him the damn hundred dollars."

Sally's face was ashen as she reached under her mattress and pulled out a purse. With trembling fingers she fumbled with the drawstrings and counted out a stack of bills. She held them out to Alf.

Alf had never felt like this in his life. He was terribly ashamed but at the same time terribly angry. There was so much hurt in him he was almost out of his mind. He wanted to kill both of them so much that he trembled. He started to put pressure on the trigger, but something in the back of his mind told him it would be the wrong thing to do. He paused to think and then slowly holstered his Colt. He picked up the money and stuck it in his shirt pocket. He stared at her face in silence for a minute, and then turned to see Marty and Si standing behind him. Alf couldn't think of anything to say to them. He knew he had been played for a sucker, but he could still hear her telling him she loved him as they'd made love. His heart felt like an anvil sitting in his chest. He fought to hold back the tears but knew he couldn't for long. He stepped around the brothers and fled down the stairs and out of the saloon. Tears began streaming from his eyes as he jumped on Blackjack and galloped out of town.

CHAPTER 28

Alf rode for hours with little regard for where he was going, or anything else for that matter. Blackjack ran until he got tired and then slowed to a walk. Alf wasn't directing him, so he just kept going in the same direction. Eventually he came to a small running stream with pools of clear water and green grass growing on the banks. Blackjack stopped and drank, then went to grazing. With a bowed head, Alf sat on Blackjack for a while before he finally dismounted and sat down on the grass. For a second he envisioned him and Sally lying in the grass, but reality set in and he threw himself on the ground and began to cry again. For hours he lay there, sobbing for a while, thinking, and then sobbing again. It became dark but he didn't move except to wipe his eyes.

The cold night finally forced him to gather firewood. When it was burning steadily, he sat beside it and stared into the flames. His mind was still churning, trying to make sense of what he was feeling. He still saw Sally's face in his mind and couldn't understand why she would want to live that way. He knew about whores but he had always thought they whored because they had no other way to make a living. He couldn't comprehend a woman wanting to be a whore. It was almost midnight, when Alf finally unsaddled Blackjack and rubbed him down. He had almost accepted the fact that Sally felt nothing for him, but when he crawled into his blankets he cried again. He dreamed of her that night, but it was of her inner ugly self, not the beautiful girl he had loved.

When Alf woke up the next morning, his mind had cleared somewhat, and as he ran his mind back over what he had done since he'd met Sally, he began to recognize his stupidity. The more he thought about it, the more he realized how big a fool he had been. Head down, he closed his eyes and vowed he would never be fooled by a woman again. He sat there for a while longer until at last he rose, determined, and put out his fire. He saddled Blackjack and climbed into the saddle. He sat there for a few minutes as he pondered how his fascination with Sally had made him forget the reason he had come to Tascosa. His search for Jude Brown had been interrupted, but now it was the only thing that would keep his mind off Sally. This time nothing would stand in his way as he searched for the last murderer of his parents.

The day was half gone by the time Alf spotted Tascosa in the distance. When he had left the small stream, he had no idea which way to go to get to the JA ranch. He figured the stream would run into the Canadian River, so he followed it and two hours later came to the Big Sandy River that flowed across Oklahoma and on to the Arkansas River. He followed it west until he saw Tascosa in the distance. Alf knew where he was now and he turned Blackjack toward the JA ranch.

With big grins on their faces, Marty and Si ran to greet Alf as he rode through the ranch-house gate. Alf rode up to them and dismounted.

Marty patted Alf's back. "We were worried we wouldn't ever see you again, Alf. Where did you go?"

"I had some thinking to do. I needed to be alone."

"We didn't say anything, but there's talk all over the ranch that Sally stole money from you and you had to shoot Johnny Maley to get it back."

Alf picked up Blackjack's reins and started walking toward the corral. "Thanks, boys. I did a fool thing and I'd rather not have everybody know the real truth."

Si moved closer and spoke softly. "You mean about thinking you and Sally was going to get married?"

Alf swallowed. "Yeah, I feel like a fool, but I don't want to be hurrahed by anyone."

Marty grinned and shook his head. "Ain't nobody going to hurrah you, Alf. They all know how fast you are with a gun."

Goodnight was waiting at the corral when the three men arrived. He patted Alf on the shoulder. "I'm sorry things didn't work out, Alf. If you still want your job, we start for Dodge City in the morning."

"Thank you, Mr. Goodnight. Yeah, I'm ready to leave this place for a while."

The next morning at daylight, Alf and the cowboys of the JA began pushing the cattle north. A cattle herd could make ten miles a day if they didn't run into a storm or renegade Comanche. On this drive they were lucky. The rain was sparse and the creeks and rivers never flooded for more than a day. The season was still

MindSpring; the days were warm and the grass was plentiful all the way. They encountered no raiders, but when they got into Kansas, some of the farmers had put in fences, so when the herd couldn't go around them, they had to cut the fences and plow through. They made the two hundred and twenty miles to Dodge City in thirty days. Alf, being the new hand, rode drag most of the way. It was night when the herd reached the Arkansas River, and Alf didn't realize they were there until he saw the lights across the river. They bedded the herd down and then Goodnight crossed the river and went into town. Alf and the rest of the cowboys were left to watch the herd. This close to town, thieves would try to steal a cow or two to eat and Goodnight had told Randy to double the guards. Alf pulled his guard duty early and decided to catch up on his sleep instead of going into town. All that would be open would be the saloons and he didn't feel like seeing painted women selling their love to any cowboy who had a dollar.

The next morning Alf woke up to the rumble of a locomotive and an engineer blowing his steam whistle to warn everyone the train was arriving. He arose from his bedroll and looked across the river. Smoke from the train engine caught his eye first, then the vast number of buildings that lined the riverbank. People and wagons were already scurrying in all directions along the streets. Alf quickly dressed and headed to the chuck wagon. He hadn't heard Cookie ring the dinner bell, but he saw other cowboys filling their plates so he grabbed a plate and slipped in line behind Si.

Si turned to him. "Did you go to town last night?"

"No, I rode herd then went to bed. How about you?"

"I went in to Dodge after my turn at night watch, about midnight." Si paused. "Alf...I saw something last night. I saw a man wearing those boots you been looking for."

Alf stiffened. "Where did you see him?"

"He was at the Texas Saloon with a bunch of cowboys I seen around Tascosa." Si raised his hand to his chin. "Oh, and one of them was that fellow we met out on the trail when we first got into Tascosa. His name was Jimbo."

Alf's skin began to tingle. It had to be Jude Brown. "What did the man wearing the boots look like?"

"He looked a lot like Jimbo but his mustache was bigger and turning gray—his hair too."

Alf took a deep breath. "I can't look for him until we get these cattle in the pens."

Si scratched his head, and then spat. "We might run into him at the stockyards."

"Yeah, we might at that."

Alf and Si ate, then saddled their horses and waited for Randy to start the drive over the river to the pens. A few minutes later he rode over and told them to ride drag and make sure none of the cattle drifted down the river. He rode back to the front of the herd and raised his arm.

"Move 'em out, boys. Let's get 'em across the river."
The cowboys began to ride toward the longhorns, yelling and popping their whips. The cattle began moving toward the river. When they got to the bank, they hesitated, but others crowded up behind them and forced them into the water. Randy went in with them and led them to the far side. Most of the cattle crossed with no problems, but a few tried to turn back. Cowboys in the river used their whips to turn them back to the herd. A few made it back, but Alf and a few other cowboys roped them and pulled them into the river again. When the errant longhorns finally noticed most of the herd on the other side, they headed toward them.

It was midafternoon by the time all the longhorns were across the river and into the pens. When the last steer went through the gate, Alf breathed a sigh of relief and rode over to the loading shoots where Randy and Goodnight were adding up the tally sheets. The rest of the JA cowboys drifted in until all of them were standing around waiting for their pay and talking about what they were going to do with it. Finally another man came up to Goodnight and shook hands with him. They talked for a few minutes and then Randy walked over the cowboys.

"The boss said for us to go over to the Texas Saloon and get a whiskey on his tab. He'll join us later, after he gets paid for the cattle."
Alf got on his horse with the rest of the cowboys. He rode up beside Marty and Si. Marty pulled out his gun and turned to Alf. "Get your gun out, Alf. We're going to give them our Texas hello."

Alf frowned. "Do what?"

"We ride fast and shoot up in the air. Everyone expects us to do it."

"Yeah, it's a Texas cowboy tradition," Si added as he pulled his Colt.

Alf smiled as he pulled his pistol. "Well, I guess I'm a Texas cowboy now."

"Let's go, men!" Randy shouted as he spurred his horse. He raced toward town, the rest of the JA cowboys close behind him, racing to see who would be first behind him. When they came to the first building, they began yelling and shooting into the air. Alf was silent at first but then got caught up in the excitement and yelled out his own Texas yell as he rode through the streets of Dodge City.

When they reached the Texas Saloon, Randy pulled back hard on his reins and slid his horse to a stop. The rest of the riders followed suit and a huge dust cloud rose around them. Somehow they all found a place to tie their horses close to the saloon, and dusting off their clothes with their hats, they crowded through the door and up to the bar.

"Whiskey for my men," Randy shouted over the noise. The bartender rushed to line up shot glasses in front of the men and then filled them from a large bottle. The cowboys waited until he was finished and then all raised their glasses together and downed the whiskey. Alf had tried whiskey before and didn't care for it, but he went along with the rest and poured it down his throat.

"Whew," he gasped. "What is this stuff?" He turned to the bartender. "Give me a beer, quick."

The cowboys all laughed and Marty patted him on the back. "Now you are a true Texan."

Alf took a drink of the beer the bartender handed him. He leaned back against the bar and looked around the room. He felt good being part of this bunch of rowdy cowboys. He liked working off the back of a horse, and the excitement and danger helped him forget the bad things in his life. As he took another drink, one of the working girls walked up to him.

"Buy me a drink, cowboy?"

She was young and good looking and her smile reminded him of Sally's. His heart quickened a second but he quickly pushed the feeling aside. He was through with taking women seriously. If he felt the urge for love, he could always buy the remedy for a dollar. He pulled a dime out of his pocket and pitched it on the bar. "Bartender, give the lady what she wants."

It was an hour later when Goodnight arrived at the saloon. He found Randy and told him to send the men up to room twenty-five at the Dodge City Hotel and he would pay them. Randy gathered up all his cowboys and they went to Goodnight's room.

"The price on cattle was higher than I thought, so I'm giving all of you a bonus," he told the men, and began handing them each a hundred dollars. "You boys have fun, but try not to spend all of your money."

Alf got his money and went back to the saloon. He began to ask around about Jude Brown. Most people he asked didn't know him, but finally he asked the bartender at one of the hotel saloons.

"I don't know Jude Brown, but Luke Brown was staying at this hotel. His bunch checked out yesterday. Luke said they were going home to gather up another herd. Said he would be back before it got cold."

Alf walked out of the saloon, disappointed that Jude was already gone but glad he knew where to find him. He would start out for Tascosa in the morning.

CHAPTER 29

It was late afternoon on the seventh day out of Dodge when Alf crossed the Canadian and rode slowly into Tascosa. He headed for the livery stable, but as he rode past the Hog Town Saloon he noticed three horses with Luke Brown's brand tied up in front. Alf stiffened and almost pulled the reins, but instead he gritted his teeth and rode on. He had been pushing Blackjack hard and his horse needed feed and a lot of rest. Jude Brown could wait a few more minutes. Besides, he might not even be there; maybe it was just some of the ranch hands. Alf paid the stable boy and walked back up the street to a hotel. He was tired too and he hadn't eaten anything but a handful of beef jerky all day. He rented a room and went to a café next door. He ordered beef stew but his stomach was queasy and he only ate a few bites. His mind was on Jude Brown and his brothers. He wanted Jude to draw on him, but what if he yellowed out and wouldn't draw? Alf didn't know if he could just shoot him down in cold blood. If he tried to have him arrested, it would be his word against Jude and his brothers, and they would just call Alf a liar. Another thing worried Alf. What if Jude did go for his gun? Would his brothers stay out of it? Alf didn't know if he could shoot all three of them before one of them shot him. But he did know he had one more man to kill to avenge the murder of his mother and father, and it wasn't something he could let go of. He had to finish it.

Alf stepped out onto the boardwalk. There was a slight breeze in the air and he could smell the sweet fragrance of apple blossoms. His mind went back to another day when the scent of apple blossoms was in the air. He had smelled them when he'd walked home from school that day. He had smelled them when he'd watched the four horsemen with the red star boots ride by with their sacks of loot. He had smelled them when he'd seen the smoke from his burning house. Suddenly the horror he'd felt as he watched his home being consumed filled his mind. Again he watched and waited for his father to appear and comfort him, but he never came. Alf grimaced, closed his eyes, and forced the scene from his mind. He took a deep breath, and then pulled his Colt to check his rounds. He adjusted his holster and headed for the Hog Town.

The Brown ranch horses were still swishing flies when Alf reached the dance hall. He pushed through the batwing doors and stepped into the smoky room. The dance floor was full of painted ladies and grubby cowboys dancing to some fast-paced waltz played by a four-member band. Several frowning cowboys sat at tables, playing poker with well-dressed card hustlers. The drinking men lined the bar; some were jolly, laughing and smiling, while others sulked over their beer and whiskey. Alf took it all in before he saw someone he knew. Jimbo was sitting at a table with two other men. One of them looked a lot like Jimbo but older. Alf dropped his eyes to the man's boots. A big red star stitched into the leather glared back at him. Alf flexed his fingers and took a deep breath, then began to walk toward the table.

Jimbo was the first to notice him. He glared and then recognition settled in. "I know you. I met you and two other boys outside of town a few months ago. I saw you at the roundup too. You ride for Goodnight."

"I thought I recognized you too. You're Jimbo, right?"

"Yeah, I'm Jimbo."

Alf nodded toward the other two men, "Your brothers?"

Jimbo nodded toward one of the men, "Yeah, that's Luke, and the one with the fancy boots is Jude." Jimbo frowned. "What do you want?"

Alf backed up a step. "I was admiring Jude's fancy boots. I've seen a few other people wearing fancy boots like those."

Jude glanced at his boots and then back at Alf, and a sneering smile appeared on his face. "Not like these you haven't. There were only four people who had boots like these and they are scattered all over Texas." Suddenly he frowned, and then his mouth flew open as he scooted back in his chair. "Who are you, mister?"

Alf's eyes narrowed and his skin began to tingle. "I'm the twelve-year-old boy you and your three friends rode by up in Clark County nine years ago."

People sitting close by paused what they were doing and turned to watch. Jude glanced at Luke and Jimbo and then back at Alf.

Alf backed up another step. "It was me, my brother, and my two sisters walking home from school. We all saw the sacks of loot from our home hanging on your saddles, but we didn't know that then."

The music stopped. Everyone in the saloon was watching.

"We saw you talking and laughing like nothing had happened, but back down the road were the dead bodies of our mother and father. You and your three friends murdered them. You set our home on fire to cover your tracks and make it look like an accident." Alf took another step back, tears welling in his eyes.

Jude glanced around the room. "No, that wasn't me. I ain't never been in Illinois."

Alf clenched his teeth. "Willy James was with you. He tried to kill me but I got him first. Before he died he got religion. He confessed everything to me, the preacher, and the county sheriff." Alf backed up another step. "You murdering coward. Get up and face me like a man."

The noise of sliding chairs and scrambling boots filled the room as people got out of the line of fire. Several ran out the door screaming.

Jude turned to his brothers. "Willy was crazy. I wasn't there."

Alf glared at Jude. He was ready to end it. "Stinky Sholt confessed too. Both of them said you were the leader."

Luke looked at his brother. "Are you going to let him talk to you that way? Kill the son of a bitch."

Jimbo nodded. "Get up and face him. We'll back you up."

Jude's mouth slowly turned up into a smile. He grabbed a bottle of whiskey on the table and took a long swig. He wiped his mouth, glanced at his brothers, and nodded. They all stood up. Jude glared at Alf. "If you accuse one of us, you have to face all of us." All three brothers went for their guns.

Alf had watched in silence as Jude stood and he didn't care. He didn't think he could get all of them, but he was going to kill Jude. If he was lucky, they might miss and he would have a chance. He saw Jude go for his gun and he went for his.

Gunfire exploded in the saloon. Bottles on the shelves rattled and smoke filled the room.

Alf looked for movement but the brothers were still. Jude was lying on the floor, his gun beside him, unfired. Luke was crumpled up beside him, his gun in his hand. He had fired, but only into the floor. Jimbo was up against the wall behind them, a huge hole in his body oozing blood and guts. Alf's ears were ringing but he heard steps behind him and he turned. Sheriff East walked up beside him.

"Did you come to arrest me?"

"No, I've been here the whole time."

"You heard everything?"

"Yep."

"Why didn't you stop it?"

Sheriff East held up his still smoking double-barreled shotgun. "Some men need killing. We've been suspecting the Browns of rustling for a long time. I just got a wire from Goodnight saying he had proof that some of their cattle's brands were changed. I came over here to arrest them."

"So I'm not under arrest?"

"As far as I'm concerned, you did me a favor. I wasn't looking forward to bringing them in." Sheriff East walked toward the Browns' bodies. "You go on about your business."

Alf holstered his pistol. "Thanks, Sheriff. I guess I'll be going on out to the JA tomorrow or maybe the next day. If you ever need someone to cover your back, let me know. I plan on being around for a long time."

Alf turned and walked out of the saloon. He felt different now. The festering wound in his mind had healed. It had made a scar, but he could live with it. Now he was free to do whatever he wanted and to go where ever the wind blew him.

Author's notes

Alf Smith was a real person who was born in 1859 in Clark County, Illinois. He had a brother, Charley and two sisters, Cordie and Jenny. When Alf was twelve his parents died and he and his siblings were put in foster homes. Around 1880 Alf arrived in Texas and worked on the docks in Galveston. Later he worked as a cowboy and made several cattle drives. He was known to play the guitar and the banjo. He knew the constellations in the sky.

The historical Samuel Clements and Horace Bixby, of course were real people. The time period of Mark Twain's two most popular books is correct.

Sam Bass was a real outlaw in Texas. In 1878 he was shot during an attempted holdup in Round Rock, Texas by Texas Rangers George Herold and Richard Ware.

The Karl Steinheimer story of the ten jack loads of gold has been mentioned in dozens of accounts of buried treasure for years. Years ago my daughter Vickie and I searched the hills just east of Reed's Lake looking for the buried treasure but we were unsuccessful. The gold bars may still be there, waiting for someone to find them.

All the towns and communities in the book were real. Belton, Texas was founded in 1850 and is located by the Leon River and Nolan Creek. Streets names and some of the buildings named are correct. The first ice house was opened there in 1875. Ice sold for ten cents a pound. In 1879 Belton had a telegraph office.

Temple, Texas was first settled when the Santa Fe railroad was laying tracks toward it from Galveston. It was incorporated in 1882 and by 1884 the population was over 3000 people.

Tascosa, Texas was founded in the late 1870's after the Comanche were defeated and placed on reservations. The ranchers moved in and by 1880 it was a thriving but wild town full of saloons and dancehalls. It was reported that a lot of the bad men of the day were seen there including Billy the Kid and John Wesley Hardin. In 1886 the railroad came but missed Tascosa by 20 miles. With the cattle drives over, the town soon died and today the only building left standing is located on the Cal Farley's Boys Ranch.

Harrison Roberts was a real person as are all his family mentioned in the story. He did live in Texas at the time and owned land just outside Belton Texas. Any actions or dialog by Harrison or his family is fiction although Sarah Elizabeth, {Becky} did marry Jack

Houston. They had no children and Jack died in 1894. In 1898 she married Rufus Light.

Today hundreds of the descendants of Harrison and his Children still live in the area.

Mary Francis Kendrick was a real person and Alf Smith did meet her through her brothers Marty and Si. Did Alf Smith ever see her again? That is a story for the next book.

Dwight Hood Roberts

ABOUT THE AUTHOR

Dwight Hood Roberts lives in Belton, Texas on a small country estate. He has rode horses, herded cattle, and fixed fences. When he writes about cowboys he has been there and done that.

www.ingramcontent.com/pod-product-compliance
Lightning Source LLC
Chambersburg PA
CBHW070813120626
46556CB00002B/478